KNOX

LIGHTHOUSE SECURITY INVESTIGATIONS

MARYANN JORDAN

Cover by Graphics by Stacy

ISBN ebook: 978-1-956588-07-1

ISBN print: 978-1-956588-08-8

❀ Created with Vellum

1

"I'm pregnant."

Knox jolted, eyes widened, shock hitting him. "What the...?" He glanced down at the glass of water in front of her, having ignored how she bypassed the beer earlier.

An uncharacteristic expression of nerves crossed the beautiful woman's face. She'd always exuded self-confidence, but now her lips were pressed together as though waiting for his response.

"Seriously?"

She nodded. "Yep."

Feeling gut-punched, he shook his head, still stunned. "But how..."

"Honestly, Knox? You have to ask that? Um... it happened in the usual way." She didn't give him a chance to ask another stupid question. Jerking her head to the side, she added, "Looks like Flyboy knocked me up."

A smile spread over Knox's face, and he shot a look

toward his brother, whose broad grin and sparkling eyes gave evidence Knox's sister-in-law's news was the most extraordinary announcement in the world. Jumping up, Knox pulled her to her feet and wrapped his arms around her, kissing the top of her dark hair tipped in red, murmuring, "Babs, that's fuckin' amazing. I can't believe you and *Robert* are going to make me an uncle."

She leaned her head back and looked up, laughing. "You and your parents are the only ones who call him Robert! It makes me feel like I got pregnant by a stranger!"

Knox rolled his eyes, pretending irritation. While getting used to his older brother going by their last name was weird at first, he'd slowly started calling Robert by the name Drew also. But he'd still get his digs in whenever he could. "Hell, he was Robert until he went into the Air Force. Those lazy-ass fuckers were the ones who started calling him by his last name. Considering you're married to him, making you *Mrs. Drew*, I think you'd be used to it!"

Her nose crinkled as she nodded, then startled. "Oh, my goodness. I just realized that when you get married, she'll be Mrs. Drew, also!"

Before Knox could think of a retort, Drew took to his feet and puffed out his chest. "What? No congratulations for me and my super swimmers?"

"*Your* super swimmers?" Babs bit out, twisting her head around. "How come this impending little Drew-baby is due to *your* swimmers? Maybe I just had exceptionally potent eggs."

2

Knox lifted his brows and wisely decided to keep his mouth shut as he gently turned Babs toward his brother. He grinned while Drew wrapped his six-foot, seven-inch frame around her, and he could've sworn his brother's embrace was even warmer than any other time he'd ever witnessed. Babs had him wrapped around her finger, something Knox never thought he'd see happen to Drew. When Knox was younger, he was often in awe of his older brother. Drew had always been cocky, a man sure of himself, and didn't mind letting everyone know. But now that Knox was living in the same area and able to forge a renewed relationship, it was easy to see how Babs completed him. A strange mixture of elation, pride, and envy slid through Knox as the two cuddled in the middle of the room.

As Drew finally shifted her to his side, tucking her under his arm, Knox stepped forward with his hand extended. "Bro, congratulations. Have you told Mom and Dad yet?"

"Not yet. Babs wanted to tell you first. We're going to call them tomorrow."

"Then I'm honored. But I'll go ahead and warn you to wear earplugs. Mom probably won't stop screaming with joy."

The trio settled into the comfortable living room again, Babs still tucked into Drew's side as they lounged on the sofa and Knox in their kick-ass, deep-cushioned chair. Their conversation was easy as it always was.

They were not only related by blood and marriage but all three worked together for Lighthouse Security Investigations. Their boss, Mace, hired former special forces and CIA ops to create a business that offered security contracts, security installations, and investigations for private and government agencies. Known as Keepers, they were often out of town on assignments, so it wasn't like he saw them every day. Plus, Drew and Babs had been working for Mace for a couple of years. Knox had only recently left the Navy as a FIREHAWK, piloting special operators, excited to continue his career in the private sector.

As the conversation continued, he noticed Babs' eyes began to droop, and soon she was fast asleep, her body reclining on Drew's.

His brother chuckled, and even though Knox knew the position wasn't comfortable, it was obvious that Drew wouldn't move and disturb her rest.

"Still can't believe you're going to be a dad," he said, keeping his voice low.

"Tell me about it," Drew replied, for once, his face serious. "I'm scared shitless and thrilled all at the same time."

"You'll be great. Both of you will."

"I figure we had good examples, so if I just do what Dad did, then hopefully, I won't screw the kid up too bad."

Babs stirred, and Knox pushed himself to his feet. "Damn, I've got to get a chair like this. One I can sink down into when I've got the game on."

"Hell, bro, you can have that one."

Knox's brows lowered. "Are you getting rid of it?"

Nodding, Drew replied, "Babs has already said she wouldn't be able to get in and out of it when she gets larger and then later with a baby in her arms. I thought I'd get her a nice, comfy rocker to go in here instead."

"I'll take it. My apartment needs all the help it can get."

Not expecting Drew to get up, he was surprised when his brother slid away from Babs, gently laying her on the couch and covering her with an afghan. Standing, he said, "I'll walk you to the door."

Once there, the brothers hugged and slapped each other's backs. He was considered tall at six feet, four inches, but he still had to look up at Drew. "Thanks for the invite. You'll have to give Babs my thanks when she wakes up." Inclining his head toward her, he added, "I'm really excited that you guys are making me an uncle. It'll be great being so close that I'll be around for everything."

Drew rubbed his chin and nodded. "To be honest, Knox, I thought you might follow Carson out to California. I just have to say that Babs and I are really glad you didn't."

Knox had been based in California with the Navy but had eagerly moved to Maine to join the LSI Keepers. Recently, Mace had partnered with a man he'd known with Special Forces, Carson Dyer, who was in charge of LSI-West Coast. One of the other Keepers also had a brother that had started working for Mace and had decided to move to California and work for Carson there. Knox had a feeling that it was speculated by more than one of their coworkers that he might do the same.

When he was younger, he was often torn between

emulating his older brother and wanting to do his own thing. It wasn't hard to imagine Drew wondering if Knox would want to strike out on his own, but age had brought him to a place where he craved more family time and was now content with their relationship.

Seeing Drew's appraising gaze, he shrugged, shoving his hands into his pockets. "I thought about it. Mace talked to me, as well. I guess it would've seemed like a natural place to move back to, but I spent years living in California and was excited about moving to the East Coast. Staying here means I get to not only do the job I want to do but can work with you and Babs. And now that I know I'm going to be an uncle, that gives me another reason for wanting to stay."

He could've sworn that Drew's expression registered relief, and even though his brother would often joke, it seemed he was serious when he held Knox's gaze and grinned. "It'll be fuckin' awesome, won't it? Keep working together. Mom and Dad can see both of us when they come to visit. We'll raise families together—"

"What? Whoa!" He jerked his chin back. "You're getting ahead of yourself. Not only am I not ready to become a dad but I'm not even dating anyone!"

Drew waved off his objections. "Yeah, but you will. It's just a matter of time."

Knox lifted his brows. Before getting with Babs, Drew could throw drinks back and shut down a bar with the best of them—and didn't often go home alone. "Who are you, and what have you done with my brother?"

Drew barked out a laugh, then jerked his head

around to make sure he hadn't woken Babs. Looking back, he grinned but lowered his voice. "Just keeping it real, man. Not many of us Keepers are still single. Remember, that shit happens when you least expect it."

Throwing up his hands in surrender, Knox opened the door and stepped out. "Not sure it's in the cards for me. I've got a tiny-ass apartment that I like because I don't have to do anything with it and a widescreen TV that I can watch anytime. I've got a job where I can travel when I want to without worrying about someone else's schedule. Right now, I can't see how I could fit someone into my life. Although, picking someone up at a bar for a night no longer holds any appeal."

"That's the beauty of meeting someone on a mission. They *get* us. They just fit into our lives without trying."

He started to reply but couldn't think of a comeback. Maybe Drew was right. With a last wave, he turned and walked to his pickup truck as the sound of Drew's front door closed. He imagined Drew waking Babs gently, taking care of her. *My brother is gonna be a dad.* Once again, a shot of envy mingled with the happiness he felt.

It only took about twenty minutes to drive to his apartment, and walking inside, a strange sense of isolation struck him. He flipped on the light, and instead of the comfort he normally enjoyed with the small, minimalistic-furnished apartment, it seemed too quiet. He tossed his keys and phone onto the kitchen counter directly to his left, jerked off his boots, and dropped them next to the door. Giving his head a shake, he tried to dislodge the odd feelings.

I can leave my boots out when I want. I can drop my shit

on the kitchen counter. I can watch whatever I want anytime, day or night. Eat whatever I want whenever I'm hungry. Sleep whenever I want. But tonight, the bachelor mantra wasn't ringing true, and he still felt disquieted.

Scrubbing his hand over his face, he headed through the only bedroom and into the bathroom. *Must be because I've just been a front-row witness to my brother and his wife's cuddling, happy life.* He flipped on the water in the shower and quickly stripped. Stepping under the warm water, he scrubbed his body but couldn't scrub the thoughts from his mind. Finally drying off, he pulled on some clean boxers, brushed his teeth, and crawled into bed. But sleep didn't come easily. He tossed and turned, then finally ended up on his back, staring at the ceiling.

I'm going to be an uncle. He couldn't keep the grin from his face. The truth was the news made him exceedingly happy. Not only did Drew and Babs deserve to have their dreams come true but he was struck with the idea that happy endings can actually happen. *Is that what I want? Am I looking for a happy ending and have no idea if it's going to happen?*

His years as a Navy pilot for special operations had been a high-stress, often out-of-the country job with no set hours. The few women he'd attempted to date hadn't been able to handle that lifestyle, so he'd opted for the occasional nameless bar hookup only to find them unsatisfying. Sure, he made sure they both got off, but there was no conversation. No sharing. No jokes or stories or making memories. Before meeting Babs, Drew had always been a ladies' man, shunning relationships and commitments. Knox preferred getting to know someone, but that took time, something he had little of.

Rolling over, he groaned as the sleepless minutes continued to tick by. Most of the other Keepers had found their mates, doing so in the middle of missions. Drew's words resounded in his head. *"That's the beauty of meeting someone on a mission. They get us. They just fit into our lives without trying."* Mace had just told him of a new mission coming down the pike, guarding an elderly man who was a brilliant scientist while on a cruise vacation. In fact, when Mace gave him the assignment, everyone had chuckled, especially his brother and Babs.

"Oh, perfect," Babs had quipped, winking at her brother-in-law. "The perfect place for romance."

Knox had scowled as he shot her a glare. "If I recall, you didn't exactly enjoy your cruise." Babs had often referred to her cruise experience as the vacation from hell.

She'd laughed, shaking her head. "Nope. Spent the whole time trying not to barf all over the place. God, it was awful."

"But babe, we got together because of that cruise," Drew had called out, his brows lowered as he stared at his wife, much to the amusement of the others in the room.

"Best thing about it, Flyboy!" She'd turned back to Knox. "And I'll be fascinated to see who reels you in!"

"Not me," he'd said, leaning back and stretching his arms over his head. "No rocking the boat when on assignment. And a cruise is hardly where I'll find someone who'll get their hooks into me."

Now, thinking back on that conversation, his answer was right. *I'll be there to do a job, not chase after women in bikinis looking for their next umbrella drink along with a single man.* Even a shipboard romance held no appeal considering the idea of a one-night stand was to not see the other person again. *Can't accomplish that on a ship.*

Finally giving up on finding sleep, he flipped on the light, piled the pillows up behind him, and grabbed the book lying on his nightstand. He preferred paper instead of e-books, therefore needing the light. *This is something else I can do whenever I want—read in bed, even in the middle of the night.* And yet, in truth, that lonely thought didn't bring him joy.

Knox sat with the other Keepers in the main conference room of the LSI compound, located in the caverns below the lighthouse Mace owned. The room was massive, and the walls, ceilings, and floors were reinforced with steel beams and panels. It was sealed, environmentally protected, and filled with computer equipment and stations. Everything they could need on a mission was contained in other rooms that branched out, and the area held a fully equipped gym, a locker room, and a secure passage to get to the water where the ocean waves crashed against the rocks.

After Mace had gone over his agenda and given out more assignments, he turned toward Knox. "I've got your mission information on your tablet. Security assignment is Dr. Curtis Spinosa. He's currently a professor emeritus at Georgetown University with an educational pedigree a mile long. According to James Celini, the director of the Department of Homeland Security, Dr. Spinosa is the head of a government biomedical warfare think tank. He's a private citizen currently living in Virginia Beach. He's seventy-four years old, in good health, widower with no children. Taking a five-day trip along Central America, several ports-of-call."

"And the need for security?" Knox asked.

"There's no threat against him, but his knowledge, not only with biological warfare but also with the inner workings of the think tank, has DHS contracting with us to have him watched. Now, this will probably be a vacation for you because, honest to God, there's no overt threat. He lives a normal life in Virginia Beach, travels to D.C. when needed, and that's it."

The newest Keeper, Cole, slapped him on the back. "Damn, man, a week's cruise. That's a primo assignment. They've got casinos, shows, bars, swimming pools, hot tubs, rock climbing walls, surfing pools, zip lines, and all kinds of shit on those big cruises. I know you're there to work, but your downtime will be full!"

He nodded, uncertain how many of those activities he'd have time to do but was looking forward to checking some of them out. *Maybe that's what I need, a mission that feels like a vacation.* Mace ended the meeting, and everyone began filtering to their stations, a few leaving for security equipment installation evaluations. Knox stayed at the table, his gaze riveted on his tablet. He'd already looked at the preliminary information on Dr. Spinosa, glad that the man knew he was going to have a private security escort. Knox had discovered that it was much easier to work with an assignment that expected him.

Pulling up the cruise itinerary, he noted they'd depart from Norfolk, Virginia, with ports of call in Mexico, Costa Rica, and then Belize before sailing back to Norfolk. He'd been to all the locations before except for Belize. Just as he started to look up information about that country, Sylvie called out, "Knox? If you're ready, I can go over your trip details."

Nodding, he stood and walked over to Sylvie's desk. An integral part of LSI, she was not only their administrative manager but was also Mace's wife. Taking a seat next to her, he looked at the computer screen as she tapped away, efficiently pulling up everything he'd need to know.

"You'll fly to Norfolk tomorrow morning and go directly from the airport to the dock. You won't have a long time to wait before they begin boarding. You probably won't have a chance to meet Dr. Spinosa before you board the ship. The accommodations are very nice on this cruise. All rooms have windows and balconies. Your room will be next to his. The cruise will leave tomorrow evening. The cruise includes all meals as well as all amenities." She twisted her head and smiled at him. "Any questions?"

Shaking his head, he smiled in return. "I can't think of any. As usual, Sylvie, you're on top of everything." Standing, he bent to kiss her cheek, then turned and waved to the others.

Mace called out, "Let us know if anything happens or you need us. Hope like hell you don't, but keep us apprised."

Knox nodded, knowing that was business as usual. It

wasn't unusual for an assignment to go sideways, and the Keepers would all pull together to make sure every mission was successful. "Will do," he threw out. With a final hug goodbye to Drew and Babs, he headed upstairs. His flight left early the next morning, and he figured he'd spend the evening packing and studying up on Belize. *Sunshine. White sand beaches. A cruise full of activities. Some downtime to enjoy.* Those might be just the things to shake him out of his doldrums.

Mace walked over to Sylvie, placed his hands on her desk, and leaned forward. He never got tired of seeing his beautiful wife, either at home or work. She looked up and tilted her head slightly to the side.

"Did you tell him?"

Her lips curved, and if he thought she was beautiful before, her smile punched him right in the heart.

She slowly shook her head. "No. I thought I'd let him find out on his own."

Mace's smile met hers, and while he usually kept things professional at work, he leaned forward and touched his lips to hers. Standing again, he winked before turning back to his desk.

Knox stood under the long awning on the concrete dock, waiting in line at the security checkpoint. Looking around, it dawned on him that he didn't see any children running around or in the line. No harried parents trying to lug their belongings and keep up with their little ones. Being much taller than most, he scanned the area, surprised to see very few young adults, as well. Certainly, no college-age and very few that looked to be below the age of thirty. The crowd was mostly middle-aged and older couples, small groups of seniors standing together, and a few travelers like him standing alone in line.

The youngest people he observed seemed to be working for the cruise line. Up ahead, he spied a woman with wheat-blonde hair in a ponytail, a clipboard in her hand, and a large bag over her shoulder seeming to steer several older persons together. Too far away to see if she was wearing a cruise line jacket, she soon passed through the doors with her group.

Another woman walked nearby, her gaze landing on him and her lips curving in a slow, seductive smile. Heavy makeup, an unnatural color of deep red hair. Gold jewelry on her fingers, wrists, neck, and ears. And a predatory gleam in her eyes. Not interested, he looked back down at the paperwork in his hand, glad when she moved up in the line and disappeared through the doors as well.

Once through security, he walked down the dock. The ship would be impressive to most, but having seen much larger vessels in the Navy, the smaller cruise ship seemed dwarfed amongst some of the other cruise lines docked nearby. Coming to the entrance ramp, he made his way up toward the red-jacketed crew at the top. Greeted by a blindingly white-toothed blonde whose eyes lighted when they landed on him and a tall man with an equally white smile, he was welcomed aboard. He and the others nearby were ushered into a comfortable room for the basic safety instructions.

Finally able to make his way through the various staff greetings, he began to understand why a few of the women were eyeing him like the last lollipop in the candy store: the number of single men he'd seen that was close to his age were few and far between.

"If you'll follow me, sir, I'll take you to your room." He followed the young man down a hallway, the plush carpet under his feet softening any footsteps, keeping the sounds inside muted. Taking one of the elevators down a floor, they moved into another carpeted hallway to his room, where his bags had already been placed.

"We hope you enjoy your cruise, sir," the smiling purser said as he opened the door and ushered Knox inside. "The cruise information is on your desk, and if you need anything at all, please call. My name is Randolph."

Thanking the purser, he glanced around, inspecting his room. A king-size bed in a large stateroom. Much bigger than he'd anticipated. Fully stocked and equipped bathroom and full closet. His room also included a desk and a settee that looked to be much more comfortable than what he had in his apartment. *Wow, Sylvie really outdid herself on these reservations.*

The back wall was entirely glass, and walking to the sliding glass door, he spied a small private balcony. One side had a wall and the other had a door that could lead to the balcony next door. Twisting his head, he spied the connecting door between the rooms, sure that they'd be locked. Uncertain if Dr. Spinosa was already in his room, he decided to wait before contacting him.

Pulling out his phone, he searched the cruise line website. He'd spent the previous day researching his assignment and packing, never considering the particular cruise. The words "No Children Under 18 Years Old" popped up. Then he looked up cruise amenities. Described as a luxury line for the mature traveler. Fully stocked library and computer lab. Spa. Swimming Pools. Lounges. Gym.

Mature traveler? That's why the cruise is filled with mostly retirees. A rueful chuckle slipped out. No casinos. No pizza or hamburger joints. No rock climbing. No rollerblading. No shipboard bungee jumping.

Unpacking his suitcase, he blinked at the box of condoms shoved under his shirts. Pulling it out, he read the message taped to the top.

These might come in handy for your "mature" cruise! Drew

Barking out a laugh, he couldn't believe Drew had managed to slip these in when he took him to the airport. "Looks like these won't get used," he muttered aloud, already thinking of how to get his brother back. *Guess it's a good thing I wasn't after anything other than my mission and some downtime.*

3

The cruise hadn't begun, and Libby was already exhausted. Tucking errant tendrils of hair behind her ear, she slung her purse and work bag onto her shoulder. Now that the luggage had been taken, she was only marginally less encumbered. But she wasn't going to complain. Oh no, not her. She was well aware that this trip of a lifetime would never have been possible if not for her job. That, and the fact that Terrence Baldwin broke his leg. It wasn't that she was glad he'd broken his leg, but always taught to find the silver lining, she couldn't help but revel in the fact that she was about to walk onto a luxury cruise ship due to his untimely decision to prove to his teenage son that he could still play football.

Terrence was the assistant administrator for Windsor Village Independent Elder Living Facility and had planned this cruise for the residents who had expressed a desire for the trip. He'd ended up with only ten who'd eventually signed up and paid for the cruise, and Terrence had been thrilled for months about going. But his broken leg two weeks ago and impending surgery were what brought her into the administrator's office. She'd stared in dumb silence as Mr. Snyder had not only offered her the position of overseeing their group on the cruise but had insisted upon it.

"You're the perfect replacement for Terrence," he'd said. "As activities and recreation director here, you're in the perfect position to work with the cruise activities director to make sure the residents have the best cruise possible."

She'd tried to tell him that she could not afford a luxury cruise, but he'd quickly waved away her concerns, informing her that all her expenses would be paid. With that golden nugget dangled in front of her, she couldn't say yes fast enough. Growing up, her family vacations were either camping in the mountains or at the beach. Her parents worked hard, but their modest jobs didn't allow for luxuries on vacations, including hotel rooms. But they had a large tent and sleeping bags, and Libby certainly didn't miss what she'd never had, and considering their vacations were full of fun and adventures, she had no complaints.

When she'd told her brother about the cruise, he'd launched into a safety lecture about a woman traveling alone to a foreign country. Looking at her group, she held back a grin. *If he could see me now... I'm hardly alone!*

When she'd told her parents that she was taking this trip, they'd been so excited for her, and she'd promised to send them pictures each day. Staring at the thick carpet, beautiful artwork on the walls, and glass windows with etched scenes, she couldn't wait to start taking pictures, but with her arms full, she knew that would have to wait.

Determined to make Mr. Snyder proud that he'd chosen her, she intended to do everything possible to make sure the residents enjoyed their trip. She'd even gone so far as to contact Andre Flambre, the cruise activities director, to make sure she knew all the amenities that would be offered to her group.

Now, juggling the papers in her hands, she glanced down her list. "Mrs. Carlton—I mean Cynthia, you need to sign the form that says you attended the safety meeting." She was accustomed to calling the residents by their surnames, but as a group, they'd informed her that during the cruise, they'd prefer that she use their first names. "This is a cruise! A vacation! First names only!" Cynthia Carlton had declared, and the others nodded their heads with enthusiasm.

Once she'd secured Cynthia's signature and scanned the other forms to make sure she had them all, she turned to hand them to the purser. "Here they are," she said, glad to have one more item to check off her to-do list. "I think you'll find everything in order."

The purser scanned each form, then smiled as he looked up at her. "Except for you. I don't have one signed by you."

"Oh, yeah. Sorry," she mumbled, shifting the items in her hands once again so that she was free to sign the form on the clipboard he held.

He looked down at the paper and then lifted his gaze, still beaming his smile toward her. "Well, Olivia, it's nice to have you on board. I'm Randolph, but also known as *Randy* to my friends."

She started to tell him that everyone called her Libby but stopped. The way he emphasized Randy had her do a double-take, still finding his smile aimed directly toward her. Instead, she opted for what she hoped was her most professional smile. "Thank you, Randolph." Turning to her group, she announced, "Okay, we're ready to find our rooms—"

"I'll take care of that, Olivia," Randolph said. "It's not only my duty but my honor to escort all of you to your cabins." He held out his elbow with a gallant air to Cynthia, who giggled as she slid her hand through his arm.

Libby watched as they started down the hall, hearing Cynthia's voice carry all the way back to her. "You know, Randolph, the safety film told us how to get to the boats in case of emergencies, but on the Titanic, they didn't have enough."

As they continued, she could hear Randolph rush to assure Cynthia. Bringing up the rear, she fell into step with one of the other women.

"Hmph. You know I like Cynthia and would never talk ill about anyone, but she's already flirting."

Looking to the side, Libby chuckled. "I'm sure she's just being friendly, Sally."

"Friendly? In my opinion, she should be less friendly, and you should be more so. She ought to leave the young men for you to pick up—"

"Sally, I'm not here to pick up anyone!"

Sally sniffed. "That's your problem. You need more spunk, and then you'd get a man."

Libby watched as Sally moved ahead to join up with the others and sighed, her shoulders slumping. *More spunk. Who has time for spunk?*

"Don't mind them, Libby."

She turned to the voice next to her, and a genuine smile slid over her lips. "Dr. Spinosa," she greeted.

"Curtis. You can call me Curtis."

Sighing, she nodded. "I know, Doc—um, Curtis. It's just hard for me to break the habit."

"Well, that's what vacations are for," he declared, patting her arm, his eyes twinkling. "I, for one, have decided to break my normal routine while on this trip. Instead of reading first thing in the morning, I'm going to go for a swim. And instead of a nap after lunch, I'll visit their excellent library. That way, I can make sure to be ready for the shore stops that we'll make."

As the recreation director, she'd gotten to know everyone in her group very well over the last several years, and the doctor was well known for keeping to his regimen, so even if he made small changes, she knew they were important to him. Laughing, she said, "Well, I want you to have fun on this trip, so whether you follow your routine or break it, do whatever feels right."

His gaze held hers as he tapped her arm with his fingers. "Yes, but make sure you have fun, too. This trip is a chance for you as well, you know."

She smiled and nodded to satisfy him, but knew she was there to work. *And first things first... get them all into their rooms.*

By now, they'd caught up to the others, and she carefully noted the room numbers on her list as Randolph showed everyone to their rooms. She heard the 'oohs' and 'aahs' from the others as they entered their staterooms and was excited to see hers.

Randolph turned toward Curtis and waved him toward room 313.

"Oh, we'll be right across the hall from each other," she said, already turning her attention to her side of the hall.

"Oh, dear. Oh, dear," he began to mutter. "This will never do."

Turning quickly to see what the matter with his room was, she saw that he had not even entered. Glancing at Randolph, it was obvious from his wide-eyed, opened-mouthed expression that he was surprised, as well. "What's wrong?" she asked, moving to Curtis.

"Oh, Libby, I feel so foolish. But I simply can't have the thirteenth room. I know I'm a scientist, but I'm also superstitious. I don't know what to do. I don't feel right asking someone to switch with me."

"My room is just across the hall. I'll switch with you," she said with ease, glad that there was a simple solution.

"I can't possibly ask that of you," he protested.

Stepping closer, she placed her hand on his arm, concerned with the tension now lining his face. "Curtis, you're not asking anything of me. I'm volunteering. I'm not superstitious, and even if I was, I was born on June 13. So, if the number thirteen is bad luck for me, I think it would've shown up by now." She turned toward

Randolph and said, "Whatever you need to do, please make a note of our room switch."

"Of course, of course! The staterooms are identical, simply on different sides of the hall!" Randolph seemed pleased that a satisfactory solution had been discovered so easily. "In fact, I'll take care of the luggage right now."

It only took a few minutes for him to switch their luggage, and then he escorted Curtis into his new room. Walking back out into the hall, he pulled out a tablet and quickly entered the information before looking up at Libby. "Olivia, I can't thank you enough for making that so easy."

She shrugged, following him into her newly assigned room. "I was happy to do it. It's my job to take care of the group as much as possible, and this was a simple fix." Allowing herself to look around, she was unable to keep her smile from widening. "Oh, my goodness. This is more lovely than I could've imagined!"

Randolph took extra time to show her around her room although she hardly needed a guided tour. "And you'll find the cruise information in the notebook on your desk. I'm sure you'll find there are lots of things to do to make your cruise more memorable." He lifted his brows suggestively, but she just wanted him to leave so that she could take it all in without seeming like a cruise-newbie.

When he finally left after going on and on about the bathroom amenities, she quickly walked to the sliding glass door and stared out over her balcony. The view was not extravagant yet considering they were still at the dock, but she could only imagine sitting here, drinking coffee in the early mornings.

"A cruise," she whispered, her words carried away with the breeze. "I can't believe I'm actually on a cruise! And a luxury cruise, at that!" Giving in to the urge to twirl, she danced around the room, stifling her desire to scream in delight.

The king-size bed was covered in a deep burgundy comforter, and four pillows were piled near the head-board. The walls were light-colored, and the furniture was dark wood. The room included a desk, a comfort-able chair, and a small sofa covered in a burgundy and navy pattern. A television sat on an armoire across from the sofa.

Sucking in a deep breath, she let it out slowly. *Okay, time to get to work.* She walked to the desk and placed her notebook next to the one Randolph had indicated. She double-checked the itineraries, mealtimes, and activities provided by the ship, then glanced at the clock. There was still a little bit of time before she would take the group to the deck to watch the ship move out to sea.

Unpacking her clothes, she carefully hung up each garment. Her hand smoothed over the material, hoping the few wrinkles would fall out. She'd splurged on several new outfits and dinner dresses, knowing her typical clothing of choice for work was what she called *comfortably professional*. The cruise line's website specifi-cally mentioned that the dinners were casual, which had surprised her. Of course, it was Cynthia who'd explained that casual didn't mean jeans, but it also didn't mean black tie. Hoping she'd chosen correctly, she looked down at her slacks and decided to change into something cooler, reaching for one of her new sundresses.

She stripped off her pants and pulled her shirt over her head, halting when the material snagged on her earring. With her head covered and her arms twisting as her hands worked to disentangle the earring, she heard a knock and then a door opening.

"Hello? Dr. Sp—"

The voice was deep, definitely male, and unknown. She squealed as she jerked the material over her head, then cried out in pain as it tugged on her ear. Unable to dislodge the shirt from her ear, it dangled to the side of her head as she whipped around to see a man standing in the doorway, his eyes wide as his body jerked.

"Oh, shit! I'm sorry! Excuse me!" He dropped his gaze to his feet and backed through the doorway, appearing to scramble to get his hand on the doorknob to pull it closed behind him.

Libby blinked, her chest heaving in surprise and embarrassment. Staring at the now-closed door leading to what she assumed was the room next to hers, she swallowed audibly. She turned and looked into the mirror and blinked again. Her T-shirt was still caught on her earring and dangled unceremoniously from the side of her head. Her hair was falling out of her ponytail. Her face was bright red with the heat of blush. And she was wearing nothing but her bra and panties.

Oh, my God. Did that just happen? A strange man just saw me almost naked? Looking back in the mirror, she shook her head slightly, letting out a long exhalation. A snort followed as she noted her bra and panties covered more than most women's bikinis. *Thank God, I was wearing something besides granny panties!* As soon as that thought crossed her mind, she snorted again. Hearing a noise coming from the hall, she mumbled, "Nothing I can do about it now," and jumped into action.

Leaning closer to the mirror, she managed to get her T-shirt untangled from her earring. Pulling the sundress over her head, she settled it over her hips and then slid her feet into low-heeled sandals. The shoes weren't new, but then, with the splurges on clothes, there'd been little extra money left over.

She glanced at the clock again and realized there were several more minutes before she needed to gather the group to go up on deck. Sitting on the edge of the bed, her mind replayed the few seconds of shock as the man entered her room.

Tall. *Way taller than me.* Muscular. *That was evident just by his forearms showing from where his dress shirt sleeves were rolled up.* Dark brown hair, cut short. *Not styled like he preps in front of the mirror but enough that he looks like he cares about his appearance.* And piercing blue eyes that had held her gaze before he backed out of the room. *Blue eyes that will be hard to forget. He's the most gorgeous man I've ever seen, has a room right next to mine, and we're stuck on a ship together for almost a week.*

The sight of him scrambling backward hit her. *Oh, great. He's embarrassed. I'm embarrassed. And I'll probably see him every time I leave my room.* She dropped her chin to her chest and sighed. *I wonder if I could stay hidden from him for the next six days...* Sally's words came back to her. *Maybe I do need more spunk!*

Pulling herself together, she stood quickly and walked over to flip the lock, jiggling the doorknob to make sure it was secure. She still had plenty of time before gathering the group to head to the deck. Determined to make the most of her free time, she grabbed her phone and began taking pictures of her room. Stepping out onto the balcony, she saw that a doorway between her balcony and the man's cabin was closed. Checking to make sure it was locked as well, she rolled her eyes. *I hardly think he'll be back!*

She turned toward the water and harbor, taking more photographs to send her parents. Her father used to say that a vacation wasn't complete until something unexpected and exciting happened. *Looks like I've already had my dose of unexpected!* Glad that she could now simply focus on taking care of her group, she headed back into her room.

4

Knox stood in his room with his hand still on the doorknob, leaning forward with his forehead pressed against the door, his face flaming with heat. *Holy shit! What just happened?* Trying to process how the messages had gotten confused, he'd walked in on a half-naked young woman and hoped he wasn't going to get kicked off the ship for the accusation of being a Peeping Tom.

Shoving away from the door, he grabbed his phone and looked down at the messages. A few minutes prior, he'd sent Dr. Spinosa a message, having been given his phone number.

Dr. Spinosa – this is Knox Drew, your security detail for the cruise. I'm in the room next to yours. We need to meet at your earliest convenience.

Mr. Drew – I'm in my room now. You can come on. The door is unlocked.

So how the hell did that young woman get into Dr. Spinosa's room? He hadn't been told that the doctor had a traveling companion.

Typing again, he sent, **What room are you in?**
314

What the hell? He knew the mix-up was not due to
Sylvie considering she was exemplary with all details,
especially with the Keepers' travel. Not wasting any
more time attempting to figure out what had happened,
he shoved his phone back into his pocket and stalked
out of his room. Glancing at the room next to his, he
winced, then moved to room 314 across the hall.
Knocking, he breathed a sigh of relief when Dr. Spinosa
opened the door with a smile.

The scientist was several inches shorter than Knox
but with a trim body that belied his age. His gray hair
was cut short, and his blue eyes peered up at Knox from
behind his wire-rimmed glasses. Dressed in a blue polo
shirt and khakis, he looked every bit a man ready for a
cruise.

"Mr. Drew, how nice to meet you. Please come in."

"Thank you, sir. And you may call me Knox. While
you know I'm here for your security, to everyone else,
I'll just be an acquaintance."

"That makes sense. And please call me Curtis. Of
course, I have no doubt that the need for security isn't
warranted, but James Cellini at DHS was insistent.
Hopefully, this will be a delightful cruise for both of us."

"To start with, Curtis, I have to ask how you ended
up in this room. My information had you in room
three-thirteen. I was given the room next door since
they were connecting rooms."

Curtis's eyes widened. "Oh, I didn't even think about
that. I'm afraid I asked to trade rooms." He threw his

hands up to the side and shook his head. "I know it sounds ridiculous, but I've always been superstitious about the number thirteen. So, our delightful Libby traded with me."

Cocking his head to the side, his brows lowered. "Libby?"

"She's the wonderful recreation director at the facility I live in. Windsor Village. It's an independent living facility. Not a nursing home," he rushed. "But I'm able to have my own large apartment with a full kitchen, and yet I don't have to take care of the house at all. And when I want to have company, there are plenty of people around. To be honest, cooking isn't my favorite pastime, so I'm able to eat in the dining hall. But Libby is so good about coming up with things for us to do besides play bingo. You know, Knox, not everybody likes to play bingo!"

Knox's lips twitched at the rambling explanation. He'd already read the dossier on Curtis, having learned that Windsor Village was luxury accommodations for seniors. But what he didn't know anything about was someone named Libby. "I was given a list of people in your group, but I don't recall someone named Libby."

"Olivia Cook is her real name. And she was only added to our group recently. But I must tell you, we were all thrilled that she could come. Smart, funny, and such a sweetheart. She'll be much better company than the man who was originally going to travel with us. She'll be up on deck as we set sail, and you'll have to meet her."

It was on the tip of his tongue to announce that he'd

already done so but he remained silent on that, hoping she would, also.

Not noticing his discomfort, Curtis continued. "Now, Knox, you'll have to let me know how this works. I've certainly had security when I was in D.C., but when in Virginia Beach, I'm used to being on my own."

"The best backstories are those that are the simplest. If it's all right with you, I'll simply be the son of a friend you haven't seen in years. That way, we can be seen together but it won't be odd if we don't know everything there is to know about each other."

"Excellent," Curtis agreed, rubbing his hands together.

"That will give me the opportunity to be around you at times but won't require that I stay right with you. I want you to go about the cruise as you would normally, and it'll be my job to simply keep an eye on you. DHS ran a check of the cruise staff and passengers and nothing alerted them at all. Where I will stick closer to you will be at the ports when we leave the ship. That will be the riskiest, even considering that, as you say, there's little risk."

Voices were heard in the hall, and a light knock sounded on Curtis's door. Knox, closest to the door, opened it and came face-to-face with the woman he'd walked in on, now fully dressed and blinking up at him, her face as red as he had been earlier.

"You?" she squeaked. Blinking again, her eyes narrowed and she reached out to push him out of the way.

She would never have been able to move him if he

wasn't willing, but he quickly slid to the side as she stalked past, not stopping until her gaze landed on Dr. Spinosa. A delicate floral scent wafted by as she hurried past. She was much shorter than him, the top of her head only coming to his shoulders, and yet he had the impression that if he hadn't moved of his own volition, she would have continued to push until she made it into the room.

"Curtis? Are you okay?" she asked.

"Of course, I am! Is it time to go up on the deck?"

Her head swung back and forth, her gaze moving between Curtis and Knox, giving him a chance to study her. The thick, blonde hair that had been sticking out at odd angles earlier was now tamed into a neat ponytail at the base of her neck. Dressed in a modest sundress, he knew the curves that lay underneath. Her brown eyes were dark, probably more so due to her anger.

Opening his mouth to diffuse the situation, she beat him to it.

"Who is this man? Do you know him, Curtis?"

"Yes, yes. This is Knox. Quite the funny thing, actually. I knew his father. He recognized my name and came over to introduce himself to me. We've just been getting acquainted." Turning toward him, he said, "And this is Libby."

Knox observed her staring at Curtis for a few seconds before swinging her head back to him.

"Oh! I see. That's why... um... oh. Yes, well, uh..."

Stepping forward, he reached out his hand, making sure his face gave away no recognition, hoping to abate her embarrassment. "As Curtis said, I'm Knox. It's nice to meet you."

She swallowed deeply before lifting her hand and placing it in his. Her hand was small, and as he gently wrapped his fingers around hers, a strange tingling moved up his arm. If her widening eyes were any indication, she felt it, too. Releasing her hand reluctantly, he stepped back.

She glanced up at him again, her lips pinched tightly together, then turned her attention to Curtis, her voice softening. "The ship will be pulling away from the dock soon, and I'm gathering everybody to go up onto the deck."

"Excellent! Let me get my phone so I can take pictures," Curtis said.

The door opened, and Knox swung his head around to see who the new arrival was. A woman with a violet stripe in her gray hair leaned in and shouted, "Are you all coming? Shake a leg before we all die of old age waiting on you!"

"Cynthia, we're coming!" Libby called out. Looking back at Curtis, she said, "If you're ready, we'll go now. I'm not sure Cynthia will wait much longer." Glancing up toward Knox, she offered a polite nod.

"Knox, you must join us!" Curtis said.

From the tight-lipped expression on Libby's face, he had no doubt that she'd rather he not come along, but with a mission to accomplish, he pushed ahead. "That sounds great. I'd love to."

The three of them stepped out into the hall, and he watched as Curtis closed his door then jiggled the knob to make sure it was locked. Glad that his assignment was security conscious, he turned toward the group.

"Okay, everyone," Libby said, smiling at the group of ten elderly persons gathered around. "Let's head upstairs to the deck." She started down the hall with several of her group trailing along, leaving a few glancing back and forth in confusion.

"Excuse me," he called out, drawing her attention to him. He pointed in the other direction from where she was going. "The elevator and stairs are this way."

Her brow furrowed as she looked up and down the hallway, then sighed. Moving past him, she mumbled her thanks and began leading the group forward. He fell in line with Curtis, looking down as the man next to him chuckled.

"Our Libby is directionally challenged," Curtis said.

"You can say that again," said one of the women walking nearby. She looked up at Knox and continued, "She's good as gold but couldn't find her way out of a paper sack if her life depended on it. Never seen anyone get so turned around." She stuck out her hand as they walked. "Sally. Sally Pepper. Are you single?"

Shaking her hand, he introduced himself. "Knox Drew, ma'am. Nice to meet you. And, yes, I'm single, but—"

"Are you dating someone? Are you engaged? Are you gay?"

Her sharp eyes and clipped manner of speaking while interrogating him were reminiscent of drill sergeants in the Navy. "No, and no, and no."

She pinned Curtis with a hard stare and jerked her head toward Knox. "How do you know him?"

"He's the son of an old friend that I haven't seen in years."

"So, you can vouch for him. Are you going to set him up with her?"

"Oh!" Curtis said, his brows lifted. "I... well, I don't know. Should I?"

"What's there to think about?" Sally huffed. "Close to the same age. Both nice-looking. Both single. Nothing to think about." With that, she walked faster and caught up to a group of women just ahead.

"The women have a tendency to take over," Curtis said, heaving a sigh.

An elderly gentleman, slowing his pace to walk beside Knox, smiled up at him. "I'm Roger." Nodding toward two other men who were just ahead of them, he added, "That's Barney and William. Curtis is right. The women will rule the cruise, so we men have to stick together."

Knox was surprised at how easy the setup of the mission was falling into place. He'd made contact with his assignment, they'd quickly established a backstory that others would accept, and he found himself surrounded by a group of older men that seemed to have enveloped him instantly into their camaraderie. Of course, he was no longer sharing a connecting door with his assignment, but being across the hall was the next best thing. Somehow, he would need to discourage the idea of being set up with Libby. Not an easy task considering he'd be spending time in her presence.

By now, they'd made it up to the deck but didn't see the women. Turning to look behind him, a red-faced Libby came along, the women trailing after her. Stifling a grin, it seemed she'd taken another wrong turn, but far be it from him to incur her wrath by mentioning it. So far, stumbling into her room was the only hiccup of the day. *Okay, maybe just a hiccup for the mission, but a bigger deal for her. I'll just be polite, avoid her as best I can, and it'll all be forgotten.*

The redhead with the predatory gleam in her eye wandered by, her gaze raking over him. She had changed clothes also, now wearing a too-tight, too-low top. She started toward him, but just then, Sally and Roger maneuvered him to walk with them. Grateful, he managed to stay with Curtis' group.

As he moved to the rail with the others for the traditional goodbye wave to no one in particular, he glanced to the side. Libby was standing with her hands on the rail, her face raised to the sun, which was giving her cheeks a glow, and her eyes were closed. Her lips slowly curved, and she breathed deeply, which had the effect of drawing his eyes down to her chest. The memory of her satin-covered breasts hit him, and he jerked his gaze back to her face, thankful her eyes were still closed and she hadn't witnessed him staring at her.

There was no doubt about it, Libby was beautiful. Fresh, delicate, beautiful. Turning back to the view over the rail as the ship moved away from the dock, he felt a strange melancholy at the idea of avoiding her. *I'm kidding myself... there's no way I'll be able to forget about the woman on the other side of the connecting door.*

5

Knox. *What kind of name is Knox? Not only is he movie-star gorgeous but he's got a name to go with that body and face. A name like from a superhero movie. Or a rom-com. Or a romance novel.* She rolled her eyes as she leaned against the deck rail, hyper aware of his presence nearby. Her plan to avoid him for the rest of the cruise was dying a fast death considering Curtis had invited him to spend time with them since he was traveling alone. And he appeared more than willing to do so. She'd seen a few women on the deck eye him as though he were the last fish in the sea and they had the biggest net. *God, I sound like Sally. I'm surprised she doesn't tell me to get a bigger net!*

Now that they had officially set sail, Libby needed to put some distance between her and Knox for her own peace of mind. After telling her Windsor Village group that she'd see them later, she finally felt as though she could breathe as she walked away from Knox, who was still chatting with Curtis.

She headed inside to find the cruise ship's activities

director. Even with the ship's map on her phone app, she knew there was no way she could locate it on her own.

She immediately looked for one of the crew wearing the signature red jackets and asked for directions. Thrilled that they walked her to the activities director's office, she thanked them profusely. Lifting her hand to knock, she tapped lightly.

"Come in," came a voice from the other side of the door.

She opened the door and peeked in, seeing an office much larger than she'd anticipated. Plush carpet. Wooden desk and credenza. Leather chairs. The man sitting behind the desk looked up, the smile on his face widening as his gaze swept over her before meeting her eyes. He jumped to his feet and walked around his desk, his hand extended.

"Hello, hello! I'm Andre Flambre. How may I assist you?"

She placed her hand in his to shake but he continued to hold it as he ushered her to the chair. Tugging slightly, she freed her hand as she sat. "My name is Olivia Cook, the recreational activities director for a group of seniors that I'm traveling with from Windsor Village Independent Living—"

"Oh, Olivia! Yes, yes. I've been looking forward to meeting you since we communicated by email." Instead of walking back behind his desk, he sat in the other chair angled toward hers, his knees touching hers as he leaned forward.

Shifting so that they were no longer touching, she

kept her smile plastered on her face. "Mr. Flambre, I wanted to obtain a list of all the activities for each day. I know my group has already decided for themselves what excursions they'd like to take, but I want to go over the list with them so that they don't miss anything. That will also let me know what activities I might suggest for them based on their individual likes and needs."

"Olivia… I hope I may call you Olivia? Please call me Andre."

"Yes, of course."

"I'll be more than happy to provide you with anything that assists with your traveling companions' pleasure on the cruise. I would also deem it a great honor to work with you on creating activities that would be suitable for them, as well. But please, don't think that our activities are only for your group but for you, also. There are lots of activities that would be more suited for a woman of your age that I'm sure you'd enjoy."

"Thank you," she replied. "I'll make sure to avail myself of the ship's wonderful accommodations."

He stood and walked over to a credenza and picked up several brochures and collected several printed pieces of paper. Handing them to her, he explained, "The brochures contain information that I'm sure you've already discovered from our website and what has been sent to you, but it's nice to have extra copies. What I'm also giving you are the planned activities that will be announced each day." He leaned forward, his smile wide as he lowered his voice. "You're very special,

Olivia. No one else has a copy of these. But since we'll be working side-by-side, I'll give them to you so that your group may plan a little bit ahead of time."

"Thank you," she repeated, uncertain if he had something in his eye or actually winked at her. She took the papers from him and scanned through the activities.

"Can you tell me what your group likes to do?" he asked.

She laughed. "They are as diverse as you can imagine. I know of at least two or three that would love to go to the gym to exercise but don't want to join a class. The stretching yoga will be perfect for several others. I have one that will spend time in the library and computer lab. At least three of them will want to spend as much time walking on the decks as possible. All are looking forward to the shore excursions to the Mayan ruins." She looked back down at the list. "Oh, the wine and dessert pairing class will suit most of them, also. Several like to play cards and will easily join a game in the lounge."

"And you?"

She looked up from perusing the list. "I'm sorry?"

"What do you look forward to enjoying?" He leaned closer, his gaze fully on hers.

Shrugging, she said, "I really hadn't thought about it. I only found out I was coming a couple of weeks ago, so I haven't spent much time perusing the list for myself."

"Well, we must remedy that. I'll make sure you have a memorable voyage." His gaze dropped to her chest.

Jumping to her feet, she rounded the chair, putting some space between them. "Thank you. Well, I must be

44

going. I'll let you know if I need your assistance." Before he had a chance to take her hand again, she darted out the door and down the hall.

Lips tight, she finally breathed easier as she rounded the corner and headed down another corridor. Shoulders slumping, she leaned against the wall. She hated conversations where she wasn't sure of the other person's motives. *Was he just friendly or flirting? Is he used to close quarters on a ship, or was he purposefully getting in my space? Was he indicating he wanted to see me socially or just professionally?* Reading men had never been her strong suit. She preferred to know what someone was thinking instead of having to guess. Wincing, she thought of the occasional times of embarrassment when she'd thought a man was interested only to find out he wasn't. And it wasn't any less embarrassing with the last man she'd dated for a few weeks only to find out that he'd already told his parents that he'd found the woman he wanted to marry. *Not the same feeling I'd had at all.*

Pushing off from the wall, she looked up and down the corridor, uncertain which way led back to her cabin. Finding a doorway leading to stairs, she opened it and walked up a flight, throwing open the door at the next floor, still disquieted. "Ugh!" she groaned, rushing through the door and slamming into a wall that grunted.

"What the he—"

As she careened backward, the papers flew from her hands as her arms windmilled to catch her balance. She shot her gaze up to the talking wall, and hands snatched out to catch her arms, keeping her from landing on her ass. She blinked up at the face attached to a body and not a wall. *Oh, God... it's Knox.*

By some miracle, she'd managed to keep her dress from flying upward as she'd flailed, but now that he had her feet firmly underneath her, it struck her that there was little he hadn't seen already. As much as she would have liked to have avoided another embarrassing moment with him, she knew she owed him an apology for rushing through the doorway without looking. "Thank God it was you that I nearly ran over," she said.

His head jerked slightly at her words, and she replayed them in her mind. "No, that's not what I meant. I'm so sorry. What I meant was that it was better to be you instead of someone more feeble. Not really *more* feeble since that would imply that you're some-what feeble. I'm sure you're not feeble at all. In fact, I know you're not. I thought I'd run into a wall." Forcing her gaze to stay on his, she watched as his eyes widened. "I'm sorry, that didn't come out right, either. It's not that I thought you were a wall. Well, actually, I did, but not in a bad way. More in an immovable object sort of way."

The expression on his face remained, and she decided to give up any pretense of apologizing further. Dropping her gaze, she spied the brochures and papers scattered about the floor. Bending quickly, she realized too late that he'd had the same idea as their heads bumped. "Ow!" she cried out, this time falling on her ass before he had a chance to grab her. Looking up, his hand was holding his head, as well. Her knees were cocked, and her sundress was resting at the top of her thighs. "Oh, God, I'm sorry," she managed to moan.

Deciding that any other words would only lead to more embarrassment, she jerked her skirt down and closed her legs.

"No, no, don't apologize. Are you hurt?" He bent low, and with his hands under her armpits lifted her easily back to her feet. Dropping his hands to her waist, he kept them there, keeping her steady. Of their own volition, her fingers clutched his biceps, holding on as though in fear of landing on the floor again.

Barring the ability to travel back in time, she knew there was no way to avoid him. Lifting her gaze to his intense blue eyes, she sighed. "I really am sorry. I'm fine. Are you okay?"

His lips curved slowly, and the heat of his gaze moved over her face. "Please, Libby, don't apologize." His hands stayed on her waist, their bodies close together. "To be honest, I wanted a chance to speak to you alone. To apologize for earlier. I thought about not mentioning it and just pretending it didn't happen. But that didn't feel right. I owe you an apology, and I hope you accept it."

Her face had flamed with embarrassment when she ran into him and now heated anew. She nodded in haste. "It's fine. You thought that you were entering Dr. Spinosa's room."

"Yes, I did. I had texted him, and he told me to come on in. It never dawned on me that he wasn't in his assigned room."

"I'm sure the door was supposed to be locked, and housekeeping must have missed that. Anyway, no harm done."

His fingers flexed slightly, reminding her that they were still clinging to each other. She dropped her hands from his arms and stepped back, suddenly missing the warmth of his touch. Clearing her throat, she shrugged and attempted a nonchalant tone. "It was surprising, but you hardly saw anything that wouldn't have been worn to a swimming pool."

"I'd still like to know that you accept my apology."

His words, spoken softly, forced her to hold his gaze once again, feeling their sincerity. She smiled easier, no longer forced. Nodding, she said, "Absolutely, I accept your apology as long as you accept mine for flying through the door without looking first and then slamming into you."

He laughed, the sound rumbling from deep inside his chest. Inclining his head slightly to the side, he replied, "I do."

For a few seconds, she felt time stand still as this handsome, well-mannered, kind man looked at her while saying the words *I do*. Jolting, she blinked out of her musings. "Well, good," she rushed. "I'm glad we have that out of the way." Glancing down at the floor, she could not keep the grin from her face as she added, "I'm going to bend down now and pick up my papers. I'd advise you to continue with your walk to avoid another head injury."

Laughing heartily again, he placed his hand on her arm and shook his head. "I'll take care of the papers." He bent and quickly gathered them before standing, offering them to her. "If you don't mind my asking, where are you heading?"

"I'd been to see the cruise activities director to get an early jump on helping my group understand the activities they might like to do each day. I had a crew member show me the way to his office, but I was in a bit of a hurry when I left and became confused. I knew my room would be on a higher deck, so that's why I came through the stairs." She looked up and down the hall, not recognizing anything. Sighing, she admitted, "I actually have no idea where I am."

Smiling, he pointed in the direction he'd come from. "The library and spa are down this way. Our rooms are on the next deck."

"Oh!" She said, still looking up and down the hall.

"Did you know that each level of this ship has a different color carpet?"

She jerked slightly as she looked up. "Seriously?"

"If you memorize them, it'll help make it easier to find your way. Our rooms are on the blue floor. This is obviously green, and the floor you came from is red." He turned and waved his arm forward, saying, "But, if you'll allow, I'll walk with you back down to our rooms. I was heading there anyway."

Deciding to forgo her original idea of avoiding him at all costs and ignoring the warmth she'd felt when his hands rested on her waist, she nodded. "Thank you."

"So, Libby—"

"So, Knox—"

They laughed, and he said, "Please, you go first."

"I was just going to ask if you had taken one of these cruises before."

"No. First time. You?"

She nodded. "Yes. Truthfully, I would never be able to afford a cruise like this. Perhaps one of the bargain ones where there are tons of people and bars where they make their money. But this?" She spread her hands out toward the artwork displayed on the walls. "Never." She cast her gaze upward toward him. "For your first cruise, did you specifically want a... um... tamer version?"

"You could say that. I might not fit in with the geriatric crowd—"

She snorted, then blushed. "Sorry, but you definitely aren't in the geriatric crowd! Please, go on."

"I was just going to admit that crowded pools, umbrella drinks, college spring break crowds, and kids running rampant... not my scene. So, I thought I'd try this."

Nodding, she agreed. "I can understand that. And to think that you've met an acquaintance of your father's. How fortunate!"

"Yes, it was."

She hoped he would talk more, but he fell into silence as they made it to their hall, and she wished she'd paid more attention to the directions they'd taken. Stopping at her door, she clutched the sheaf of papers in her hand and smiled. "Well, I'll see you around."

"At dinner, I'm sure," he added.

"Yes, I'm sure I'll see you there sometime."

"No, I mean I *will* see you at dinner. Curtis has invited me to eat with your group."

"Oh! Well, then I guess I'll definitely see you later."

She smiled, glad that they had moved past the embarrassment of earlier.

"We could walk together if you'd like. I'd love to escort you there."

Facing him, she cocked her head to the side. "Are you sure you aren't just afraid I'll get lost?"

He laughed and shook his head. "While I want to make sure you make it to eat, I really would be honored for your company."

"Fine then," she agreed. "I'll see you at about six." With that, she entered her room, closing the door. Walking over, she sat at the desk and looked at the papers, trying to push Knox from her mind. "Focus on the job, not the man," she mumbled aloud. It didn't take long to arrange the information for each member of her group, making sure they not only had the activities that they were interested in but also some that they might find exciting.

Leaning back in her chair, she grinned, thinking of Knox joining her group for dinner. *Day one... didn't start so well, but it's ending perfectly.*

6

While Curtis took a nap, Knox had decided to explore the ship, both shocked and pleased when Libby literally ran into him. While the cruise was filled with a variety of adults, many in couples or groups, there were definitely some singles looking to mingle. In the first half hour of his ship touring, he'd had to avoid or disentangle himself twice from women who'd approached, hoping to become better acquainted in a way he had no desire to know them. And that didn't include the looks thrown his way from a few of the staff.

The redhead had managed to catch him coming out of the library, her step determined as she closed the distance between them. Learning her name was Renée, he'd managed to get out of her invitation to be her dinner companion by telling her he had other plans. She didn't look pleased, but a more determined expression crossed her face. Irritation filled him. *I've got a job to do, and avoiding certain entanglements is a pain in the ass.*

Running into Libby was like being hit with a fresh

breeze. Plus, it gave him the opportunity to apologize. He hadn't planned on inviting her to walk with him to dinner, but since Curtis agreed that it would be good for him to appear with his group often, it made sense to make sure she knew he was going to be there, and entering the dining room with a beautiful woman might go a long way in keeping the stalkers from approaching.

Thinking of her wide eyes staring up at him after they'd cracked heads, her dress skewed and legs splayed, looking adorably stunned, he grinned. *Definitely a breath of fresh air.*

So far, he'd detected no imminent threat to Curtis but knew the trips to shore would be the most likely place for a problem. Deciding that he'd manage to be on each shore excursion with Curtis, he wondered if that would put Libby in his path more often, a thought that didn't displease him. Just for company, not anything else. He doubted she had any inclination for shipboard romance, which made her the perfect companion to hang out with while he kept an eye on Curtis.

Sitting at his desk, he looked over the list of activities that Curtis had already signed up for, then decided to make sure he had the most up-to-date list after Libby went over new possibilities with her group. Their stops would include Cozumel, Mexico, which they would reach tomorrow morning, and they would be allowed to go to shore during the day. They'd then travel to Costa Rica tomorrow night and have a chance to see the sights there the next day. Then one more trip back north to Belize, where they'd have their last shore excursion.

He'd looked up Cozumel, Costa Rica, and Belize

City before he left, gathering all the intel possible. Each was known for tourism, white sandy beaches, historical sites, exotic food, and crime. If the average tourist knew what the crime rates were in the cities, he doubted anyone would go. For a long time, most of the crime centered on their own citizens, the beach resorts near the cruise ship ports often left alone. But strapped economies, poverty, and cartels created thieves and murderers who now saw wealthy tourists as perfect prey. So, he not only had to consider that Curtis might be the target of a kidnapper but also random criminals.

That thought had him thinking of the other ten members of Curtis' group, especially Libby. Brow furrowed, he wondered how it would be possible to extend protection over all of them. Scrubbing his hand over his face, he leaned back in his chair and sighed. *I can't. No way. It's just not fuckin' possible even if it was my mission.*

He had to admit this was a new situation for him. Usually, the assignment for a single-person security detail was just that—one person to guard with no other distractions. But here on the ship, Curtis had a group of friends that were in the process of befriending Knox. Added to that was the delightful Libby. *Shit.*

Making the decision to talk to them after dinner, he'd offer a better lesson in port-of-call security measures than what they were receiving from the ship. He'd emphasize the need for togetherness when in a port, keeping their phones charged and with them at all times, and checking in with each other. *That's the best I can do.*

Looking at the time, he changed into running clothes, feeling the need to pound the track that ran along the upper deck. He'd have just enough time to go for a run before hitting the shower and getting ready for dinner. And the idea of meeting Libby had a smile spreading across his face.

Knox walked down the carpeted hall toward the wide staircase, his hand resting lightly on Libby's back. When he'd met her outside their doors, he'd felt a bolt of lust. Not surprising considering how beautiful she looked. Seeing her in a jade green dress, the material wrapped in a way that only gave a hint of cleavage but managed to cinch her waist before flaring out over her hips, had his eyes widening. Then, when another male cruise passenger walked by, staring at her, Knox wanted to bark at him to keep his eyes to himself. Instead, he'd flung a possessive glare toward the other man, who'd wisely kept walking in the other direction.

She had missed the exchange while looking down at her phone. Looking up, her brow was lined.

"Is everything okay?" he'd asked.

"I thought everyone was going to meet here at six and walk to the dining room together. But looking at the text, it appears that they've all gone before us. I'm sure they'll save us a seat, though."

Surprised that Curtis had not told him of the change of plans, he led her to the staircase, and they ascended to the next floor. For lunch, the dining room had been casually set, but seeing it now at dinner time, it was elegant. While the cruise was luxury, they'd emphasized that it was not a black-tie-for-dinner experience. They wanted their passengers to be comfortable at all times.

As they waited in the short line to be shown to their group's table, she glanced up at him and smiled. "I'm glad you're with me. I always feel weird walking into a place by myself. I'm not shy, but when I walk in by myself, I have this irrational fear of everyone staring at me."

"They probably are."

Her head jerked slightly. "Why would they?"

"Because you'd be the most beautiful woman there."

She rolled her eyes as an indelicate snort slipped out, which then led to laughter. "Yeah, right."

"No, Libby, I'm serious." As her mirth slowed, she stared at him as though trying to determine if he was telling the truth. "I'm not exaggerating. The men would be staring at you because you're the kind of woman most of them can only dream of. The women would stare at you because you're their biggest competition."

Before she had a chance to retort, they made it to the hostess, who greeted them with a wide smile. "Ms. Cook, Mr. Drew, you'll be at table fourteen this evening."

Libby had already seen the members of her group and started into the dining room as Knox followed. Arriving at the two tables next to each other, it was obvious there were no extra chairs. One table held six members of her group, and the other table held four, all seats filled.

"We'll need to ask them to bring more chairs," Libby said, twisting her head to look for a server.

"Oh, no," Cynthia spoke up. "I'm left-handed and can't stand to have someone sit on that side. And of course, Jeanette is deaf as a post and needs to be next to Helen. Marcella was already going to sit with Roger to find out more about Mayan ruins. We got here a little early, and so we were able to choose seats that worked best. I believe they have a table over there for you two."

While Libby stood blinking in surprise at Cynthia's explanation, Knox glanced toward Curtis and Roger, seeing the two men covering their smiles. Hiding his own chuckle, he shook his head. With his hand resting on Libby's back again, he nodded toward the table for two close by.

"Thank you all for making sure we had a place to eat. Libby? Are you ready to sit down?"

"Um, yes. That'll be fine." Turning back to her group, she added, "Make sure we're all together for breakfast tomorrow. We'll be leaving for our Cozumel excursion together. I don't want to lose or forget anyone."

With that, she turned her attention back to Knox, and he guided them over to their table. Not surprisingly, he noticed other men in the room had their eyes trained on Libby and once again felt the urge to bark at them to stop. It also didn't miss his notice that several women glared her way. Turning his attention back to her, it was obvious that she had no idea of the effect her beauty had.

After ordering, she turned her gaze to him, her face lit by the flickering candle in the center of the table. She sucked in her lips and fiddled with her napkin for a few seconds before blurting, "This is kind of awkward."

He chuckled. "Then ask me a question, and it won't be so awkward anymore."

"Oh, okay. Um... I hate to start with the most boring question of all, Knox, but where are you from?"

"It's not boring if I'll be able to ask you the same questions." Seeing her nod, he replied, "Alabama."

She blinked, her head tilting to the side. "Really? You don't sound like you're from the south. Well, that's not really true. You do have a little drawl."

Chuckling, he said, "You should hear my brother. He really has the deep-southern accent. I was always able to pick up dialects easily, and after years of being in the Navy, I gave up the southern accent, but it slips out sometimes."

"Did you move back to Alabama after the Navy?"

"Oh, no." He shook his head with emphasis. "My parents are still there. Dad is a high school history teacher and head football coach. Mom is an English teacher in the same little town. My sister is there, married with a couple of kids. But I live in Maine now."

"Maine? Wow, that's a long way from Alabama," she laughed. "But then, after traveling the world with the Navy, I suppose you could have your pick of great places to live."

"What about you?"

"Oh, I'm boring." She hefted her shoulders in a slight shrug. Before she had a chance to say more, their appetizers were served.

He wanted to know more, so as they ate, he prodded, "Please continue. You aren't boring to me." He forced his gaze to stay on her eyes and not her mouth as she dabbed her lips with her napkin.

"I grew up outside of Baltimore. Sort of between Baltimore and Washington, D.C. My dad works for the city as a bus driver, and my mom is a receptionist for an accounting firm. I have a younger brother who joined the Marines a few years ago."

"And how did you end up in Virginia Beach?"

"I had a full-ride scholarship to Old Dominion University—"

"Wow, that's impressive," he said, barely glancing at the server as their empty plates were whisked away.

She waved her hand dismissively. "Oh, don't be too impressed! Some were for my grades, but I also qualified for financial need. My parents made decent salaries, but taking care of my grandmother was more important than saving for college at the time. So, between the two kinds of scholarships, I was able to graduate with no debt, thank goodness!"

He was struck with her honesty and the way she spoke candidly, not sugarcoating anything and yet not looking for pity either. "Hey, don't knock however you had to do it. Getting through is still a huge accomplishment and worthy of your pride."

She smiled her gratitude, and once again, the moment was broken as their food arrived. He watched in pleasure as Libby ate with enthusiasm although the little moans that escaped her lips were a distraction considering each one sent another flare of lust through him. *What the fuck?* He'd been around beautiful women before and had never felt such a jolt. As a pilot for special operations, he'd had to learn to control all bodily functions, but there was something about her that continually caught him off guard.

He glanced to the side, then back to her. "Don't look now, but we seem to be the center of attention from your group."

Her eyes bugged as she swallowed. "Seriously?" she whispered, holding his gaze as though afraid to twist her head around to look at the culprits.

"The women's heads are together, and occasionally, they look over here. The men are just shaking their heads although both Roger and William have offered winks. Curtis is simply grinning. Although maybe that's from gas." A bark of laughter erupted from her, quickly followed by her cheeks flaming and her fingers over her mouth. Unable to keep from laughing himself, he shook his head. "I should apologize for my sophomoric humor, but seeing you laugh was worth it."

"You goof," she said, dabbing her eyes with her napkin. "Now I'm sure we're being looked at after I made such a barking noise. Someone's going to think we have a dog in here."

He continued to shake his head slowly, trying to remember if anyone had ever called him a goof before... and came up empty. "No. No dog. Just a beautiful woman enjoying herself." He watched as more color tinged her cheeks and wanted to find out more about her. "So, tell me more about your work. Is it what you've always wanted to do? Your dream job?" As soon as the words left his lips, he was fascinated with the combination of her lips smiling with the pensive specter in her eyes.

"Would it make sense if I said yes and no?"

"I think you can answer the question any way you want," he replied, his interest piqued.

"When I was about eight, my mother became ill, and my grandmother came to live with us to help out. She was there when we needed her, and I loved having her live with us. Even after Mom got better, she stayed. So, I grew up with her love on a daily basis as well, and I think that's why I enjoy working with the elderly so much."

"You don't see it as work, do you?"

Her eyes widened and a little smile crept over her face. "No, I don't. Some people look at their wrinkles and white hair. Their stooped bodies. And they become impatient because they don't walk as fast or think as quickly. But there is so much to learn from someone who has lived their life. My grandmother taught me that."

"They're very lucky to have you," he said, loving the way his sincere compliment made her eyes sparkle even more.

"And I'm lucky to have them, as well." She took a sip of wine and continued. "My degree is in recreational therapy, and I specialize in the elderly. I love the people at Windsor Village, and I know I'm so lucky to have the position." She glanced over her shoulder before looking back at him with a grin. "How can I work for these people and not love my job? They're so much fun."

"And yet, I hear a *but* coming."

She cocked her head to the side. "Am I that transparent?" Her shoulders slumped. "I should learn to hide things better."

"No," he insisted. "You should never hide things that you feel." She held his gaze for a long moment, the intensity making him fight the urge to squirm. He had the feeling she didn't miss much, and that thought made him want to turn the spotlight back to her. "I'd really like to know."

She sucked in her lips, growing quiet as the server brought their dessert, complete with a dessert wine. Once they were alone, she tasted the light cheesecake, closed her eyes as though in ecstasy, then smiled again. "It doesn't feel right to complain about a job that pays well, gives me benefits, is a beautiful facility to work in, and I really enjoy the people." She rolled her eyes as she took another bite, then tasted the wine. "In fact, to complain when I have all that going for me makes me sound like an ungrateful wretch!"

"But there's obviously something about the job that doesn't feel quite right," he prodded.

"When I was in my graduate program, I completed an internship in a nursing home in a very poor area. And while the people that I assisted had very little money, many of them having worked hard all their lives and then relying on subsidies and Medicare, I loved working with them. I felt like I was truly helping them with physical activities, games, and mental exercises. Anything and everything I could do to add joy to the later years of their life. But after I graduated, I applied to lots of places, and Windsor Village was the first to come through. I toured their facilities and was floored! Honestly, Knox, walking through Windsor Village is a lot like this luxury cruise ship. Plush carpet, art on the walls, beautiful furniture, excellent cuisine. And, of course, the opportunity for lectures, travel, even this cruise."

Brows lifted, he nodded. "So, it's the disparity between the two that made the difference."

"Exactly! I mean, people are the same. I loved the people in the nursing home, and I love the people at Windsor Village. But when I looked at the salary and benefits package from Windsor Village, I talked to my parents, and while they told me to do what was best for me, I could see that they were excited about the offer." She toyed with the last of her dessert, sighing once more. "The truth is that I felt more useful to the nursing home patients. Like I had an opportunity to really make a difference in their lives. With these wonderful clients, they'd still go to the opera even if I wasn't around."

He could see the frustration and possible guilt written on her face and wanted to erase the lines from her brow. Reaching out, he placed his hand over hers. "Regardless of where you're working, what you're doing is important. But the great thing about your career choice is that you can always make a change. It's not like you're locked into the same place."

Her gaze jumped from their hands up to his face, and he watched as the light shone in her eyes and her lips curved upward once again.

"You're right. You're absolutely right. I have to admit that the experience I'm getting while working at

Windsor Village is amazing. But I'm not locked into them forever. When the time is right and another position comes along to work with clients who have greater needs, I can always make a change."

Strangely thrilled that his words had brought the bright expression back to her face, he smiled in return.

"But now, it's your turn. I don't know what you do for a living, Knox."

He hesitated for a second. Keeping to his mission and staying on target had never been a problem, and yet the idea of not being completely truthful sliced through him. Pushing that uncomfortable feeling down, burying it deep, he smiled. "I'm a pilot for a private company."

"Oh, I didn't even ask what you did in the Navy. So, you were a pilot for the Navy?"

Nodding, he said, "That's where I got a chance to do something I love... fly."

"So, you don't work for a major airline?"

"No, I fly smaller passenger planes for employees of a company."

By now, most of the diners were leaving the room. Standing, they walked out together. They'd almost made it to the door when she stepped back to make sure everyone in her group was taken care of.

Renée took the opportunity to approach Knox. Elegantly coiffed and dressed, she leaned closer. "I was too late in inviting you to be my dinner companion." Her eyes cut to the side toward Libby, then back to his. "But hopefully, I'm not too late to ask you for a drink tonight."

"I'm sorry," he said, taking a step back. "I have other

plans." At that moment, Libby turned to walk toward him, her gaze darting between him and Renée, uncertainty filling her eyes. Lifting his elbow toward her, he asked, "Are you ready?"

She smiled and stepped forward, sliding her hand through his arm. She offered a slight nod toward Renée, then lifted her gaze back to his. "Absolutely."

Offering Renée a nod as well, he escorted Libby out the door. An idea quickly formed as the perfect way to stay close to Curtis and Libby but keep other women away. A stab of guilt pierced him, but he shoved it down. *I wouldn't be leading her on... just two adults enjoying each other's company.* Glancing down at the beautiful woman, he slid his arm downward, freeing her hand so that he could clasp it in his own.

7

Libby was uncertain how long Knox planned on holding her hand as they walked out of the dining room. It was obvious that he wanted to get away from the other woman whose face was a combination of predator and entitlement, but as they made their way down the main staircase, his hand still firmly clasped hers.

"Olivia!"

Startling at her name, she looked to the side and halted, seeing Andre waving his hand as he approached.

"I hoped I would see you tonight. I— oh..." His words stumbled as his gaze dropped to her and Knox's hands.

Knox's fingers tightened slightly around her hand and didn't let go.

"Hello, Andre. How are you?" Turning to Knox, she said, "This is the activities director for the cruise ship, Andre Flambre. Andre, this is my friend, Knox Drew."

Knox lifted his right hand and shook Andre's. "Nice to meet you."

"Yes, yes," Andre nodded. His smile was wide but didn't reach his eyes. Turning to Libby, he added, "I'd hoped that you had time to go over some activities with me concerning your group. I thought we might share a drink this evening as we explored some possibilities."

"Oh... um... well, I..."

"Ms. Cook already has plans this evening," Knox said smoothly, his smile aimed at her.

Unable to keep from smiling in return at his verbal rescue, she held his gaze then turned back toward Andre. "I'll be going ashore tomorrow with my group. You can send any suggestions to me, and then we can chat later about shipboard activities."

Andre inclined his head, his smile still firmly in place. "Certainly. I look forward to it. Good evening." He continued past them down the hall.

She stayed locked in place, her gaze lifted to Knox's face as he stood close to her. Uncertain what to say, she was glad when he spoke first.

"I know that I should apologize for being presumptuous, and if you really want to work with him tonight, I won't stand in your way."

The intensity in his blue eyes was so strong, and she was mesmerized, not sure she could have walked away even if she wanted to. But she definitely didn't want to. Shaking her head slowly, she replied, "No, I had no desire to work with him this evening. I approached him earlier today to see if there was any information I should pass on to my group, but his interest was a little... over the top. I would have turned him down even if I was by myself, but it was nice that you were here."

"I'm glad I was here, too."

"And the woman in the dining room?"

He also shook his head slowly, his gaze never leaving hers. "I would have turned her down even if I was by myself, but it was nice that you were there."

Her lips curved as he used her own words.

"Would you like to walk out on the deck before turning in?"

"Absolutely."

With her hand still firmly in his, he guided them toward the doors that slid open, allowing them to step out into the night breeze. The moon glistened on the water, creating diamond sparkles. They passed several groups and other couples, eventually stopping along the rail where no one else was standing.

He opened his mouth then closed it quickly, and she waited, but nothing came forth. Giving their hands a little shake, she drew his attention down to her. "Is there something on your mind?" she asked.

Chuckling, he nodded. "Actually, yes, but after having already been presumptuous once tonight, I find myself holding back."

"I'm intrigued," she laughed. Shrugging, she added, "Come on, Knox. Just ask whatever's on your mind."

"I know your group is going into Cozumel tomorrow and I wondered if you'd mind if I tagged along."

A shot of excitement hit her at the idea. Trying to

not show her enthusiasm, she said, "Not at all. But I should warn you, the tour was arranged more for seniors, so you might find it a bit tame."

"I don't think I'd find it too tame, not with the company I'd be keeping."

Her tongue darted out, moistening her bottom lip. "Of course, it would give you more time with Curtis, but it would take you away from the other women on the cruise... the ones who would prefer you spend time with them instead of our group. I'm fairly sure the woman we just left would be devastated to lose your company."

He chuckled and shook his head. "The truth is, Libby, I have no interest in her or any other woman on the ship other than the one I'm standing with right now. I want to spend time with Curtis, and at the risk of being presumptuous again, being with you is a bonus."

"I don't think that's presumptuous at all, Knox. I'm enjoying your company, too."

He smiled and squeezed her hand again. She wished she could ignore the tingles she felt as the warmth traveled up her arm. While spending more time with him would not be a hardship, she hoped her heart wouldn't make the leap from friendship to something more, knowing disappointment would lie at the end of that path. They both turned, leaning their forearms on the rail, their gazes out on the water.

The movement of the ship was calming as they glided along. The sound of low voices from further down the deck mingled with the water slapping against the sides. She tried to ignore the way Knox's forearms next to hers made her feel strangely protected. There was the barest space between them, but the hairs on her arm seemed to tingle with electricity. Earlier, she'd hoped to avoid him for the rest of the cruise, but now, it seemed she was destined to be in his company, and that thought didn't bother her. Stifling a grin, she had to admit the idea of spending more time with him made her happy. Keeping her eyes forward so she wouldn't be tempted to stare at his face, she murmured, "You must have seen this sight so many times before."

"What?"

His voice sounded surprised, and she twisted her head to find his gaze pinned on her. "Um... the water at night. Since you were in the Navy, I assume you've looked at this kind of beauty a lot."

"The water, yes," he replied, but his eyes never wavered from hers to glance out over the ocean. He lifted his hand to tuck a breeze-blown tendril behind her ear, his finger lingering for just a few seconds over the shell of her ear. "But seeing this kind of beauty before... no."

Not breathing for fear of the moment passing between them disappearing, her fingers gripped the rail tighter. He leaned in closer, and she wondered if he was going to kiss her. *Yes, please...*

"Breathe, Libby," he whispered, and she gulped in air.

The moment passed, and they both turned back to the rail, the conversation flowing once again. He shared stories from the Navy, and she entertained him with stories of their traveling group.

By the time they'd made it back to their rooms, they

stood outside their doors. She lifted her hand and placed it in his. "Thank you for a lovely evening, Knox."

"Libby, it's been my sincere pleasure."

"See you tomorrow, bright and early. And you'd better have walking shoes on because my group is determined to see the ruins near Cozumel!"

Laughing, he said, "Oh, don't worry. I'll be there. And I'll be ready."

They said good night, and she entered her room. It didn't take long to shower and change into her pajamas. Sliding underneath the covers, she discovered the linens were as luxurious as the rest of the cruise line. Rolling over, she stared at the wall and realized Knox was sleeping only a few inches away. Feeling ridiculous, she couldn't help but grin, even knowing she was playing with fire before the gentle movement of the ship rocked her to sleep.

"While the Mayan ruins at San Gervasio are not nearly as complete as some of the other archeological discoveries, its ruins were once a hubbub of worship to the goddess Ix Chel, a deity of fertility and medicine. Most pre-Columbian Maya women would travel to San Gervasio at least once in their lives to make offerings to the goddess."

Libby listened with great interest to their tour guide while keeping an eye on her ten charges. She'd been assured by Andre that morning when she saw him that the excursion would not be too strenuous for her seniors. The tour had been specifically arranged just for the members of Windsor Village, and so far, she was exceedingly pleased with their guide's slow pace and raising his voice slightly so that all could hear.

Glancing to the side, she caught sight of Knox standing near Curtis. Her eyes had continually sought him out during the tour, but she had tried to keep her distance, not wanting anyone else to see her interest. *I'm here for a job, not a man!* But as her heart leaped at the sight of him, it was hard to keep her job in mind.

Discreetly staring, she was surprised that he paid little notice to the ruins or the guide. While his aviator sunglasses hid his eyes, it seemed his attention was on their surroundings as though monitoring something unseen. It had been his insistence that he wanted to come with them on the tour, but she now wondered if the ancient ruins really held his interest.

"I'm glad we're not here in the middle of the summer!" Sally said, wiping her brow as she moved closer to the shade.

"I keep trying to get the others to stand in the shade, but I don't want to keep them from seeing all the sights," Libby replied.

They were not the only visitors around, and as they walked along the stone paths through the ruins with their guide, she walked over to Knox, who was carrying the water. She'd filled a rather large backpack with necessities, but as soon as Knox had seen her this morning, he pulled it from her shoulders and carried it himself. She'd scrunched her nose as she looked up at him and said, "I was going to carry that."

"I know," he'd said while smiling as he reached out and tapped the end of her nose. "But my mama would have my hide if I allowed a lady to carry a heavy pack while I walked around with nothing in my hands."

She'd laughed while the others in her group nodded in approval. "Well, we can't have your mama mad, now, can we?"

Now approaching him, he smiled down at her. "I think I can lighten your load since it's time to hand out the water."

The others gathered around as she unzipped the backpack and made sure everyone in the group was hydrated. Turning to them, she asked, "Are you glad you're on this excursion?"

"Absolutely," Cynthia said. "The beach looked beautiful, but we'll have other beaches to sit on tomorrow. Plus, I can do that back home. This trip was for seeing something I've never seen before and won't ever see again."

Helen drank deeply, then nodded. "Love the ruins, but I don't like all the lizards!"

"Those aren't lizards," William said, shaking his head. "Those are iguanas."

"Are they scaly?" Helen asked, her hands on her hip. "Do they have a long tail? Do they have a tongue that sticks out?"

"Well, yes," William nodded.

"Then they're just big lizards!"

"If you're ready," the guide called out, "we can board the bus and will stop at El Cedral on our way back to Cozumel. It's the oldest Mayan site on the island."

Libby hung back as the others boarded the comfortable, air-conditioned bus. Turning, she spied Knox as he faced away from them, his gaze on a group of young men arriving in several open-topped jeeps. She walked toward him, her eyes on him as she approached. "Hey, Knox—"

He quickly turned and jerked his toward the bus door. "Hop in, Libby. Now."

She blinked at his low but sharp tone. Doing as he asked, she pinched her lips together. As she settled into her seat at the front, he spoke softly to the driver. "Let's get going." The driver didn't appear to be surprised by Knox's polite but authoritative command. The bus doors closed, and since the engine was already running to get the bus cool, the driver put it into gear and they pulled onto the road. Knox slid into the seat next to her, and she battled the urge to ignore him in a pout or to find out what had him so grumpy. The latter won out. Twisting slightly to face him more fully, she asked, "Are you okay?"

He whipped his head around and shoved his sunglasses up on his head. "Yeah, why?"

"Because I'm not sure you listened to one thing that the tour guide said about the ruins. In fact, I'm not even sure you looked at the ruins. And furthermore, you seemed to be staring around as though you expected aliens to drop down on our heads and spirit us away."

His lips twitched ever so slightly. "I did hear what the tour guide said. San Gervasio is the only Mayan archeological site designated a UNESCO World Heritage Site. It has nine temples, and Mayan women would travel to pay homage to the goddess of birth and fertility. On top of that, I looked at the thatched roofs made of palm leaves that were over some of the current digs, noted the size of some of the stones and how the arches were built, and even took note of the iguanas that Helen was so averse to. And furthermore, I don't believe in aliens."

Unable to help herself, she rolled her eyes. Lifting her hands in a sign of defeat, she said, "Okay, okay, I concede that you were listening." Still twisted toward him, she continued. "So, why did you speak so sharply to me?"

"I needed you to get on the bus."

Jerking slightly, her brows lowered. "But I was coming to get *you* to get on the bus. I knew we were ready."

"I didn't want you out there with those men who'd arrived."

"Huh?"

Now his brow lowered as he shifted closer. "Those. Men. Jesus, Libby... didn't you see them?" His words were whispered, but they were still growled.

"I saw a couple of jeeps pull in but didn't notice anything."

"You were walking toward me, and their eyes were on you. And not in a good way, babe."

In another circumstance, she would have loved the

little endearment that slipped from his lips, but the way his razor-sharp tone was pulled from deep inside of him had her huff. "Are you pissed?"

"Uh, yeah."

She blinked. "At me?"

"Libby, I want you safe. I want all of you to be safe. And if that means that I'll keep watch while you and your group tour the area, fine. But I need you to be vigilant, as well. Those men had been drinking, already throwing out beer bottles as they drove up. They had trouble written all over them, and I needed you out of the way in case something was about to get ugly."

Uncertain how to respond, she pressed her lips together and sighed. The truth was, she hadn't paid any attention to the men. Her attention had been riveted on Knox.

He leaned closer until their shoulders were touching and whispered. "I know you're very observant. You keep your eyes on the group to make sure they're all okay. You care about them, and it shows. I suppose it was my years in the Navy that taught me to be very aware of my surroundings. Crime might not touch most tourists, but it's definitely around. I want your group to be able to enjoy themselves fully, so it gives me peace of mind to keep a watch out."

As understanding hit, she reached over and placed her hand on his arm. "Oh, Knox, I'm so sorry I questioned you. The talk you gave to the group this morning before we left the ship about being security conscious was really good. It's so sweet of you to watch over the group, but I don't want you to spend your cruise vacation trailing after us out of a sense of duty—"

He placed his forefinger over her lips, shushing her. "When I'm watching out, I'm just doing what's natural to me. But believe me, I'm here with you because I want to be."

As she stared into his eyes, the feel of his finger against her lips had her fight the urge to dart her tongue out and taste him. She knew he was referring to wanting to be with all of her group, especially Curtis, but the way he stared at her right now, it almost sounded like he wanted to be just with her. Swallowing, she nodded, and he dropped his finger. She immediately missed his touch.

El Cedral was small compared to the ruins they'd just left. They were the oldest ruins, but the guide explained that little was left of the temple after the Spanish came through in the 1500s and then the Americans tore down more to build an airplane landing field during WWII. But it didn't matter to Libby that the ruins were less impressive as her attention continued to focus on Knox. Frustrated that she was so easily diverted, she walked over to her group, determined to make sure their needs were met.

By the end of the afternoon, her group had re-boarded the ship. She was exhausted and had no trouble seeing how tired they were, also. Andre met them at the top of the entrance, effusively asking everyone how they enjoyed their excursions.

When his eyes alighted on hers, he stepped closer.

"Olivia, how marvelous to see you again. I trust everything was to your satisfaction."

"Yes, but would it be possible for some of my group to have dinner served in their rooms? A few of them have expressed the desire to eat in peace and go to bed early."

"Absolutely!" he enthused. "They can order room service, or if it would be easier, you can take their selections and order as a group and just give the dining service their room numbers."

Breathing a sigh of relief, she said, "That's what I'll do. Thank you so much."

He stepped closer after sending a glance over her shoulder. "And perhaps I can persuade you to have dinner with me tonight."

A hand reached from the side and linked fingers with hers. "Hey, Libby. Are you ready to head down to the cabins?"

Seeing Andre's tight lips, she glanced toward Knox and noted the twinkle in his blue eyes. "Yes, I could use a rest."

"Did you get dinner settled?" he asked.

"Yes, most of them will order room service, and then they can rest up for tomorrow's excursion into Costa Rica."

Knox leaned closer. "What would you like to do for dinner?"

She was uncertain what he meant. *Just me... or us?* "Um... I don't have any plans."

"Then we'll do room service, also." Looking back at Andre, he nodded, and she barely managed to say goodbye before they were swept up in the group as they moved along toward the cabins.

Surrounded by the tired but chattering seniors, she smiled, knowing that once she had them settled in and taken care of, she'd have dinner with Knox again.

8

Knox had been on edge all day as though his skin was too tight for his body. Even with no overt threat against Curtis, he didn't consider it to be a waste of his time or LSI's resources. DHS had hired them to make sure things went smoothly for the valuable scientist while he was on vacation, not unlike some other missions LSI had undertaken. He would keep a vigilant watch over Curtis like so many other missions he'd successfully completed.

And yet, despite being aware of Curtis and their surroundings, the desire to continually check to see where Libby was and what she was doing constantly pulled at his attention. He'd discovered yesterday how much he enjoyed spending time with her but wondered about the idea of pretending they were getting together. Certainly, it gave him great cover, but the more he was around her, the harder it was to stay objective. And when the men in jeeps had arrived at the ruins, he'd felt sure they weren't there for tourism... more likely to scope out the unsuspecting tourists. And Libby had easily gained their attention.

He'd thought she'd gotten on the bus with the others, and when she'd walked straight to him, putting herself into their line of sight, he'd nearly bitten her head off. *I owe her another apology.* Sighing heavily, he thought about the way she'd obeyed his instructions immediately without arguing or pouting but then demanded an explanation when they were safely on board. *It was like she understood what I was doing.*

Drew's words haunted him. *"That's the beauty of meeting someone on a mission. They get us. They just fit into our lives without trying."* He scrubbed his hand over his face, hefting a sigh. *But she doesn't know this is a mission. She doesn't know she's part of my cover.* He'd met other women while on an assignment and felt nothing. And yet, with Libby, it was as though he couldn't get enough of her. The fear of fucking up his attention on Curtis caused his gut to burn. *I need to keep my mind on him, not Libby!*

His phone vibrated, interrupting his turbulent thoughts, and he looked down at the message. **Unlock the doors between our balconies.**

Stepping through the sliding glass door, he moved to the gate in the wall between their two balconies and flipped the lock. Swinging it open, his eyes widened at the sight in front of him. Libby stood on her balcony, facing him. The sun, dipping lower in the sky, was at her back, casting a glow all around her, creating an ethereal vision. Her blonde hair was waving past her shoulders, silky and shiny. Her freshly scrubbed face, with just a hint of makeup, bare shoulders, and long legs showed the evidence that the sun had kissed her skin. Wearing a tank top and khaki shorts with flip-flops showing off her painted toenails, she was a vision as beautiful as any woman he'd ever seen.

Her hands swept to the side like a game show hostess, showing the set dinner table on her side of the balcony. A smile lit her face as she said, "I took the liberty of ordering. I hope I did okay."

He caught the hint of uncertainty and stepped closer. He wanted to assure her that he'd eat anything just to be in her company but held back the words. *We're just friends, that's all, but damn, I can't seem to stay away from her.* "You don't have to worry about me, Libby. I've eaten all kinds of things, but I have a feeling that anything you ordered from their menu will be perfect."

Her smile widened, and she turned to lift the stainless domes off the plates. Huge hamburgers piled high with lettuce, tomatoes, and cheese greeted him at the same time as the scent of grilled beef hit his nostrils. His stomach rumbled, and she laughed. Patting his belly, he said, "Damn. You couldn't have picked any better."

"There's more!" With barely contained excitement, she lifted several more domes to expose crispy french fries, onion rings, fruit and cheese platters, and chocolate mousse covered in whipped cream. He stepped closer, but she'd headed to the side, bending over an ice bucket.

He didn't even pretend not to check out her ass that was presented to him so perfectly. Blowing out an unsteady breath, he'd just managed to lift his gaze when she twirled around, holding two longneck bottles of beer high in her hands.

Forget game show hostess. The dinner, the beer, and her body and bright smile had him thinking of movie scenes that were definitely hotter than a simple TV show. Calling upon the good upbringing his parents had instilled, he complimented, "The best meal with a beautiful woman on a cruise ship with the sun setting in the background. I've died and gone to heaven!"

Her hands stilled as her eyes widened. Then her lips curved even more. "Wow... and here I was afraid I'd either overstepped my bounds or ordered the wrong thing!"

He stepped closer, pulled by an invisible magnet, unable to keep from closing the distance between them. Stopping when he was right in front of her, gazing down at her face, he breathed her in. He lifted his hand to brush a wisp of hair behind her ear, his forefinger trailing along the soft skin of her neck. "The dinner. You. Everything's perfect."

Her tongue darted out to moisten her lips, and his gaze zeroed on her mouth, plump and pink. *Christ, he wanted to taste them.*

Suddenly, she jumped, her chest heaving as she sucked in a deep breath. "Um... we should eat while it's all hot."

He was hot, all right, but nodded, determined to get through the meal without pulling her onto his lap. She stepped back and moved to a chair, sitting before he had a chance to hold it for her. Tamping down the urges that raced through his body, he sat across from her, glad that she couldn't see the way his cock was pressed against the zipper.

Focusing on the food, he picked up the burger and took a bite. He groaned at the perfectly cooked beef and all the flavors of the condiments and toppings on his hamburger. She watched him and smiled, then took a huge bite of her own. If her wide eyes as she chewed were any indication, she liked it as much as he did.

Little conversation passed between them as they devoured their burgers and munched on their french fries and onion rings. As they slowed their eating, he took a long swig of beer. "Before you texted for me to come over, I realized I owed you another apology." Hefting his shoulders, he added, "It seems like I keep having to apologize to you."

She dabbed at her lips, her head tilted to the side. "Apology? What for?"

"While my intent earlier was good, I shouldn't have barked at you to get onto the bus."

She waved her hand dismissively, shaking her head. "You were looking out for me. You needed me to act quickly and without question, and while your tone surprised me, it had the desired effect."

His admiration for her lifted even more. "You're very perceptive."

Shrugging, she toyed with the fruit on her plate before popping a piece of pineapple into her mouth. Once again, his gaze locked in on her lips, and he was glad the table kept her from seeing that he needed to shift slightly in his seat as his cock reacted to the sight. Seemingly unaware of his thoughts, she continued to nibble at the fruit. When her tongue darted out to catch a dribble of strawberry juice, he groaned.

Her gaze jerked up to his. "Are you okay?"

Clearing his throat, he nodded. "Yeah, I guess I'm getting full."

She looked down at his plate that still had fruit and dessert. "Oh, I probably ordered too much."

"Oh, no. Believe me, I can still put it away." To prove he wasn't lying, he picked up his fork and began eating more.

"Anyway, Knox, I'll accept your apology, but you didn't have to offer it. With your military background, I'm sure barking orders or obeying orders that were barked at you happened all the time. I don't get to see my brother very often, but I know that in the Marines, he does the same."

He laughed and nodded. "I'm sure he does. My brother was in the Air Force, so we're used to ordering each other around."

"Is he older or younger?"

"He's two years older."

She eyed him carefully, then asked, "Do you guys get along, or are you competitive?"

He chuckled. "Honestly? Both."

Smiling in return, she leaned back in her seat and propped her feet onto the railing. Taking her cup of chocolate mousse with her, she dragged her spoon through the thick cream. "Okay, now I'm intrigued. Tell me about you and your older brother."

His chuckles turned to laughter. Copying her movements, he shifted his chair so that it was closer to hers and leaned back, his legs stretched out, his feet resting near hers. The sunset-over-the-ocean scene in front of them was one he'd seen many times over the years, but as the light shone behind her, it was hard to think about anything other than Libby. She glanced over at him, and he remembered he was supposed to answer her question. "He's a great older brother."

"Boring."

His spoon halted on its way to his mouth as his brows shot to his forehead. "What?"

"The word 'great.' It's boring. It's the kind of word you use when you like something well enough but you're not really going to dive in to truly describe it. Come on… tell me about your older brother."

Wincing, he thought of times he was envious of Drew's easy charm and the way women would sometimes go through Knox to get closer to his brother. Dismissing the emotion as ludicrous, he still asked, "Why are you so interested in him?"

She playfully slapped his arm. "I'm not! I'm interested in what *you* have to say about him because that tells me more about *you*."

And just as quickly as the jealousy hit, it passed only to be replaced by the uncomfortable realization that he was thrilled she was interested in knowing more about him. Refusing to analyze that emotion any more than he would the jealousy, he took a bite of the mousse, thinking about her questions.

"Okay, he's two years older than me. I always looked up to him, figuratively as well as literally. He jumped up in height, and I was slower to gain mine. Even now, at over six and a half feet tall, he towers over most men. But growing up, he was always a good friend. Sure, we battled like most siblings, but we were always in each other's corner when it really counted."

"Tell me a story about the young Drew brothers."

He opened his mouth, then snapped it shut as her simple request gave him pause. Then a memory, long forgotten, slipped back into his mind. Grinning, he shook his head at the thoughts. "When I was a sophomore and he was a senior, I was convinced I was in love with Kenzie. Kenzie Rolland. Cheerleader. A year older. Long blonde hair. Built. And she seemed to be interested in me."

"Oh, no... I hear a *but* coming."

"Yep. She came over to get help with math, and I was sure that was going to be the chance for me to finally kiss her. Then she kept asking about Robert. When was he coming home? Could she see his room?" Shaking his head, he said, "I was getting pissed, and then he walked through the door. She nearly knocked me down to get to him. Asked him out right in front of me."

Leaning forward, she stared wide-eyed. "Please tell me he didn't go for her."

"One thing about him... we might be competitive sometimes, but my parents raised us to be brothers first in all things. He told her he wouldn't go for her if she was the last girl in the school."

Libby barked out a laugh and he joined in. "Good! Serves her right." As their mirth ended, she asked, "Since you both went into the military, are you alike?"

A huff left his lungs as he shook his head. "Not at all.

Well, that's not really true, I guess. I mean, our person-alities are different. He was always a jokester. Funny. Sometimes you'd think he wasn't taking anything seri-ously, but in reality, he was smart, intuitive, intense. I think he surprised people when they mistook him for a good ol' boy then found out he was wicked brilliant. For me, I was serious. I think I must be the worst joke-teller in the world. I have to think about things carefully, and he reacts."

"But that's how you're alike," she said. "Because you're also smart, intuitive, and intense."

"Damn, you're good for my ego."

She laughed and shifted slightly. A wince crossed her face as she wiggled her toes.

"Are you okay?" he asked.

"I'm embarrassed that my feet hurt. I should've taken my own advice and worn better shoes today. I won't make that mistake tomorrow."

Finished with his mousse, he set his cup on the table then turned to grab her feet and lifted them, placing them on his thighs. His hands began to knead her feet, immediately eliciting a moan from her. "Oh, my God, that feels so good."

Making sure to keep her feet away from his crotch so that she wouldn't discover just how good it felt to him as well, he kept massaging her ankles and feet.

"Keep going. Both with the massage and telling me about you and your brother. There has to be something that drives you crazy about him."

Chuckling again, he nodded. "When he was in the Air Force, everyone started calling him by his last name.

Drew. Which is one of those names that can also be a first name. It wouldn't really matter, except that he and I now work for the same company as pilots."

"Really? You guys work for the same company?"

Nodding, he said, "Yeah. But everyone calls him Drew. To me, I always knew him as Robert. It sounds stupid, but part of me feels like by him going by our last name, it sort of takes a bit of me with him." He shrugged and shook his head. "Now that I said it out loud, it is stupid."

Her gaze was intense as she shook her head with vehemence. "No, it's not! I don't think it's stupid at all. You obviously have a great deal of affection for him, and it sounds like he has for you, too. I mean, you guys would have to get along to work for the same company and live in the same area. And that makes you a lot closer than most people are with their siblings! But you guys are definitely different, and let's face it... as the younger sibling, you'll always feel the urge to live up to what he's done. Considering he's sort of hijacked your last name and uses it as his first name would irritate anybody."

She leaned forward with difficulty considering her feet were still in his lap, but she managed to shift so that her hand landed on his arm, and he loved the warmth her touch brought.

"His jokes and good ol' boy mannerisms probably are often used as a way to divert attention. I have no doubt there are things he wishes people didn't see in him. What's important is that you love your brother. The name he goes by doesn't overshadow any of your accomplishments. I think you should be proud of every-thing you've done and who you are, Knox Drew."

The air felt heavy as he dragged it into his lungs, and yet as his chest expanded with the effort, he felt lighter. *She sees me. She gets me... or the part of me that I've shared.*

The sun had set over the horizon, casting the sky into brilliant streams of blue and purple, orange and red. A glow still offered a halo around Libby's head, and Knox couldn't take his eyes from her. How the hell she could have pegged both him and his brother so accurately was beyond his imagination, and the fact that she did felt like a vice grip on the left side of his chest.

He was mesmerized by her dark eyes pulling him in. Her pink, moist lips were slightly open. Her curves were evident in her simple vacation clothes. Her dark blonde hair shone in the sunset. As he stared, he couldn't remember having ever been in the presence of a more beautiful woman, one that seemed to see deep inside, understanding who he was.

His body moved of its own volition. For a man totally in control, he was sailing in uncharted waters but didn't care. All he wanted was her in his arms. Setting her feet gently onto the deck, he stood and reached down to pull her up. Wrapping his arms around her, he drew her body toward his, inch by inch. If she'd protested, he would have stopped even if every cell in his being would have screamed in protest. But she simply smiled.

As they stood at their private railing, he lowered his head. Not wanting to rush a moment, he touched his lips to hers. The barest hint of a touch… just enough to see if they were as soft as he'd imagined. They were.

Then she clung to him and moaned. And he was a goner. He angled his head and took the kiss deeper. Falling overboard on the sensations, he didn't care if he drowned.

9

Libby was drowning. That could be the only explanation for the way her breath was stolen, the burn in her lungs, and the inability to drag in enough oxygen to keep her brain working. And yet, the feel of muscular arms wrapped around her, holding her breasts against a rock-hard body, let her know that what she was drowning in was the best kiss she'd ever had in her life.

Ever since she'd first laid eyes on Knox, he'd seemed sculpted from the finest marble, and yet his lips on hers were so soft. The kiss had started slowly, the barest touch. So light that if she'd closed her eyes, she might have thought it was simply the breeze brushing over her face. But with her eyes open as she watched his lips come closer to hers, she knew the delicate touch was from him.

She didn't remember her arms moving but suddenly found her fingers clinging to his shoulders, uncertain if the swaying of her body was caused by the ship or the kiss. A moan fell from her lips, and as though a match had been tossed onto tinder, he angled his head, sealed his lips over hers, and took the kiss deeper. His tongue traced her lips, and as she eagerly opened, praying that he'd follow her silent invitation, the deity of kisses answered. He thrust his tongue into her mouth, dragging it over every crevice, setting off tingles that traveled along every nerve in her body.

For a moment, she allowed his mouth and tongue to do all the work, her brain barely catching up to the sensations. Finally, wanting to offer the same pleasure to him that she was feeling, she lifted on her toes, clutched his square jaws with her hands, and tangled her tongue with his. Another groan sounded out, but this time, it came from deep within his chest.

Emboldened by the sound, she lightly bit his bottom lip then soothed it with her tongue. This time, the sound that erupted from him was a deep growl. His arms tightened around her waist, and he lifted her up. Uncertain if he was going to carry her off to bed, she was almost disappointed when he sat back down in his chair, keeping her tucked closely in his lap, turned so that their mouths were still sealed together.

She knew what this was, or rather, what it had been: a shipboard romance as they enjoyed their cruise. And yet, the feelings were real. This was... *what?* The idea that he could be truly interested in her as something more fired through her. *Would he kiss me like this if this was a fling?*

Giving in to every fantasy she could imagine about Knox, she squirmed in his lap, feeling the evidence of his arousal, tightened her arms around his neck, and pressed her breasts against his chest as his arms stayed encircled around her.

The kiss seemed to last forever, and yet time ceased to matter. Cocooned in their own little world, existence was only the two of them, the rocking movement of the ship, and the tail end of the sunset. Their only witnesses were the stars that now appeared in the sky.

She clung to him, her lifeboat in the swirling sea of sensations. He alternated between licks and nips, his tongue dancing throughout her mouth. Her nerves fired off signals that should have indicated warning bells but instead just made her over-sensitive skin more receptive to his touch.

Barely aware that while one arm supported her back as she sat across his lap, the other moved, allowing his hand to slowly explore down her side, resting just below her breast, this thumb sweeping the underside.

The men she'd been with had varied with foreplay, from virtually nothing to mostly doing what they needed to do to get off. Some had cared about taking care of her, but no one had ever kissed her the way Knox was kissing her. No one had ever teased or tempted her the way he was.

Just when she was ready to suggest they take the evening's activities into her room, imagining what he could do to her body as they burned up the sheets of her king-size bed, he dragged his lips away, pressed his forehead against hers, and sighed. "I think it's time I call it a night."

The gravelly tone of the words pulled from his chest gave her pause. Uncertain of his meaning, she held his gaze, ran her tongue over her kiss-swollen lips, and dug her fingers into his shoulders, wishing the material of his shirt was out of the way. She may have discovered everything about his mouth but couldn't wait to discover more about his body.

He stood and gently held onto her waist as her feet found purchase on the deck. Still clinging to his arms, he bent and placed his lips on her forehead, leaving them there for a moment, the warmth of his gentle touch still encircling her, whispering against her skin, "Good night. I'll see you in the morning."

Her fingers loosened as she realized he was saying good night in a way that meant he wouldn't be waking up with her in the morning after having shared a bed the night before. Disappointment speared through her, and she swallowed deeply.

She held his gaze, searching his eyes. The blue was dark with lust, and if she wasn't mistaken, a touch of regret. But regret about what, she had no idea. Stepping back, she forced her lips to curve upward. "Good night, Knox." He glanced down at the plates scattered over the table and reached for them. "No, no, it's fine," she insisted, not sure that she could handle staying in his presence after the most life-altering kiss she'd ever had and not drop to the deck to beg him for more. Determined to preserve what shred of dignity she could summon, she waved her hand dismissively over the mess. "The server said they'd come back to clear it away. I just have to call them."

He hesitated, and she kept her eyes down, fiddling

with the bottom of her T-shirt, no longer sure what to do with her hands.

"Dinner was amazing, Libby."

Her gaze shot back up to his and her smile came easier. "Yes, it was. Thank you for sharing it with me."

He turned, and she could not keep her eyes off his retreat as he made his way back through the gate to his balcony, hesitating before closing it behind him. Blowing out a long breath, she walked on stiff legs to the rail and peered out over the ocean. *What just happened?* She knew the answer to her question—*the kiss of a lifetime. A mind-bending, spark-inducing, incinerating-flame, life-altering kiss.* And then nothing.

She lifted her face upward, seeing the stars against the inky sky. They almost seemed to wink, but she wasn't sure if it was because they were encouraging her or laughing at her. Overcome with the desire to seek shelter, she turned and moved back inside her cabin, no longer wanting to be in the space that Knox had shared with her. After a quick call to room service to arrange the dishes to be picked up, she walked toward the sofa, glancing into the mirror, almost not recognizing the reflection staring back.

Mussed hair. Clothes slightly skewed. Pink cheeks. And swollen, rosy lips. Well-kissed lips.

Plopping down onto the sofa, she closed her eyes, recentered her focus, and breathed deeply. "We're just two people on a cruise getting to know each other. But damn. That shot way beyond a friendly dinner. More like an almost-friends-with-benefits dinner." With that realization, she understood why he stopped. *He's honor-*

able and doesn't want to take advantage of the situation.
While she accepted what had happened, she was still left
pressing her thighs together at the thought of what
she'd wanted to have happened.

She lost track of time and jumped at the knock on
the door. Leaping to her feet, she wondered if it might
be Knox, then realized he could have knocked on their
connecting door. She threw open the door to the hall
and welcomed in the server pushing the empty cart.

He made his way to her balcony, and she helped load
the dishes onto the cart, brushing away his protes-
tations.

"Thank you so much for bringing the dinner to me
and also to the others in my group. I know they were a
bit tired after today's excursion. It was very kind of
you."

"It was my pleasure, Ms. Cook."

He smiled but not in a flirty manner, and she readily
smiled in return.

"I hope the dinner was to your satisfaction."

"Oh, yes! It was delicious. I probably should have
been embarrassed to just order hamburgers and french
fries instead of something fancier."

He laughed. "No, ma'am. One of the things I like
about the chef on this ship is that he believes all food is
good and should be enjoyed. Scrambled eggs are just as
good as a fancy dish!"

"I believe that too. And there's a time for all sorts of
different meals. But tonight was definitely a hamburger
and french fry sort of night."

"Well, I hope whoever your dinner companion was enjoyed it as much as you did."

Her words halted, uncertain how to answer. Finally, seeing the young man waiting, she nodded. "Yes, I think they did. I shared dinner with a friend, and we had a lovely time."

They continued to chat for a few minutes as they loaded the cart with empty dishes, and he unfolded a broom and tidied the deck. She closed the sliding glass door behind him and then watched as he rolled the cart into the hall, bidding her good night. Now, alone once again, she decided to take a shower and hoped that the shower head would provide the right stimulation to take the edge off what she'd desperately hoped Knox would have accomplished. Otherwise, it was going to be a long night.

"I'm an idiot."

The words Knox whispered were carried away on the night breeze. He'd stood in the opened door of his balcony and listened to Libby's sweet voice as she chatted with the server who'd come back to take away their dishes. He could hear the pleasure in her voice and had no doubt that the server was enchanted. He was also able to hear the hesitation when her dining companion was mentioned. *Dinner with a friend. Had a lovely time.*

"Christ, I'm a fucking idiot." It had been a lot more than dinner with a *friend*, and he'd had a fuck of a lot more than just a *lovely* time. It was laughing, talking, enjoying… then sharing a kiss that rocked his world, and he knew it knocked her off-balance, as well. He'd become more lost in that kiss than ever in his life. *Lost and then found.*

And then he'd stopped. Ignored the questions and the hurt in her eyes. And walked away. Walked fuckin' away.

It was the right thing to do but the wrong way to go about it. *I'm here for a job, not a shipboard romance. I'm supposed to keep an eye on Curtis, not set the sheets on fire with Libby.* And yet, even as those words moved through his mind for the millionth time, he knew Curtis was safely locked in his room. The threats were at the ports. *If there is a threat.*

Fuck, I should have just come clean with her. It was the whole reason he stopped their kiss before it went further. He couldn't give in to the attraction without her knowing who he was and why he was there. His honor wouldn't allow it.

Now, she just thinks I'm a jerk that ran hot and cold on her. Dropping his chin to his chest, he stared at his feet, his hands on his hips. *Looks like I owe her another apology. Shit, it seems like that's all I do. Fuck up and then apologize.*

Heading into the shower, he let the hot water pound against his body. Tempted to grab his aching cock and rub one out while thinking of her, he refused to give in to the urge. The first time he came with her on his mind, he wanted to be balls-deep, not alone with his own hand.

Climbing into bed a little later, he leaned against the

headboard, trying to read, but the only thought he had was of the beautiful woman lying in bed on the other side of the wall. His tumultuous feelings continued for most of the night, torn between knowing they should just remain friends and wanting to explore how far their feelings could go. By the time the dawn began to streak across the sky, he'd barely slept. For a man who normally made rock-solid decisions, he was no closer to figuring out what to do about the beautiful Libby.

10

Knox stepped out of his room just as his phone vibrated. Hoping it was Libby, he swallowed back the disappointment of seeing Curtis' name.

Had breakfast early. In library at lecture.

"Dammit," he cursed under his breath. Since sleep had been elusive, he'd gotten up early and gone for a run, sure he'd have plenty of time to shower and dress before meeting the others for breakfast. Hustling down the hall, he was glad there was a continental breakfast station for passengers on the go. Fixing an available travel mug full of coffee and grabbing a bacon and egg croissant, he wolfed it down as he headed toward the library. Stopping just outside the doors, he wiped his mouth and tossed away the napkin, taking a few seconds to gather himself so that it didn't appear as though he'd raced to get there.

Stepping inside, he easily found Curtis and the others sitting together, listening to a young man at the front offering a lecture. His gaze fell upon Libby, noting her strategic position of being right in the middle of the group, surrounded by the others, not giving him the opportunity to slide in nearby. Her gaze was fixed on the man speaking, seeming enraptured by the photographs he displayed on the screen. At least, Knox hoped her gaze was fixed on the photographs—and not on the man speaking. Recognizing the envy, he sighed and slid into a chair near the back.

They were visiting Costa Rica today, and he knew that many of her group had decided to relax at one of the resorts near the port, enjoying the beach and nature there. Most were resting up for their sojourn to Belize the next day. After that, they'd head back to Norfolk. Only a couple more days of making sure that Curtis was safe. *And then, I can see if there's any way Libby would want to see me again... unencumbered with a mission.*

As the others left the lecture, he waited for a moment with Libby only to find the lecturer making his way over to her. Knox scowled as Libby smiled at the young man.

"I hope you found the program interesting," the man said.

"Yes, Dr. Logan. Your work in Costa Rica sounds fascinating."

"Will you be going on the excursion I'm leading today to the rainforest? I'd love to make sure you have a personal tour with me."

She shook her head. "No, I'm sorry. I'll stay at the resort with my group. They plan on resting more today so they can take in the Mayan ruins in Belize tomorrow."

Dr. Logan sighed dramatically, his hand landing over his heart as he leaned closer to Libby. "Oh, I'm despondent you won't be able to accompany me, and I'll be lost of your company."

Knox had had enough of the lecturer's flirting. Stalking over, he casually placed his hand on her back. She startled as her head swung around, her eyes widening and cheeks pinking as she peered up at him. "Hey, Libby. You ready to head over to the resort?"

"Um… yes… um…"

"We need to go so we don't miss getting a good lounge on the beach," he said, applying gentle pressure to her back.

She allowed him to steer her out but looked over her shoulder. "Goodbye, Dr. Logan. Thank you!"

Once they were out of the library, she stepped away from his touch. "What are you doing?" she asked.

"I wanted to make sure you didn't miss the boat. I thought you might take a wrong turn."

Her eyes narrowed. "Very funny," she groused, hurrying down the hall.

"Libby," he called softly.

She stopped and turned toward him. "Yes?"

"We take these stairs," he said, pointing to the side.

Pinching her lips together, she stood for a moment, then sighed, her shoulders slumping. "Thank you," she said, walking back toward him, and they descended the staircase to their floor together.

They walked in silence until she finally glanced up at him and asked, "Why did you interrupt me talking to Doctor Logan?"

He shrugged, uncomfortable with the truth and not willing to admit it. "I knew the boats to the resort would be leaving soon, and I didn't want you to lose track of time."

She nodded, saying nothing more, and he inwardly grimaced. *Christ, why can't I just tell her that I really like her?* He fought back the snort. *Because I'm not in fuckin' middle school, and I'm here for a job.* Those words were beginning to sound a lot more like an excuse than a reason. Wanting to repair the breach in their budding friendship, he started to speak, but they were in their hall, and her group was leaving their rooms.

"Knox! Libby!" Cynthia called out. "Hurry, so we don't miss the boat!"

"I just have to grab my things out of my room. My bag is ready, and I'm already wearing my bathing suit under my clothes," Libby called out.

Offering a chin lift toward Curtis, Knox entered his room, gritting his teeth. The idea of spending the day with Libby in a bathing suit after pissing her off for running hot and cold had him imagining that his day was going to be hell. *Nothing more than I deserve.*

Only an hour later, Knox *knew* he was in hell. Libby was polite, even talkative, but it was evident that was all he was going to get from her—the friendzone. *Exactly what I wanted... originally.* Well, originally, he just wanted a cover. Then friendship sounded good. Then that kiss made him want a helluva lot more.

They'd left the ship on a smaller boat, landing at the port. While many other passengers headed off to the excursion buses, her group climbed onto the bus taking them to one of the local resorts that allowed cruise passengers to pay a daily fee to use their facilities. Once there, they'd wandered through the large lobby that included shops filled with local crafts mixed with the typical overpriced tourist purchases. Several restaurants were at their disposal as well as the swimming pools. He needed to stay close to Curtis and was glad when the entire Windsor Village group found beach lounge chairs that were under a wide, shaded awning surrounded by palm trees.

Determined to stay near her as well, he snagged the lounge chair next to her as she was turned away helping apply sunscreen to Helen's back. When she turned around and settled into her lounger, she blinked in surprise, met by his grin. A slight huff escaped her lips as she spread her towel over the lounger, and his smile widened. *Score one for me.*

Lifting a brow, she cocked her head as she jerked her sundress up her body and over her head, now standing in nothing but a two-piece bathing suit. It had a lot more material than a bikini but still left nothing to the imagination. With a wide smile of her own, she settled into her lounger, her eyes hidden behind a pair of sunglasses and a wide-brimmed hat perched on her head, looking more beautiful than any barely-there clad woman around. *Fuck, score one for her.*

The group lounged, chatted, read, and snoozed. Several wandered down to the water, but she remained on her lounger. Unable to take the silence any longer, he finally rolled his head to the side and stared at her profile. "I think I owe you another apology."

She rolled her head toward him but said nothing.

"My stopping... um... leaving last night was... it was sudden. And that was... well, it wasn't—"

She reached up and slid her sunglasses down her nose, her eyes pinned on him. He suddenly felt as though he could breathe, being able to see her eyes. They were not full of anger or hurt. She appeared more curious, perhaps resigned.

Continuing, he knew he was fumbling, definitely in uncharted waters. "Stopping what we were doing wasn't because I didn't want to. It was just that I... well, I guess I wanted to do the right thing. Sometimes, trying to do the right thing doesn't come across very well."

She shifted on her lounger so that she was facing him more fully. "Thank you for telling me that, Knox."

Her voice was soft, and just like the first time he heard her speak, it pulled him in. "I don't like feeling... disconnected." He grimaced at his choice of words, wishing he had his brother's gift of gab and easy way of speaking. Their mother used to say that Robert had never met a stranger and could talk to anyone. Knox had never found either of those to be a trait he possessed. It had never mattered before—until now.

"I'm glad you didn't just feed me a line but told me what you were thinking."

Her words soothed over him, and he chuckled. "I was just thinking that I wish I had my brother's ability to glibly say anything to anybody."

She shook her head, causing her ponytail to swing over her shoulder, the strands in the sunlight catching his attention. "Oh, no! If you had tried to play everything off in a glib, cavalier manner, I would've been insulted. You explained that you were just trying to do the right thing and not take things too far, which tells me a lot about you as a man. And what I know, I like."

Now it was his turn to stare, her words reaching in and wrapping around his heart. No games. No coy plays. No avarice. Just honest truth straight from her.

She smiled. "I get it, I really do, Knox. You get to spend time with your dad's old friend, Curtis. I'm sure a man that looks like you often has women throwing themselves at you. I think it's honorable that you aren't taking advantage. And what happened last night between us was just... um..."

He could see her cheeks turn a rosy blush and felt certain it wasn't from the sun. "What it was was me giving in to the attraction I feel for you. And that kiss— that kiss that was the best I've ever had and shook me up."

Her lips parted as her eyes widened. "Really?"

"Hell, yes. But I pulled back from you because I didn't want you to feel pressured. I didn't want to take advantage." Her dark eyes glowed like melted chocolate, and he was drawn closer against his better judgment. Lowering his voice, he added, "I still don't want to take advantage of you, but I want to spend time with you."

She leaned forward until there were only a few inches between their lips. Her gaze dropped to his mouth before lifting back to his eyes. "I—" she croaked, then cleared her throat. Trying again, she said, "I want to spend time with you, too. And I promise I don't feel taken advantage of."

She was flashing a green light, but it was like waving a red flag in front of the bull. It was only by the strength of his commitment to the mission and his honor as the kind of man his parents raised that he didn't toss her over his shoulder and carry her up to the resort, paying for a room that they wouldn't leave until it was time to get back onto the cruise ship, kissing every inch of her body and discovering what the rest of her looked like without any clothes. Instead, he swallowed deeply and nodded.

Still smiling, she closed the distance and gently touched her lips to his. A barely-there kiss, but as she pulled away, he instantly missed the warmth. She'd slid her sunglasses onto her face and shifted to settle back against the lounger when Sally called out, "Who wants to order lunch?"

Jumping to her feet, Libby bent to grab her sundress, gifting Knox with a perfect view of her cleavage. Jerking his gaze away, he closed his eyes, grit his teeth, and counted in an effort to keep his hard-on from tenting his shorts. By the time he'd managed to control his erection, Libby was making her way around to the others to find out what they wanted for lunch. Finally making it back to him, she sat on the edge of her lounger, her smile beaming toward him.

"What would you like? I'll place one order, and they can bring everything out all at one time."

He looked over the menu and made his selections. He'd kept his gaze sweeping around while they were there but saw no evidence of anyone but tourists and hotel staff. He doubted someone would try anything in broad daylight with so many people around but never let his guard down. He'd even called Mace this morning, letting him know that he felt guilty: he was on a cruise watching over a man with no threat hanging over him, and so far, none appearing. Mace had laughed and told him to enjoy himself. "That's how a lot of security missions go, a lot of watching and not a lot of anything else." He remembered Blake's security detail to French Guiana had resulted in a boring conference attendance for days. It wasn't until Blake's duty was over and he was ready to leave that he'd witnessed a woman kidnapped and rushed after her. Of course, he and Sara were now married.

Before Knox had a chance to fall down that rabbit hole of musings, Libby jumped up quickly as several servers approached carrying large trays.

He followed suit, helping her hand out the food to their group. There were several tables nearby under the sunshade, and the gathering was soon enjoying lunch. The group laughed and talked, bringing him into the conversations as they had since he'd first met them. If anyone had suggested to him several days ago that he would be enjoying his first cruise with a group of elderly seniors that he didn't know, he would've scoffed. But now, he enjoyed the camaraderie.

He'd managed to sit next to Libby again, and glancing to the side, he watched her sharp gaze as it moved over the group, anticipating their needs. He realized she possessed a gift for working with the older people. She managed to assist without making them feel like they needed assistance. She treated them like friends, like family. She smiled easily and laughed heartily. And even her dark, watchful eyes shone brightly. Then she'd turn her gaze his way and smile a little knowing smile, and he was gut-punched once again.

He'd never met anyone like her. Fresh, breezy, sweet, and so fuckin' sexy. He wanted to know more. What made her happy, and what made her laugh? What scared her, and what made her angry? Favorite food, favorite color, favorite movie, favorite book. What her skin tasted like. How she'd feel with her legs wrapped around him. Did her eyes shine when she came? He knew some, but hell, he wanted to know everything.

And there, on a beach in Costa Rica, surrounded by ten older men and women, watching a woman he'd only known for a few days, it hit him… he was falling for her. *How the hell did that happen?* All he knew was that it had. And he no longer wanted to fight the feeling.

11

Libby walked to the water's edge with Knox, their fingers brushing against each other's. She stared out at the crystal blue water lapping against the white sand, the tall man at her side in her line of sight as well. While the scenery was postcard beautiful, it was Knox that held her attention.

The body of a Greek Adonis. With no shirt on and his shorts hung low on his hips, the muscles on display were easily the dreams of a sculptor. Square, clean-shaven jaw. Neatly trimmed hair. He walked with an air of confidence. In another man, it would seem cocky, overly self-important. But for Knox, he gave off the vibe that he was a man comfortable in his own skin, sure of his abilities, knowing who and what he was without giving a damn what anyone else thought. And holy moly, was it sexy!

When they'd shared dinner last night, she felt sure he was interested in her. It wasn't that she'd never had a man interested in her before, just not one that had captured her interest, fascinated her, and made her breathless with anticipation of what they could do between the sheets. Or on the floor. Or against the wall. Or in the shower. Not that she'd ever had floor or wall or shower sex, but he was the first man she was willing to experiment with.

And when they'd kissed, she'd felt sure it was the start of something. Maybe just a night, or a vacation fling, or maybe something more. And when he'd walked away, her ego had taken a blow. It wasn't as though she was trying to avoid him this morning, but when the group rose early and wanted to go to the library, she was relieved, feeling the need to gather herself before seeing him again. What she hadn't expected was for him to stalk up and almost possessively claim her in front of the guest lecturer. And while it had seemed high-handed at the time, after his apology, she understood.

And what an apology. A smile spread across her face thinking about the self-assured man who admitted that he'd stopped because he wanted to do the right thing.

"What are you thinking?"

She jumped, jerking her gaze up to him. "Oh, I'm sorry! My mind wandered."

He stood and faced her, his gaze roaming over her face before looking behind her toward their group still sitting under the sunshade. He dropped his chin and held her gaze again and grinned. "Maybe I need to up my game if your mind is wandering."

Laughing, she shook her head. "To be honest, I was thinking of you."

"You are honest, aren't you?"

"I think everyone should be honest," she said. "It saves confusion. I suppose I never learned to be coy or throw out the cute, flirtatious comments that others seem to use so effectively." She laughed again. "Probably the reason I would sit alone in a bar while my friends got picked up by all the guys!"

He stepped closer, linking fingers with her. Their toes in the surf were touching, and there was only a whisper of space between their bodies. His chin lowered as he held her gaze. "I can't imagine you sitting alone in a bar. I assure you, the games people play don't impress me. But you? You would be the one woman I'd want to be with."

Her lungs burned as she sucked in a ragged breath, then let it out in a whoosh. "Wow. I really hope that wasn't just a line."

He slowly shook his head, lowering his lips to hers. "Not a line. Never a line to you."

This time, he closed the distance and kissed her lightly. Her fingers tightened in his hands, forcing her body to stay still considering they were in full view of anyone on the beach, including their group. What she really wanted to do was leap up, have him catch her, and wrap her body around him like the spider monkeys they'd seen in the lobby. Instead, the kiss stayed light and gentle, but she felt sure it was full of promise.

This time as he separated, she felt the loss again but understood the reason. His gaze moved beyond her again, and she twisted her head around to see what was drawing his attention. When she looked back at him, he seemed to be scanning the area just like the previous day.

Cocking her head to the side, she asked, "Is everything okay?"

He jerked his gaze back and nodded. "Yeah. I'm just trying to make sure the group is safe."

"Isn't that my job?" she asked with a smile.

"Nope. Your job is to make sure everyone has the best time they can. And while it's not my job, it's my nature to just keep an eye on them while they're off the ship."

Accepting his answer, she stepped back. "That's really sweet of you." A muscle ticked in his jaw as though her words bothered him, but an instant later, his face relaxed, and she wondered if she'd only imagined that expression. They walked back to the group where most of them, including Curtis, wanted to take a walk and look at the wildlife near the resort. Roger declined, saying he didn't feel very well.

Knox appeared disconcerted, but she assured, "You can go with them, it's fine. I'll stay here with Roger. By the time you get back, we can all head to the ship."

He glanced around, his brow furrowed. The expression was endearing, and she stepped closer, reaching up to smooth her finger over his forehead. "Hey," she said, drawing his attention back to her. "I'll be here. I'm not going to disappear."

He bent so that his blue eyes were boring intently into her face. "You and Roger stay here. Don't go anywhere. When I come back, I want you right here."

"Knox... I'm fine. We'll be fine. Now, stop worrying and go. The gang are getting restless."

He sighed heavily, then nodded. He turned and walked with the others toward the area of the resort that promoted a rain-forest-like exhibit complete with many native reptiles and animals. She settled back in her lounger near Roger and smiled. She'd be right here when he returned.

"I wonder where they are?"

Knox barely heard Cynthia's question as he stalked toward the empty loungers where he'd left Libby and Roger less than two hours ago. His gaze jerked around as his heart pounded. A server was walking nearby, and he growled, "You! Did you see a man and woman sitting here earlier?"

The man bobbed his head up and down. "Yes, sir, they—"

"Where are they?"

Curtis placed his hand on Knox's arm. "Let the man speak," he said softly.

It was all Knox could do to keep from biting Curtis' head off, but he clamped his mouth shut, his glare still pinned on the hapless server.

"They left, sir. About an hour ago. The lady said they needed to get back to the ship."

"Back to the ship?" His voice was deceptively soft, but the underlying tone trembled, ready to erupt.

"Knox, check your phone," Curtis said.

Fuck! He'd turned the phone to silent when the guide asked them to so the ringing wouldn't upset the animals. Jerking his phone out of his pocket, he clearly saw a message from Libby.

Roger needed to go back to see the ship doc. He was feeling nauseous. See you on board. Libby

He barely heard Curtis thanking the server but looked up to see the man scurry away. He cast his gaze around, seeing the others staring back, and heaved a sigh. "Sorry, I wasn't sure if anything had happened to them. Libby sent a text that said she and Roger went back to the ship. Roger was feeling nauseous, and she wanted him to see the doctor."

"Well, I don't know about the rest of you, but I think I'm ready to go back, as well," Sally said, gaining the nods from the others.

"Me too," William added. "It's been a lovely day, but the sun takes as much out of me as the walking did yesterday. And I want plenty of time to rest so that we can enjoy the Mayan ruins tomorrow."

Since everyone already had their belongings with them, they began walking toward the resort lobby where they would meet the bus that would carry them to the port. Curtis was bringing up the rear, and Knox fell into step with him.

"You're good at your job, Knox. You take it very seriously, and it hasn't missed my attention that the concerns you have for me also extend to the others."

"Make no mistake, Curtis," Knox said. "You're my mission. But if I'm also able to extend protection and security over others in your group while not detracting away from my main assignment, I'll do so."

Curtis nodded, and they walked in silence for a moment before he finally added, "You like Libby."

He hesitated, uncertain what to say. He'd struggled to acknowledge that he had feelings for her, and the idea of admitting it to someone else was completely foreign. But as he glanced to the side, Curtis was staring at him, and Knox suddenly didn't want to deny what Curtis had already discerned. "Yes, I do."

"Well, what are you going to do about it?"

"Do about it? I'm not sure I understand what you mean."

Curtis cackled, drawing the attention of several of the others before they turned back to their own conversations. "I'm sorry, but in my day, a young man knew exactly what he wanted to do about a woman he was sweet on."

Unable to keep from chuckling himself, Knox shook his head. "I'm here on an assignment, Curtis. You know that. I need to keep things professional."

"What you need to do is not let life pass you by. There's nothing that says you can't have a relationship with someone and do your job. I could tell your eyes were on me even when you and Libby were walking on the beach. I felt completely safe with you around. Hell, son, there isn't even a threat against me. Now, while I appreciate your dedication to what you were hired to do, you'd be a fool to not at least see if there's anything worth pursuing with Libby."

It didn't take long for the gathering to board the bus

and make the short trip back to the port. Once there, he shepherded them to the boat that crossed the water so they could board the ship, and when they arrived, they clambered to the greeting crew members, all wanting to know about Roger.

The same white-toothed-smiling crew member that had greeted them when they first boarded assured them that Roger was with the doctor getting checked out. He could tell the others from Windsor Village wanted to descend upon the clinic, but Knox called out, "Why don't each of you go back to your rooms, cool off, hydrate, and rest? I'll go to the clinic and find out what's going on with Roger and talk to Libby."

His pronouncement was met with complete agreement, and he watched as they headed down the hall. Curtis was the last, walking over to Knox after the others had moved away.

"Remember what I said. Life is too damn short to waste one minute. I met my wife several years before I ever worked up the courage to ask her out. We were together for over forty-four years before she passed."

Caught by surprise at Curtis' statement, he reached out and placed his hand on the older man's shoulder. "I'm so sorry for your loss."

Curtis sucked in a deep breath, his chest heaving with the exertion. "To a lot of people, forty-four years is a long time. And don't mistake me, I'm grateful for every one. But sometimes, when I miss her the most, I think about those couple of years that she could have been mine before those. And I regret not having those minutes with her, as well." With that, Curtis dipped his head, then turned and walked down the hall, following the others.

He watched them walk away for a moment, his mind swirling. He'd planned and flown special ops for years, making instant decisions, handling complex situations, knowing what he was doing and comfortable with that knowledge. And yet, Libby had thrown him for a loop. Everything about her called to him and pulled him in. She made him think of walks on the beach, dinners at sunset, sharing, talking, laughing, and kissing. And so much more. He no longer could fight the idea that he couldn't possibly care for her since he'd only known her a few days. He knew what he wanted—and that was to not waste more time trying to stay away from her.

Hustling up the stairs, he made his way down the hall to the ship's clinic. Walking straight in, he saw a woman in scrubs. She turned, her gaze raking over him, and smiled. Not giving her a chance to speak, he said, "Is Roger Whitcomb still here?"

She blinked, then nodded. "Yes, he's in the—"

Without waiting, he stalked to the back room, spotting Libby just at the opening of a curtained area. "Libby," he called out.

Her head jerked around, and her gaze found his. Her eyes lit, her smile spread across her face, and he was struck with the realization that her expression was aimed just toward him. In two steps, he wrapped his arms around her, wanting to know for sure that she was safe. "I'm so sorry, Libby. I didn't get your text because we had to turn our phones off."

She leaned her head back, her smile still aimed at

him. "It's okay. Roger felt nauseous, and I just didn't think he should stay in the sun anymore. We thought about just going to the resort lobby, but that didn't seem right. I felt like I should get him to the ship and let the doctor see him. Doctor Hull has been great, and already, Roger feels better."

"You did the right thing. I just felt like I was going to explode out of my skin when I got back to the loungers and didn't see you."

Before they had a chance to say anything else, the curtain was pulled back, and Roger walked toward them, followed by a white-coated man that Knox assumed was the doctor.

She let go of Knox, and he immediately felt the loss as she turned toward Roger. Following her, he smiled at the older man. "How are you?" he asked.

Roger smiled, the lines in his face deepening. "The doc says I'm fine. Probably just too much spicy food at lunch. I knew I should've taken it easy with my diet, but it was so good."

"I've given him some antacids and advised him to watch his food choices for the rest of the cruise," Dr. Hull said before turning back to Roger. "Don't hesitate to come back if you need to."

Libby moved to Roger's side, looping her arm with his. The three of them left the clinic, making their way to the elevator and then to the hall where their cabins were located. Roger was soon ensconced in his room, surrounded by most of the others.

"Hey, everybody," Libby called out, gaining their

attention. "Who plans on eating in the dining room tonight?"

Knox glanced around as no one raised their hands.

"I think I'm going to order room service," Cynthia said. "But my balcony has a nice table and can hold several people. So if anybody wants to join me, they're welcome."

The group began chatting, some deciding to eat in their rooms, others deciding to gather on the decks.

Libby shrugged. "Well, if no one needs me to check reservations, then I'll let everyone order their own food." She turned to Roger and added, "I'll come by and check on you later."

"Oh, don't worry about it," he said. "The men are going to come and check on me after they eat."

Everyone sauntered off to their rooms, leaving Libby and Knox in the hall. She sighed heavily, and he reached out to place his arm around her shoulders, guiding her toward her door. "Are you okay?"

"Yeah, I guess I am. It seems a little strange that no one needs me tonight."

"Libby, honey, you need to take care of yourself. You run yourself ragged taking care of everyone else, and you went above and beyond in taking care of Roger today."

"That's my job," she protested. "Plus, I want to help them whenever I can."

Curtis' words from earlier came back to him, and he now understood more of what the older, more experienced man was trying to tell him. "Yes, it is your job, and you're good at your job. But that doesn't mean you want life to pass you by." Her top teeth landed on her bottom lip as she seemed to ponder his words. It was all he could do to not reach out and kiss the reddened flesh. Instead, he said, "How about we try last night again?"

Now, her brow lowered, her confusion evident. "I don't know, Knox. I—"

"Look, I had a great dinner with you last night on the deck. I'd love to do that again if you're up for it."

"Just dinner?"

"Dinner, conversation, fun... whatever we feel. And I'll leave that up to you."

Her lips pressed together before slowly curving upward, and she nodded. "Okay. I would love to have dinner with you on the balcony again."

"Then I tell you what. Go in, take a shower, do whatever you need to do to feel rested and refreshed. I'll order food and meet you on the deck in an hour."

Her smile widened, and she nodded. "Can't wait!" She opened her door and hurried inside her room, leaving him in the hall, staring after her with a smile on his face.

12

Libby hurried through her shower and quickly dried her hair into soft waves. Throwing on a bit of blush, mascara, and flavored lip balm, she pulled on another sundress, settling the jersey material over her hips. Forgoing flip-flops, she walked barefoot onto her deck and realized Knox had already unlocked the gate between the two balconies. And just like the night before on her side, the table was set with stainless domed platters.

The sound of voices came from inside his cabin, and she could hear him thank the server, telling him the platters could be picked up tomorrow. With a grin, she walked forward, meeting him just as he came through his door, champagne glasses in his hand.

Brows lifted, she exclaimed, "Champagne? Wow, I have a feeling your dinner plans are much fancier than my hamburgers, french fries, and beer last night!"

He stepped closer and bent, the glasses still in his hand, and placed a soft kiss on her forehead. "I have a lot to make up for. Plus, last night's dinner was great. Just what I needed. Tonight, we'll enjoy something different."

"I suppose we should. It seems like our group is doing more room service than eating in the dining room." She laughed softly, then, seeing his head tilted in silent question, she offered, "I asked Sally earlier today why they enjoyed the room service so much. She said they get to eat in a fancy dining room at Windsor Village every day with servers. She said it was so much more fun to have room service that they could share together but be on a deck or even in their room with the view outside."

"I guess it's a good thing that none of them have gotten seasick," he said.

"I know! I wondered about myself because I hate being on roller coasters. But honestly, the movement of the ship hasn't bothered me at all."

He turned and set the glasses next to their plates, then held a chair for her. He had the table arranged so they were side-by-side, staring out over the sunset-colored water. In many ways, it felt like the previous evening, and yet they seemed to be in a different place in their friendship. She had no idea what might happen between them, either during the rest of the cruise or afterward, but she had no illusions of forever. Staring at the Adonis sitting next to her, she smiled, knowing that in truth, she'd enjoy every minute with him.

He uncovered their plates, and she gasped as her senses were delighted with the sizzling steak and juicy shrimp, fluffy baked potato with butter rivers oozing over the sides, and steaming broccoli. "Oh, my God! This looks and smells amazing. If it tastes anything as I think, I'm going to be in glutton heaven!"

Laughing, he shook his head as he poured their champagne. "I've never heard of glutton heaven, but now that you say it, you're right."

Just like the previous night, they dug into their meal, eating heartily, easy conversation flowing. "You know, we've talked a lot about my job, but you said very little about yours. The only thing I know is that you're a pilot for a private company and that your brother does the same thing for the same company. I guess it would seem stupid to ask if you enjoy it. I can't imagine flying a plane if you didn't!"

He'd finished the main part of his meal and leaned back, pushing his plate slightly to the side. He glanced out over the water before turning back to hold her gaze, a smile on his lips. "I love flying. It's not the only thing I enjoy doing, but my brother and I took flying lessons when we were old enough. I think it made our parents crazy, but as soon as we could get a pilot's license, we did. He went to college on an ROTC scholarship, then joined the Air Force as a pilot. I was just two years behind him and did the exact same thing only joining the Navy."

"That sounds like such an adventurous life. I envy that sense of freedom and accomplishment." She looked down at her meal and pushed her plate back a little, as well.

"Flying planes is not the only thing to get a sense of

accomplishment, Libby. You make people's lives better every day by what you do."

"Oh, I realize the value in what I do," she agreed. "I try to come up with different activities to keep my charges engaged and interested, something that can wane in older people. But it's not very adventurous. I didn't go to college very far from where I was raised. And I didn't get a job very far from where I graduated from. This cruise is the most I've ever done to step out of my comfort zone! I'm not sure I'm very brave at all."

"Bravery isn't just for those who fly planes. Anyone in any life can be brave."

His words penetrated deep inside to the place where she sometimes wondered if she was stuck in a rut, and she smiled. Picking up her champagne flute, she lifted it toward him. "Here's to being brave."

He clinked their glasses together, and they both drained them dry. He leaned closer, and she met him halfway, their mouths touching. His tongue darted out, and she felt the warm velvet glide over her lips. Just when she hoped he would pull her into his arms, he separated. She swallowed the sigh of disappointment, then smiled as he reached over and picked up the plates of cheesecake topped with fresh strawberries and chocolate drizzle.

"Is this okay?" he asked, "I wasn't sure what you liked for dessert."

It was on the tip of her tongue to simply reply that she'd like him for dessert, but she buried that thought and inclined her head toward the plate. "That is more than okay. It's embarrassing," she began as she dragged her fork through the thick creaminess. "But I love to eat. Almost everything. And if it's sweet? I've never found a dessert I didn't like!"

He barked out a laugh. "A woman after my own heart!"

She knew his words were a throwaway, a simple phrase to mean they simply liked the same things. And yet, she couldn't help but imagine what it would be like to have his heart.

They soon finished, and he stood, gathering a few of the plates. "I told the server they can come back tomorrow, but I had him leave the rolling cart in my room. There's no reason to have dirty dishes here all night, so I'll just put them on the cart, roll it into the hall, and give them a call. They can get them anytime."

"Smart," she said, standing, as well. It didn't take long to take care of the plates, platters, and domes. He kept the champagne bucket, and she saw that he had another unopened bottle already chilling. Still smiling, she said nothing. *If he wants to drink and talk all night, that's fine with me.* Although, she'd already decided that she wouldn't mind more of his lips on hers. She hadn't come on the cruise for a shipboard romance but, with the right man, wasn't opposed to a few nights of fun. Glancing toward the gorgeous man whose sturdy profile was cast in a glow with the sunset behind him, she knew he'd be the right man. Blowing out a deep breath, she tried to still the other thoughts crowding into her mind. *And if it feels like more? How much will this hurt to say goodbye when the cruise is over?*

He went inside to call for the server, letting them

know the cart was in the hall with the wheels locked. She walked back over to her side of their connecting balconies and moved into her room. Quickly using the bathroom, she washed her hands before grabbing her lip balm. As she slicked it over her lips, she secretly hoped he'd have a chance to taste the berry gloss.

"I wondered where you went."

She squeaked as she jumped, whirling around, the hand with the balm still in it now pressed against her heart. Seeing him standing just at her balcony door, she smiled. "You scared me! How does a man so big move so quietly?"

"I didn't mean to startle you. I came out on the deck, and you'd disappeared. I didn't want to come into your space, I just wanted to make sure you're okay. And see if I could entice you to enjoy the evening with me some more."

"Absolutely. I just needed to make a pit stop but was coming back out." He lifted his hand toward her, but she said, "I need to go check on Roger first."

"I just came from his room," Knox said.

Her chin jerked back in surprise. "Really?"

"When I rolled the cart into the hall, I knocked on his door and William was there with him. He said he felt fine, and I knew he had company. I checked on Curtis also, and everyone seems to be locked in for the night."

"Well, you took care of everything, didn't you?"

With his hand still extended toward her, he said, "I hope so. And now, I'd like to take care of you."

She walked toward him, sliding her palm against his. He wrapped his fingers around hers and gently led her outside where they bypassed the chairs and stood at the rail side by side, their gazes on the horizon.

"I was scared."

His words surprised her, and she turned to stare at his profile as he continued to face the water, waiting to see what would follow.

"This afternoon when I didn't know where you were. I was scared. We got back to the sunshade, and you were gone. No trace. I had no idea where you were or what had happened."

She placed her hand on his forearm as it rested on the railing, offering soft, quiet comfort.

"I nearly chewed up a server and almost bit Curtis' head off trying to find out where you went." He sighed heavily, then turned to face her. "I don't get scared, Libby. Flew missions. Ran special ops. Never scared. Sometimes adrenaline pumped, but I always felt in control. Ready to adapt. But today... I was just plain scared."

Her heart flip-flopped at his words. "I never meant to frighten you, Knox. That's why I left you the message."

"It was my own damn fault for not turning my phone back on as soon as I could."

His body was just in front of hers, so close her breasts nearly touched his chest, but she didn't back away. She could feel his heat. If he wanted to separate like last night, he could make the move, but she wasn't going to do it for him. But tonight, his arms crept around her body and pulled her flush against his. She gripped his shoulders with her head tipped back, holding his gaze, and waited as her eyes dropped to his mouth.

His head lowered slowly until she felt each breath of his puff over her cheek. His nose glided along hers until his mouth pressed near her ear, and he whispered, "I want to kiss you."

Her chest heaved as her lungs filled with air in anticipation. "Okay," she managed to wheeze.

"And I don't want to stop and make the same mistake I did last night."

Now the air rushed out as his nearness made her dizzy with want. "Mistake?"

"Yeah, mistake. Last night, I walked away. Tonight, if we separate, it'll have to be you who leaves."

Shifting so that she could peer into his eyes, she vowed, "I won't be the one leaving."

"Thank God," he groaned, just as his mouth descended on hers.

At the first touch, she melted in his embrace, grateful for his arms' vice grip around her body or she might have puddled at his feet. Her fingers dug into his biceps before sliding up to clasp behind his neck. He was tall, and considering she was in bare feet, his body bent over hers, surrounding her, encasing her in his strength. And she loved the feel. She'd never felt so dominated by a man, uncertain if she would have liked it, but now discovered that sheltered in his embrace might be her favorite place in the world.

Just like last night, he didn't hurry the kiss, instead tasting and savoring her mouth until finally, his tongue sought entrance which she easily gave. The friction from the velvet softness he glided over the roof of her mouth sent shivers throughout her body, and she clung even tighter to remain standing. For a moment, she allowed him to explore and taste, tease, and tantalize until she became desperate to do the same to him. Lifting on her toes, she angled her head and swooped her tongue over his, hearing the sharp intake of breath before it slipped out as a groan pulled deep from his chest. Their tongues tangled, but she'd been a fool to think she could dominate the dance.

One of his large hands slid from around her waist and glided up to cup her jaw, his thumb sweeping over her cheek as his fingertips clutched the back of her head. His kiss played her like a fine instrument, tuning her to perfect pitch. He owned her mouth, and she prayed he'd soon own her body. She had no idea where the kiss was leading, but if it was all she was ever going to get from Knox, she'd take it.

As though he read her mind, he bent deeper as his other arm left her back and slid over her ass to her thighs, where he scooped her into his arms. While the night before had been hot as hell when she'd been plastered against his front with her legs wrapped around his waist, she couldn't deny that the gallant carry was equally as hot.

He turned away from the water, then halted. *Oh, God, please no. Please no. Don't stop. Please don't stop now*, she silently begged. She refused to give voice to her yearnings. If he was going to stop again, she would not put herself in this position for a third time. *He wants me... he wants this... he's got to make a move.*

Holding her breath in fear, she waited as he lifted his head and stared deeply into her eyes.

"My bed or yours?"

She blinked, his question catching her by surprise. Considering their cabins were mirror images of each other, a tiny giggle slipped out. She'd never been a giggler, but there was a first time for everything. "Um… aren't they the same?"

"It all depends."

He still held her in his arms as though she weighed nothing and yet felt like everything at the same time. Her mouth opened, then she snapped it shut, deciding to wait to see what he was going to say next.

"When I get you into bed, I want it to last all night. Make love until we're so sated, we have to sleep. And while we sleep, I'd like to be curled up with you."

His words made it hard for her to breathe, uncertain she'd ever heard anything more beautiful in her life. Certainly nothing by a gorgeous man with the most piercing blue eyes she'd ever seen, his expression so serious and sincere, rumbling the sweetest words straight to her. "That sounds like a perfect plan to me," she managed to whisper in return, sounding more like a wheeze than sexy.

"But I don't want to force myself on you," he said. "So, if you'd rather, we can head into my bed, and then, if you feel the need to leave during the night, you can."

She slowly shook her head, a smile curving her lips, tightening her arms around his neck. Holding his gaze, matching the intensity with her own, she replied, "As I said earlier, I won't be the one leaving."

Without uttering another word, he carried her through the doorway from the balcony into her room, stalking straight over to the king-size bed. He slowly released her, allowing her legs to lower until her feet touched the carpeted floor.

They stood for a few seconds, neither speaking, neither moving, both devouring each other with their eyes. Then, as though a starting gun was fired, they lurched together, hands in a flurry as though to see which of them would be the champion disrober of all times. And right now, she was determined to win.

She grabbed the bottom of her dress and shucked it over her head. Normally one to hang her clothes carefully, she didn't care that it was tossed unceremoniously to the floor, soon to be joined by his polo. She lifted her hands then halted, her eyes wide as her gaze devoured his naked torso. She'd seen it at the beach, but for some reason, in the intimacy of her room with a bed that would soon be occupied by that torso and herself, she simply gawked.

"Libby? Are you okay?" He bent slightly to peer into her eyes.

"How the hell do you get that body? It's sculpted." She reached out and dragged her fingertips over the lines, ridges, and dips of his muscles. "It's like you stepped out of a bodybuilding magazine and landed here in my room."

"How many bodybuilding magazines have you looked at?" he asked, his voice vibrating with humor.

"Don't be so smug," she cautioned, feeling his abdominal muscles quiver underneath her touch. "My brother not only had Playboy but he also had body-building magazines, determined that if he wanted to get a woman like those who posed in Playboy, he had to look like... well, like you do."

"I work out but not to get a plastic caricature of a woman. I work out for my job. For me. And if I'm lucky enough to get an honest to God gorgeous woman who looks like an all-natural beauty, laughs from the heart, cares and frets over others, and forgives with grace... in other words, you... then that's what it's all for."

Libby was no longer sure she was breathing. The effort it would take to drag oxygen into her lungs and force it back out again would divert from the words he'd just uttered that wrapped around her, enveloping her more than the embrace he'd offered earlier. After the silence dragged out, she finally managed to speak. "Wow. Um... wow."

He stepped closer, but no longer willing to waste a second before she'd be back into his arms, her hands snapped out and had his belt unbuckled with a speed that surprised even her. It had been impossible to perform the task without her knuckles grazing over the impressive length of him, and the idea that that appendage would soon meld them together caused her fingers to fumble.

It didn't appear he wasted any time to reach behind and deftly unfasten her bra and gently pull the straps from her arms. Gravity worked on her full breasts, and just as she freed his cock, her bra fell the rest of the way to the floor.

Standing in only her panties, she felt the heady sense

of power as his gaze seared over her skin and his hands reached up to cup her breasts, his thumbs circling her nipples.

"I've wanted to see you naked since the first moment I walked in on you," he confessed.

His large hands cupped her completely, and his gentle touch had her aching for more. She became aware of the need deep inside and pressed her thighs tightly together. He suddenly dropped his hands, and as her eyes flew open, she watched as he jerked his pants and boxers down and his legs kicked them to the side. Now he was the one completely naked, and she unashamedly gawked at his body. Each muscle was defined, and his cock was erect, jutting toward her, a drop of pre-cum on its tip.

"Every inch of you is beautiful," she said, her gaze worshiping.

"I think that's my line, Libby." He hooked his thumb into the top of her panties and gently pulled them down her legs.

She held onto his shoulders as she stepped each foot out, and her panties landed on top of her already-wrinkled dress. Now, both naked, she suddenly had no idea where to start.

He obviously didn't have that problem as he bent, scooped her into his arms again, and laid her on the bed. His lips kissed down her neck to each breast, tugging and sucking each nipple until she wanted to weep with need. Her core was crying for attention, and as though he could read her thoughts, or at least her body, he continued kissing down her abdomen, over her mound, then dove in like a starving man, feasting on her folds. He licked, tongued, kissed, and sucked until she writhed on the mattress, her fingers clutching the longer hair on top of his head.

Just when she felt her inner core tighten, he added a long finger deep inside and crooked it, hitting the spot that had her seeing stars. At the same time, he sucked on her clit, and fuck the stars... she saw galaxies. Crying out, her hips bucked upward as the electric vibrations jolted through her, but his assault continued until she was lying in a puddle in the middle of the bed, her body unable to move. He licked her several more times after pulling his finger from her.

He kissed his way back up her body, thrusting his tongue into her mouth, and the taste of her on his tongue almost had her begging for round two, but she was panting so hard she couldn't speak.

"You okay, babe?" his deep voice resounded.

"Guh..." she managed to utter.

He began to laugh, and she felt his mirth as it rumbled against her chest. It was the most beautiful feeling and sound she could imagine.

13

Knox couldn't remember the last time he'd laughed during sex. Maybe back in college when he'd been drinking, stumbling and fumbling around with a sorority girl. Maybe with one of his last short-term relationships, but those never ended well, and if there had been laughing, he felt sure it wasn't during sex. And sure as hell not with the occasional hookup to relieve sexual tension.

But here Libby was, not even well-fucked yet but having gotten off like a rocket with his mouth and fingers, kissing him as he'd never been kissed before, and now could barely speak. No games. No pretense. And was fuckin' adorable.

His cock was aching to slide into her slick heat, but if they did nothing more, he'd be fine. This was about her and what she needed.

"Are you going to keep staring at me, or is your cock going to get some action?" she asked.

He chuckled again, pressing his hips against hers,

eliciting a hiss from her. He buried his face in her neck, kissing the soft skin, feeling her pulse pounding underneath his lips. "Don't worry about my cock, babe. I want to take my time."

He kissed and sucked, nuzzled and licked, discovering her soft skin, the tickle points behind her knees and ribs, and was mesmerized by the little moans she emitted and held captive by her dark eyes and bright smile. She writhed underneath his weight, and the feel of her nipples pressing against his chest and the heat of her core against his cock had him almost mindless with need.

He reached over the side of the bed and snatched his pants from the floor, pulling a condom from his wallet. He shifted to his knees, but before he ripped open the foil, he needed to know exactly what she wanted.

Her gaze moved from his face to the condom in his hands, and back to his eyes. As though she understood he was handing her control, she smiled. "I know what this is, Knox. I'm not some starry-eyed girl who thinks sex comes with forever. You live and work in Maine. I live and work in Virginia. I'm not asking for anything more than tonight. After that, we'll only have one more night on the ship, and if sex with you is anything like I anticipate, I'd be a liar if I said I wasn't hoping for tomorrow night, as well."

Every word she'd uttered was exactly what he'd hoped to hear. Just sex. Parting as friends. No misunderstandings. And yet, the finality of them before they even started caused his heart to squeeze painfully. There was so much he wanted to say, so much he wanted to tell her, but even as his mind raced to plot how they could stay in contact after the cruise, he couldn't figure out how to do so without her knowing everything there was to know about him, including that he was only here as an assignment and he'd started out with her to aid in his cover. But there was no denying feelings were already forming.

Her hands lifted to his arms, squeezing slightly. "You've just been handed unencumbered sex with a naked, willing woman in her bed, telling him she has no expectations beyond tonight, and for some reason, you're hesitating."

"I just can't figure out how I got to be so lucky to meet you. To get to know you. That would be enough, Libby. But you lying here, giving me all of you, is a gift I never expected."

Her smile urged him to action, and he rolled on the condom. Lining the tip of his cock to her entrance as she lifted her knees and spread her thighs, he leaned over her and stared into her dark eyes. "Are you sure?"

She shifted upward, sheathing herself, and his eyes nearly rolled back in his head. Barely able to mumble, "I guess that's my answer," he thrust to the hilt. Her wet heat surrounded him like a glove, and he'd never felt anything so sweet in his life. They moved as one. She lifted her hips to meet his, and he kept up the rhythm while alternating thrusts both deep and shallow. He held himself off her chest with his fists planted on either side of her shoulders. Wanting to feel more of her against him, he slowly lowered his torso until his forearms were planted on either side of her head and his large hands cupped her face.

Occasionally, she'd close her eyes but then open them quickly as though she didn't want to miss anything. He felt the same, keeping his gaze pinned on her, not wanting to miss one single nuance of her expression as their bodies joined.

He had no idea what to call what they were doing. She was no fuck. And considering he planned on spending tomorrow and tomorrow night with her, she was also not a one-night stand. As their rhythm increased, all thoughts disappeared from his mind other than the feel of his cock sliding in and out of her warm, tight, slick sex. Uncertain he was going to be able to hang on much longer, a fact that shocked the shit out of him considering he had control of his body in almost all situations, he wanted her to come again.

Shifting his weight so that he was still held slightly off her chest with only one arm now, he glided his other hand down her body. Palming her breasts, tweaking her nipple, swallowing the little sounds she made, he finally reached the prize, thumbing her clit as he continued to thrust deeply.

Just as he hoped, her entire body tightened as her eyes widened before she began to quiver. Her fingers clutched his shoulders, her short nails digging small crescents into his skin. He didn't care if she left marks, he'd wear them proudly. In fact, to be marked by her would be a badge of honor. Keeping his eyes on hers, he memorized each expression that crossed her face as her body flew apart, her orgasm taking her over the edge.

As the slickness increased, he thrust harder, his balls tightened, and his lower back burned just before he roared through the most intense orgasm he'd ever experienced. Continuing until every drop had been wrung from his body, he gasped for air, wondering if he could suck enough oxygen in or would die right there in her arms. Barely able to shift to the side as he crashed half on top of her, he decided he didn't care if he lived or died as long as he was in her arms with her looking at him like she was right now.

Barely able to mumble, "I need to take care of the condom, but I don't think I can move." Her laughter met his ears, and he pretended to glare.

Her arms tightened around him, and she kissed him lightly. "I don't care if you never leave this bed."

"Be careful what you wish for."

Still holding his gaze, she slowly shook her head. Lifting her hand and cupping his jaw, she smoothed her thumb over his lips. "Anything I ever wished for just came true."

He'd never wanted to keep kissing a woman after sex. In fact, other than his few relationships, he'd never stayed in bed with a woman after sex. But this, whatever this was, was uncharted territory. Kissing her lightly, he rolled to the side and padded across the soft carpet to her bathroom. A few minutes later, he emerged to see her still lying in all her naked glory. He stopped at the bed and asked, "Do you still feel the same about me staying?"

She patted the mattress and grinned. "If you tried to leave, I'd tackle you. Considering your size, it might be one of the most unsuccessful tackles in history, but I'd certainly try."

He reached down and pulled another condom from his wallet and tossed it to the nightstand, secretly thanking his brother for the box he'd tucked into his luggage. Sliding underneath the covers, he pulled her tight, tucking her in close so that her head was resting just over his heart.

Uncertain if he'd be able to sleep with so much on his mind, she gave her weight to him as she found slumber, and he fell asleep, as well. And when the morning sun greeted them with a kiss, he still had a smile on his face considering they'd woken in the middle of the night, their bodies moving as one until they found bliss together again.

"Does anyone need more water?" Libby asked.

Knox turned toward her and grinned as she moved around her group, fussing over them, wanting to make sure they were okay.

"If I drink any more, I'm going to have to make a trip behind one of those trees over there," Sally grumped. "I prefer indoor plumbing if you don't mind!"

The others laughed, and Libby just shook her head, rolling her eyes. Knox caught her gaze and winked. He could've sworn she blushed, and he could only hope it was from the memories of what they'd done this morning in her minuscule shower. He'd never attempted shower sex before and felt sure that the small shower on a cruise ship was not the most advantageous way to begin experimenting, but one look at her body and his cock was ready to go. With her willing and able, they'd managed spectacularly.

They fell in line behind the guide, and while Mayan ruins had not been an interest to him before Mexico, after seeing them in Cozumel and now in Belize, he had to admit the subject was interesting. He still kept a sharp eye out but so far had seen nothing untoward. It looked as though DHS's concerns about something happening to Curtis were unfounded, but he wasn't going to complain. Glancing to the side at Libby's smiling face, he counted himself lucky that he was the one Mace had chosen for the assignment.

"Many of the stones that were part of the original structures were reused for residential construction in modern times. The ancient site did not come to the attention of archeologists until nineteen sixty-three. But you can see much of what remains would have made an impressive sight in its original state."

The group continued to follow the guide to a large stone pyramid. "This is the largest of the Altun Ha temple pyramids. You might recognize a drawing of the structure as the logo of our leading brand of beer."

His last comment was met with chuckles from the group. "This is so fascinating," Libby said as she looked up to Knox. "I've never traveled outside the United States although I've always wanted to. These are places that I've read about but never dreamed I'd have the chance to visit."

It was on the tip of his tongue to tell her that he

would take her wherever she wanted to go, love to show her whatever sights she wanted to see, but with tonight being the last night on the ship as it headed back north to Norfolk, he knew he couldn't make any promises beyond the cruise. *But at least we'll have tonight and tomorrow on the ship. We won't dock until the afternoon.* Already planning to make the most of that time, he smiled but remained silent, unable to make promises he couldn't keep. *But could I? Just because we live in different places doesn't mean we couldn't continue to see each other.* The thought of never seeing her again sent an ache throughout his chest.

Shaking out of his musings, he focused on their fellow travelers, still only seeing tourists around. As Libby and he caught up with the others, he looked up at the pyramid, his mind going to the stories that Walker told of when he met Julie, now his wife, at a Mayan temple in Mexico.

"The Altun Ha was occupied from about nine hundred B.C. to one thousand A.D. There is a tomb that contained the remains of an adult male who was interred with a jade and shell necklace, jade ear flares, a pair of pearls, five pottery vessels, and other shells. There are many other offerings that were similar to what is found in tombs in the Mayan ruins in Mexico, implying associations between the two groups."

"Knox!"

The alarm in Libby's voice jerked his attention back to her. She grabbed his arm and leaned up on her toes. He bent to hear what she needed to whisper.

"I don't think Roger looks very good."

His gaze shot over to Roger, who was walking with the other men but seemed to be sweating profusely. "I'm going to move up and walk with them. Make your way to the guide and tell him that we need to start heading back."

Nodding, she hurried forward to the others, and he watched as she whispered to the guide, who nodded. He walked to the men, keeping a smile on his face, and said, "I know the tour was going to last a little longer, but our guide is about finished with everything. Since I don't think we're going to be climbing to the tops of any of the pyramids, we should start heading back to the bus."

He was prepared in case any of the others were going to complain, but the two-hour-long guided tour seemed to have been plenty for their group. As they began to make their way to the parking lot, he managed to maneuver between Roger and Curtis, chatting amiably while keeping his eyes open. The bus driver had the bus running and the air conditioning going, and while he didn't want to alarm anyone, he pulled Curtis to the side as the others boarded and said, "Keep an eye on Roger."

Curtis nodded in understanding. "Will do."

It didn't take long for them to make their way back to Belize City, the bus driver taking them directly to the port where they would catch the boat back to the ship. Breathing a sigh of relief as soon as they landed, Knox could hardly wait to call Mace to report that the mission was almost over with no problems for Curtis.

He and Libby escorted Roger to the ship doctor's office again. After a few minutes, she turned to him and said, "Why don't you go back to the others? Make sure everyone is okay and see what they want to do about dinner. The past two nights, everyone has enjoyed dinner somewhere other than the dining room. If they'd like to go to the dining room, that would be good. If some of them want to just rest after today's excursion, that's fine, too. I'll stay with Roger and call you when we're ready to come back to the rooms, as well."

He lifted his hand and cupped her jaw, seeing where the sun had kissed her cheeks. "Are you sure? Wouldn't you rather be the one who goes back, and I can stay with Roger?"

She leaned her cheek into his palm, closing her eyes for a few seconds. When she opened them, she smiled. "I think it's best if I'm here with him. It still feels like my responsibility." Shrugging, she added, "I want to be here for him."

Bending, he kissed her lightly. "Okay. Let me know when you guys are ready to head back to the room. Do you want to eat dinner in the dining room or alone—"

"Alone," she rushed. She blinked as though surprised at her response. "That is if you'd like to."

"Definitely alone," he said, drawing another smile from her. Kissing her again, he breathed her in.

An hour later, the text from her nearly halted his breath. Barely able to call out to Curtis that he'd be back, he ran up to the top deck just in time to see her climb on board a helicopter. Her face was pinched with worry, and he could see tears streak down her cheeks as she turned and waved toward him.

14

Libby stood in the hall just outside of Roger's hospital room. As soon as the ship's doctor determined that Roger might be having a heart attack, he had radioed for an emergency helicopter flight to a private hospital in Belize City.

Now, as she waited for Knox to arrive, she'd just finished talking to the cardiologist, Dr. Neal.

"Are you sure?"

"Yes, Ms. Cook. From our tests, it looks like he had a mild heart attack, a non-ST elevation myocardial infarction. We'll do more tests this evening and tomorrow morning. I know you've spoken to his son in the United States, and if all goes well, he should be able to fly him back home in a couple of days."

She grabbed his hand, shaking it, tears filling her eyes. "Oh, thank you, Dr. Neal—"

"Libby!"

She turned at the shout of her name, her heart

leaping at the sight of Knox stalking toward her with Curtis following in his wake. Rushing forward, she crashed into him, burrowing into his strong embrace. She felt his lips on top of her head. Opening her eyes, she spied Curtis' worried expression.

Pulling herself together, she said, "Roger is going to be okay. This is Dr. Neal, his cardiologist."

Curtis and Dr. Neal stepped to the side and then disappeared into Roger's room.

"Babe, how are you?"

Letting out a long breath, she shook her head. "It all happened so fast. I had no idea that Dr. Hull had called for the helicopter as soon as he looked at Roger. While I was waiting for them to do some kind of evaluation, the helicopter was already on its way. By the time I was told and given permission to travel with him, I barely had a chance to text you."

"What's the diagnosis?"

"He said it's a mild heart attack, but from their first tests, they think he'll be able to travel in a couple of days. They'll do some more procedures and tests tonight and tomorrow. If all goes well, we can fly back in a couple of days."

He jerked, and she leaned back further to look into his face.

"*We?*"

Scrunching her brow, she asked, "I'm sorry... what is *we?*"

"You said *we*. You said *we* can fly back in a couple of days."

Nodding, she said, "Yes. Roger and I will fly back in

a couple of days. They said that his son has already started contacting medical evacuation planes that can take him back to Norfolk."

"But Libby, babe, I don't want you to stay here. You need to come back to the ship with Curtis and me. We'll make sure everything is taken care of for Roger—"

Her hand landed on his arm. "Knox, honey, I can't go. I need to stay here with him. It's my job. It's what I need to do. As much as I want to spend the last twenty-four hours on the ship with you, I have no choice. Or rather, I can't make that choice."

She stared as a muscle in his jaw ticked, his mouth tight. He turned and walked several feet away, his hands on his hips, his chin dropped to his chest. She felt torn, both wanting to rush to him to hold on to what she thought might be more than a shipboard romance and head into Roger's room to make sure he was taken care of.

A noise at Roger's door drew her attention away from Knox, and Curtis appeared. He moved to her, pulling her into a hug and patting her back. "Oh, Libby, I can't thank you enough for getting Roger to medical care as quickly as you did."

Tears pricked her eyes again, and she just nodded. As his arms dropped and he stepped away, Knox walked back over, but his expression was just as tight as earlier.

"Libby, we need to plan," he said.

She nodded but had no clue what plan he was referring to.

He grimaced, scrubbing his hand over his face

before leading her to the side of the hall. "I can't stay here with you," he began.

"Knox, I don't expect you to—"

"Let me finish 'cause we don't have a lot of time."

She nodded, pressing her lips together.

"I need to get Curtis back onto the ship, and I need to make sure... we need to get back to Norfolk. But then I can arrange a flight back here."

Libby shook her head. "There's no need. You dock late tomorrow in Norfolk. Roger and I will probably fly back the next morning. We'll be back in Virginia Beach less than a day after the ship gets there." His face twisted with emotions she couldn't define but she felt his anguish. Rushing, she said, "I'll be fine. I'll stay here in the hospital. I won't leave. I can snooze in his room and eat in the cafeteria."

"Christ, this is so fucked up." Heaving a sigh, he reached his hand into his pocket and pulled out something silver that glistened in his hand. "I... I bought this in a gift shop. I was going to give it to you today."

She glanced down to see a small chain with a silver charm of a lighthouse. "Oh, Knox, it's so pretty. Is this one of the lighthouses nearby?"

"Um... I don't know. But I'd like it if you'd wear it at all times. It will hopefully make you think of me."

She smiled, touched by the gift. "Of course, I'll wear it." She slipped it over her head and let the necklace settle against her skin.

His gaze dropped to the charm, and his face twisted again, almost in anguish. He opened his mouth, then closed it several times. Finally, he growled, "Goddammit! I should have thought to bring your things, but I thought you'd be getting back on the ship."

"Knox, look at me," she ordered, uncertain where his anger was coming from. Clutching his thick biceps, she stood on her toes to get closer to his face. He acquiesced, and she focused on his blue eyes. "I will be fine. You have to get back. I understand that. You have a job and a life and can't just hang around here with me. But you're so caring and honorable. You want to make it all better." As soon as those words left her lips, his grimace deepened, his face hardening into marble. "Seriously," she continued, "I know you have to go. And… maybe… maybe when I get back to Virginia Beach—"

"I want to see you." His words were firm, almost clipped as he spoke. Stepping closer, he bent to where his face was just in front of hers. "You call me and let me know what's happening."

"Knox, you know how bad reception is on the ship—"

"Don't worry about that. I've got people that can help get messages through. Just don't worry about anything except staying safe. And when you land at the Norfolk airport, I'll be there."

Her heart pounded at the ferocity of his voice and the intense way his gaze held her captive. All the crazy emotions that had been swirling for hours since Dr. Hull first exclaimed that Roger would be flown off the ship by helicopter now fell away, exposing one thought overtaking all others… *He wants to see me again!*

A movement to the side caught her attention, and she saw Curtis standing nearby, his face scrunched with what she was sure was concern for Roger. Knowing the ship would soon be leaving the port, she looked back at Knox. "I'll walk you two downstairs."

Knox wrapped his arm around her, and three entered the elevator to the first floor. As they stepped just outside the hospital lobby, the warm, tropical air hit her, but it was nothing like the heat that enveloped her when Knox surrounded her in his embrace. Clinging together tightly, bodies pressed together in an almost desperate need to connect, she blocked out the rest of the world. Nothing existed but she and him, what they'd shared, and now, hopefully, what they'd continue to share once she was back. While she'd told him the previous night that she'd take whatever she could get and had meant it, standing in his embrace right now, she knew that if she had the possibility of more, she wanted it.

She leaned back to look up, uncertain what to say, but quickly discovered words weren't necessary. His head was already descending, and his mouth landed on hers. This kiss was different. Still full of heat, but this time it felt like a brand. Still full of emotion but now felt desperate. It was claiming. Owning. Possessing. And she wasn't afraid.

They separated, but he kept his forehead pressed to hers, his large hands cupping her face. "Babe, we didn't get a chance to say everything that needed to be said. And it's fuckin' killing me, but I know I've got to get Curtis out of here." He leaned back a little bit further so that his eyes held hers. "What we started as isn't where we are now. What we are now is a helluva lot more than what either of us expected. If we'd had another day, I would've had a chance to have told you everything. But now, just know that you need to stay safe, stay in contact with me, and I'll meet you as soon as you land. If something happens and you can't leave after tomorrow, you wait for me, and I promise to come back for you."

She simply nodded, unable to find the words to assure him that she would do all he asked, including wait for him, knowing at this moment that she'd promise to wait forever for him if that was what he wanted.

He kissed her hard again as she clung to him, tears filling her eyes. Finally, tearing away, he cursed under his breath before calling out to Curtis, "I'll get a cab. Say goodbye now."

With a last look, his face full of anguish, he stormed off to the side of the entrance where the cabs lined up.

Curtis came to her, hugging her once again. "I'm so sorry, Libby. I feel like this is all my fault."

She patted his back, his words surprising him. Leaning away, she peered into his eyes. "Your fault? What on earth makes you say that?"

"Knox having to leave and not stay here with you. I know his contract says he has to stay with me until I get back, and I know if it wasn't for that, he wouldn't leave."

"Contract?" She tilted her head to the side. "What contract?"

"There's no reason not to say now, but I have to be back in D.C. the day after tomorrow, and with Knox as my security detail, he's under contract to see me safely back home in time to make my next trip out."

Her head jerked slightly, his words confusing. She knew Curtis still worked for the government in some important capacity with his knowledge of diseases, but her mind had trouble following up on what he was saying about Knox. "I thought his father was a friend of yours."

"Oh, that was the cover story we came up with as to why he was hanging with us," Curtis said, smiling softly. "He was lucky you were with us, as well. Not only did he get to spend time with you, but it made it seem even more normal to be with a beautiful woman than to just hang with a bunch of old geezers."

She jerked again, this time with her whole body. "I… I was part of some cover you two concocted?"

"Yes," Curtis confirmed, then frowned. "Well, only at first. Then, I know that boy has been falling for you. I told him earlier that he needed to go after you."

"But still… at the beginning… he was lying to me?"

Curtis' frown set the wrinkles in his face deeper. "Well, when you put it like that, it doesn't sound very good. But he had no choice… it's his job, you see. But as soon as we'd dock in Norfolk, I have no doubt that he was going to make sure you stayed in his life. You understand that, right?"

She nodded, a fake smile plastered on her face and her mind struggling to catch up with everything Curtis had told her.

She barely had time to look up as Knox came

jogging over. "Curtis! I've got someone who says he can get us to the port in less than ten minutes."

Curtis bent and kissed her cheek, but her focus was pinned on Knox as he stalked closer and grabbed her, pulling her tightly into his embrace. Cold had seeped in where before there had only been heat. Doubt now replaced certainty, and anger began to fill in the crevices where her respect for his honor had been so solid.

His hands slid from her back to cup her jaws again, and he kissed her. She didn't protest because the truth was she wanted this last kiss from him.

"Goodbye, babe," he mumbled against her lips. "I'll see you just as soon as I can." He leaned up and held her gaze, as always, his blue eyes piercing deep into her. She saw a question move through them as he stared, but was grateful there was no time for him to give voice to that concern.

"Goodbye," she whispered, swallowing back the tears.

"Fuck," he cursed under his breath as the muscles in his jaw tightened.

Her lips trembled as they attempted to smile. "Go. Please. I need to get back up to Roger."

The mention of Roger seemed to be the only thing that spurred Knox on. With a final kiss, he turned and jogged to the taxi, and she stood, watching as it pulled away from the hospital. The last thing she saw was his face turned to the window, those blue eyes still holding her captive.

On wooden legs, she made her way back into the

hospital and up the elevator. Inside Roger's room, she sat in the chair alone, having been told by a nurse that he was having one of the procedures performed and would be brought back to his room soon. She lost track of time, her mind churning, trying to make sense of everything she'd experienced, now viewed through the filter of Curtis' words.

Was everything a cover? He said he was a pilot for a private company, but he provides security? His father was never a friend of Curtis'. It gave him a good reason for being with the group. And me? Showing interest in me was part of the cover for being with the group? If so, he wouldn't have had to sleep with me. So, was that just for fun? Or real?

She stood and walked over to the window, rubbing her aching head. She had to admit that while she'd been willing to accept that they were just for fun, by the time they'd gotten to this morning and he'd vowed that they were the start of something, she'd believed him. *But how can you start something real based on a lie?* Her fingers found the lighthouse necklace, and she held it in her palm.

She looked out the window and realized Roger's room had a view of the port, and in the distance were several cruise ships. It wasn't hard to pick out the one she'd been on as it was much smaller than many of the others. And now it was moving away, taking with it the rest of her group. And the man she'd fallen in love with. A man she didn't really know at all.

Knox stood on the deck as the ship moved out to sea. His gaze was locked onto Belize City, and now that he knew where the hospital was, he could pick it out as one of the taller buildings. Knowing he'd left Libby there, his gut clenched, and his fingers curled into fists. Emotions he'd never felt before slammed into him, one right after the other, knocking the breath right out of him.

Regret. Regret that his mission had made it so that the reason they'd first met was a lie. Regret that he hadn't been able to tell her the truth. Regret that the time he'd hoped to spend with her during the next twenty-four hours would solidify the start of them so that by the time they landed in Norfolk, he'd be able to explain why he was on the cruise and how he now wanted more with her. Regret that his very being cried out to protect the woman he cared for and yet was being forced to leave her side. Regret mixed with embarrassment that he was still on a luxury cruise while she was going to sleep in a plastic chair next to Roger's bed.

He wanted to drop his head so that he wouldn't witness Belize City disappear into the horizon. Keeping his gaze trained on the now-fuzzy building in the distance where he'd left his heart, he refused to look away until the last second.

"I figured I'd find you up here, Knox."

With Belize City now out of sight, he turned to see Curtis standing nearby. Unable to think of anything to say, he simply nodded.

"But don't worry. I squared everything with Libby so she'd understand why you couldn't stay with her."

Giving a slight head jerk, he stared at Curtis. "You squared everything?"

"I figured since we were on the last leg of the cruise and nothing had happened to me, it would be okay if I let her know that you were here for my protection." Knox's eyes bugged, but Curtis continued. "I let her know that your company had a contract to keep me safe until I could make it back in time for my meeting in Washington. She asked about your dad and me being friends, and I confessed that that was your cover that we'd come up with." He chuckled and shook his head. "I let her know that she was fortunate that she was with our group because that gave you even more reason to hang around a bunch of old geezers as part of your cover."

Knox's knees threatened to give out on him, and his hands snapped to the side, his fingers wrapping around the deck rail. His chest depressed as the air rushed from his lungs, and for a few seconds, he felt so lightheaded he was surprised he didn't pitch over the rail and into the water. As it dawned on him that Libby now knew he'd lied to her since the beginning, he figured she probably wished he would end up at the bottom of the ocean.

Curtis leaned over and patted his arm. "You don't have to thank me for making things right with Libby. It's been my honor to have you pull the security detail, so returning the favor and letting her know that you didn't have any choice but to leave her was an easy thing to do."

With that, Curtis smiled and headed back into the ship, leaving Knox still clinging to the rail. His head jerked around toward the horizon where Belize City had been, now faded away. And the woman he knew he'd fallen for was not only gone from sight but for all he knew never wanted to see him again.

15

An hour later, Dr. Neal came in to check on Roger, who was sleeping peacefully. He smiled at Libby and walked over to her. "I see you're still here. You must be tired."

"I don't really have anywhere to go, so I hope it's all right for me to stay with him."

"Yes, but I can't imagine that it's very comfortable. I'm sure the hospital didn't mention it since you are not listed as family, but a resort that's a few blocks away allows traveling patients' family members to stay at a very low rate. I've been there with my family, and it's nice. You could catch a cab and stay there for tonight. It would help you to rest, and then you can be right back here tomorrow to find out what flight details Mr. Whitcomb's son has arranged."

She sucked in her lips, uncertainty filling her as she cut her eyes over to Roger sleeping.

Dr. Neal stepped closer, drawing her gaze back to him. "Ms. Cook, really, I insist. You are no good to him if you are exhausted."

Finally nodding, she smiled tremulously. "You're right. Okay, I'll do it. And thank you so much for the information."

He wrote down the name and address of the resort then handed it to her. "Get a good night's sleep, and then come back first thing in the morning if you like. At least you'll already have a room for tomorrow night to rest before the two of you fly out the next day."

With nothing else to do, she headed down to the lobby and through the main doors of the hospital again, remembering when she was here earlier with Knox. Glancing at the spot they'd stood to say goodbye, she could still feel his arms wrapped around her and his lips pressed against her forehead. Sighing, she was glad to see taxis lined up available. Giving the address to the driver, she found that Dr. Neal was right, and within ten minutes, she was in the lobby of a beautiful resort with beach access. Stunned at the low rate, she was even more surprised to discover that it was a beautiful room.

After checking out the facilities, she went back to the resort lobby, heading directly to the little shops that were part of the resort. Knowing she was paying tourist prices, she bought several T-shirts along with a full skirt in a floral pattern and another pair of shorts, thrilled to find that in the personal section of the store, she was able to pick up some panties along with toiletries. Back in her room, she luxuriated with a long shower, trying to focus on everything except Knox. As she washed, her fingers ran over the necklace around her neck, the lighthouse charm warm against her skin, and the memory of their shower sex that morning continued to steal into her thoughts.

At first uncertain if she could choke down food after the day she'd had, she looked at the room service menu. Perhaps it was the pictures and descriptions of the delicious offerings, but her stomach let her know that skipping lunch was one thing but skipping dinner also would not be acceptable. Ordering room service, she thought of the breakfast that morning on the ship with Knox and sighed for the millionth time.

She thought of walking down to the beach, but Knox's warnings about resort security stayed firmly in her mind. Making sure her door was locked with the chair underneath the knob and the windows securely latched, she piled up on her bed.

Looking at her phone, she spied numerous missed calls, phone messages, and texts. All from Knox. With her fingers hovering over the keyboard, she hesitated. Squeezing her eyes shut, she tried to ignore the ache in her chest. Finally, with a heavy sigh, she flopped back on her pillows, her phone still in her hand.

Knox sat at the desk in his cabin, letting the phone ring continuously, gritting his teeth at the voicemail greeting.

You've reached the voice mailbox of Libby. Leave a message, and I'll call you back.

The same fuckin' greeting he'd gotten every single time he'd called for the past hour. Finally sending a text, he jabbed at the keys on his phone. **You promised you'd talk to me. I know what you think, but you've got to give me a chance to explain. Please.**

Scrubbing his hand over his face, he leaned back in the chair, sighing heavily. Finally, he reached for his laptop and opened it, logging in, alerting Josh that he needed to talk.

After a moment, Pippa's face came online. "Hey, Knox. Josh is talking to Mace, but he'll be right back." Pippa was Josh's fiancée, a new employee at LSI.

"Is everything okay?"

"Yes, with the mission, but I need assistance."

The smile on her face immediately dropped with the seriousness of his words. In a few seconds, Drew's face appeared, and he knew anyone else in the room was watching, as well.

"Bro, talk to me," Drew ordered, his easy going demeanor now replaced with concern.

Suddenly self-conscious, he wasn't sure how to explain the situation, but not one to mince words, he jumped in. "Our client is fine. We've left Belize City, and as I reported, there have been no incidents or problems. As I've also previously reported, I've taken on the responsibility of the other ten people in our client's group. Roger Whitcomb suffered a heart problem this morning and was flown to a private hospital in Belize City. It turned out to be not serious, and they are keeping him tonight and possibly tomorrow for observation and testing. The doctors there have been in contact with his son in the United States and are making arrangements to have him flown back to the

States the day after tomorrow. Olivia Cook, the woman that was traveling with this group from Windsor Village, has elected to stay in Belize City with Roger and accompany him back to the States."

Drew nodded, and in the background, Knox could see that Mace had slid into a seat next to his brother. "Understood," Drew said. "You said you needed assistance? Do you need us to coordinate to make sure that Roger's son is able to procure the medical flight?"

Drew's willingness to jump in and help without question filled Knox with gratitude. "Thanks, man, and that wouldn't be a bad idea. But it goes deeper with that. It has to do with Libby—um, Olivia."

Drew's eyes widened, but all he said was, "Libby? What do you need?"

It was a tribute to all Keepers' ability to know when something was serious that kept his brother from ragging on him. Jumping in with both feet, he continued. "She was cover to begin with... gave me an extra excuse to be with the group of seniors. But she became more. Only problem is, she didn't know that she started as a cover. Now she knows, and I didn't have a chance to explain how things are different. The ship continues to Norfolk, where we'll dock about two p.m. tomorrow. I'll see that Curtis is safely on the bus provided for the Windsor Village group. I'll stay in Norfolk to meet Libby and Roger when they're flown in. If for some reason Roger and Libby can't get back, I'll fly down to Belize to get them."

"I know you're worried," Cole said. As one of the latest Keepers Mace had hired along with Knox, the two men had bonded. "If you need me or Drew to fly to Norfolk, we can easily assist."

"Just be ready," he advised. "Hopefully, all goes well, and they'll be back on schedule."

"That works," Mace said. "You can take as much time as you need. I assume you made sure she was safe before you had to leave?"

"She's staying at the hospital. It's not fuckin' luxury, but she'll be safe. I gave her a lighthouse charm before we left, but I have no idea if she'll wear it now. She doesn't know what it is."

"I'll run a check to see if it's at the hospital," Josh called out.

"Appreciate it."

Drew added, "I'll get hold of Roger's son and find out what he might need for contracting with a medical flight."

"Believe me, I've tried to think of everything before I even called. I'm still trying to get hold of her, but so far, she's not calling or texting. I don't know if it's because something is going on with Roger or she's upset and pissed at me. Neither is a good situation, and I'll feel better when I can finally talk to her."

Bray, their resident medic, moved so that his face was in the camera's view. "Chances are that a medical flight from Belize City will only make it as far as the Keys before stopping unless it originated from the States to begin with. I'll check with Roger's son to see if the company he hires can only get them to Norfolk."

For the first time in hours since the nightmare

began, Knox felt a sense of rightness. "I can't thank you all enough."

The others disappeared from view, leaving only Drew and Mace in the camera. "Anything you need, Knox, for the mission that you were assigned or the new mission with Libby, it's yours." With that, Mace offered a chin lift and stood, walking away, leaving only the face of his brother staring at him.

New mission with Libby. He hadn't even thought of it in those terms, but Mace instinctively knew.

"So, it happened," Drew said, uncharacteristically soft-spoken.

Not caring if the others were still in hearing distance, he nodded. "Yeah, it did. But bro, I think I fucked up badly."

"You were in a tough position, Knox. Don't beat yourself up for it. Look, she can stay at the hospital and stay safe until you guys can get back together. Once that happens, I know you can make it right. If her feelings are the same, you guys will be able to move past the subterfuge of how you met."

He stared at his brother, his lips twitching before they both chuckled aloud. From behind, in the room, he heard Babs' voice.

"Subterfuge! I didn't even know my husband knew a word that big! Flyboy, you got it going on, babe!"

Now, both chuckling with the sounds of others joining in, he said his goodbyes. Disconnecting, he closed his laptop, letting out a heavy sigh. Things were not right yet, but with this group of Keepers behind them, he had a feeling they would be.

Letting out a sigh of relief, he stood and walked through the doorway and onto his balcony. The gate was still open between their rooms, and his feet took him to her side. Looking out over the water, he gripped the rail and closed his eyes. *Was it just this morning that I stood right here with her in my arms after making love during the night? Was it just this morning that I knew for sure that my heart was involved?*

He turned and walked through the sliding door into her cabin. Her clothes were neatly hung in the closet. They'd left the 'Do Not Disturb' sign on her door because she'd told him that when they got back, she wanted to smell him on her sheets. He walked over to the bed and lifted the pillow her head had rested on last night while she was tucked in his arms. Her scent surrounded him. *Stay safe, babe. Stay safe for me.*

His chest ached, and he grabbed her suitcase, desperately needing something to do. He carefully went through everything in the room and packed all her belongings. Determined to reunite her with them as soon as he could, he carried them back into his cabin. Finally, lying down on his lonely, king-size bed, his mind was filled with her.

His phone vibrated with a message, and he looked down, expecting to see Drew's name. Instead, seeing it was from Libby, he almost dropped his phone in his haste to read her text.

At Fort George Resort. Hospital arranged. Locked in for the night. Libby

Heart racing, he couldn't remember being this anxious ever before, not even behind the instruments of his first special ops flight into Afghanistan. He typed several responses, deleting each one. He finally decided to keep it simple but hoped it conveyed his thoughts.

Miss you more than you can imagine. Glad you're secure. Stay in touch and stay safe. I will see you soon. Knox

He knew it wasn't much, but at the moment, he'd take anything he could get and didn't give a fuck how desperate that made him sound.

16

Where the hell is the cafeteria? Libby had wandered for several minutes down halls that all looked alike, searching for the hospital cafeteria. It was late afternoon, and once again, she hadn't eaten since breakfast at the resort. She'd thought about going back there but wanted to stay with Roger as long as possible.

He had come back from another test, a little groggy but smiling as Dr. Neal explained that everything looked good with his heart. She was there to hear his advice for Roger. "While I want to keep you one more day to be sure you're ready to travel and I advise you see your cardiologist as soon as you get back home, you should be able to leave here tomorrow. Your son is working with the hospital outpatient coordinator to get the medical flight arrangements for you to travel back to the United States."

With that good news, Libby had kissed Roger's cheek and told him to rest while she located the cafeteria to get a bite to eat. While walking to the elevator, her thoughts had slid to Knox although she had to admit he was never far from her thoughts at any time. But now, she realized that they were docking in Norfolk. *He'd said he would wait for me there. Will he? Do I want him to? Will I be able to believe what he tells me?*

Lost in thought, she'd gotten on the elevator and pushed the button to go down to the cafeteria floor. The doors opened, and she stepped out, turning to the left and starting down the hall. In typical hospital fashion, the scrubbed and waxed tiled floor gleamed and the cinderblock walls were painted a pale blue, but this floor obviously had no patient rooms. There were doors lining the sides, and as she passed by a few that were opened, she could see offices or what appeared to be labs but no people.

After wandering down several empty halls, she became turned around, uncertain where she was. The normally bustling hospital was strangely quiet on this floor. Finally, seeing a door that was barely cracked open and hearing voices, she walked forward, hoping someone could direct her to where she could find the cafeteria.

As she approached, she lifted her hand to knock on the doorframe since the door was almost shut and didn't want to be presumptuous by just stepping inside. The voices coming from the room were low but still distinct.

"How many kidneys will we get this week?" a man asked.

The strange question caused her feet to halt and her hand to stop in mid-air before landing on the door frame. Not intending to eavesdrop, she still waited to see if it was a conversation that she should interrupt to ask for directions or should keep wandering.

"Four scheduled. Cost is low. They will take minimum." This voice was a woman's, and Libby wondered how many people were inside.

A chuckle sounded. "And we get maximum," the man said. Another chuckle joined in.

"There are a few more possibilities. Two surgeries where a kidney could be taken, also."

It sounded like just two people, and she hesitated to interrupt a conversation about patients or surgeries. She started to turn away, then stopped, indecision filling her. *Oh, good grief, I can find the cafeteria myself.* Turning, their next words halted her steps.

"What about the expatriate with no family? We could harvest everything from him and make a fortune."

"No, he won't do. The hospital was contacted by a relative just this morning. If they *conveniently* die, their relatives will want their body and then possibly ask for an autopsy. We can't afford discovery."

"Damn." A sigh was heard. "Anyone else?"

"There is an expatriate coming in for a heart procedure, and the hospital has not determined any family as of yet. If that remains so, all organs could be harvested."

"The heart alone would be worth a million in American dollars."

"Depending on what we could harvest, it could be several million in total. But even the clients coming in to get paid for a kidney, we can get close to a million for all three together."

Libby stifled a gasp then slapped her fingers against her lips. *Millions? Harvested? Conveniently die?* As the overheard words being thrown around so casually finally penetrated, she realized what the two people inside the room might be discussing. *Are they selling organs? Oh, my God!* She knew that in some countries, the poor and desperate would sell a kidney for money, but the idea that someone in the hospital would cause death to sell organs caused her legs to threaten to give out. Leaning against the wall next to the door, her heart raced. The fear of being discovered in the hall threatened to choke her as her breath stuck in her lungs. Keeping her fingers pressed to her now-quivering lips, she tried to soften the sound of her breathing.

"Fool! You didn't close the door all the way when you came in."

Her eyes flew open in fright. Backing slowly from the door before turning, she hurried as silently as she could around the corner. Still on the floor where each hall looked the same, she continued to tip-toe-run until she came to the elevator that had brought her to this nightmare. Continually looking to the side as she pushed the button, she thought she heard footsteps approaching, but it might've been the pounding of her heart.

Just as she thought she'd faint from the lack of oxygen, the doors glided open, and she rushed in, whirled around, and punched the floor that she knew Roger's room was on. The doors closed, and she slumped against the wall, her legs threatening to give out from underneath her as she sucked in a gasp of air.

The elevator seemed to take forever although it was only a few seconds before it stopped and several people got on. Trying to appear innocuous, she kept her eyes on the doors in typical elevator behavior of avoiding looking at anyone.

As soon as the elevator opened, she rushed out, never so glad to see the hustle and bustle of a regular hospital wing. Making her way to Roger's room, she was glad he was sleeping, afraid that she wouldn't be able to mask her fright. Slumping into the chair next to his bed, she pressed her trembling fingers against her lips again.

Wondering if she dared to report what she heard, she realized she had no idea who in the hospital might be party to what was being discussed. *And I'm a foreigner. Just a traveler with no rights in this country. What if no one believes me?* As much as she hated to remain silent, fear slithered through her veins.

Closing her eyes, the image of Knox filled her mind. Strong. Capable. A protector. That was the Knox she knew. But now, she also knew that he worked in security, a fact that he'd kept from her, as well as used her as cover. But he was a man who'd know exactly what to do. As much as she wanted to be angry with him, she wished he was here.

The need to walk, to run, to escape filled her. Standing quickly, she decided to get away from the hospital and go back to the resort. At least there, she could be away from the claustrophobia that made the confines of the room close in. As she started out the door, she ran into someone just entering. Squeaking in surprise, she looked up to see Dr. Neal. "Oh! I'm so sorry!"

He smiled and shook his head. "Please, no apology necessary." He looked over her head. "I see he's still sleeping. That's to be expected after the procedure this morning. He should be fine to leave tomorrow morning." Peering back down at her, he continued, "Where are you off to in such a hurry?"

"I thought I'd go back to the resort. Since Roger is resting, I can do the same and be ready to go in the morning." She lifted her hand and felt his fingers wrap around hers. "I can't thank you enough for everything you've done."

He smiled and nodded. "It was my pleasure, Ms. Cook. I hope you rest well this evening."

He continued to the nurses' station as she stepped into the hall. She looked around but saw nothing different. Patients being wheeled. Nurses walking in and out of rooms. Family members doing the same. For a moment, it was as though the conversation she'd witnessed earlier was all a dream, or rather, a nightmare. *But I know what I heard.*

Hurrying to the elevator, she was glad to get in with a group of others, most exiting on the first floor. She moved with them through the lobby, and just before she exited the hospital, she stopped with a strange sense that someone was watching her. Glancing around, she saw nothing suspicious. *I can relax when I get back to my room.* Rushing out, she hailed a taxi, breathing easier when it let her out at the resort.

With so many people in the resort lobby, she felt

anonymous and safe. Stopping at one of the restaurants in the food court, she ordered room service to be delivered, then walked down the short palm and floral-lined path to her building. Once inside her room, she locked the door and double-checked the windows. Looking at the clock on the nightstand, she felt sure Knox and the others were now docked and off the ship. She wished she'd had the presence of mind to have asked Cynthia to gather her belongings from her room. *Surely, someone thought of that.* As soon as that crossed her mind, she knew exactly who would have thought of her things: Knox.

She walked to her bed and turned, falling backward. Staring up at the ceiling fan as it slowly turned, she tried to sort through the tumultuous thoughts slamming into her in the cacophony of voices that were crowding her mind.

A knock on the door had her bolting upright, her heart pounding. Groaning, she rolled her eyes. "You're being ridiculous!" she said aloud to herself. "Nobody saw you. Nobody's after you. Nobody even knows you know anything!" Grabbing some money for a tip, she stalked to the door.

With her hand on the door's deadbolt, she still hesitated in spite of the words she'd just told herself. Peeking through the security hole, she saw one of the servers with a rolling cart. *Of course, if this was a movie, the heroine would throw open the door only to have the server be a bad guy in disguise.* Dropping her chin to her chest, she shook her head. *Bad guy? Jesus, I'm losing it!*

Opening the door, unable to keep from using her

foot to stop it just in case she needed to, the bright-faced, young server smiled at her. "Room service, Ms. Cook?"

"Yes, thank you so much. Um… I'll roll it in if you don't mind." Handing the tip to the server, whose smile widened even further, she waited until they had walked away before rolling the cart into the room, quickly closing and locking the door. It didn't matter how much she reminded herself that she was in no danger, she couldn't help the desire to secure the room.

The scent of stewed chicken with beans and rice enticed her to lift the domes and sniff in appreciation. Her stomach rumbled its distress that she hadn't found the cafeteria earlier. Patting her belly and talking as though to an old friend, she said, "You and I both wish I'd found the cafeteria."

Sitting at the table near the window, she enjoyed the view through the palm trees toward the white-sand beach. Thoughts of Knox filled her again, memories of their short time together on the beach in Costa Rica. As she ate slowly, enjoying each morsel, she wished he was there with her. Crinkling her brow, she shook her head. *What does that mean that I wish for a man who'd lied to me?*

Her experience with someone working in security was limited to books, television, and movies, but she wasn't ignorant to how important it was to protect the client at all costs. She pulled her foot up and placed it in the chair seat, resting her chin on her knee. Crunching on the fried tortillas, she licked the crumbs from her lips as she continued to muse. What was it Curtis said? *"I know that boy has been falling for you."*

The way Knox held her face when he kissed her. The way he linked fingers with her, their arms pressed into the mattress as their bodies joined. The way he held her gaze when his cock slid slowly into her. The way the blue of his eyes darkened just before he came.

Her breath caught in her throat as his words slammed into her. *"Babe, we didn't get a chance to say everything that needed to be said. And it's fuckin' killing me, but I know I've got to get Curtis out of here. What we started as isn't where we are now. What we are now is a helluva lot more than what either of us expected. If we'd had another day, I would've had a chance to tell you everything. But now, just know that you need to stay safe, stay in contact with me, and I'll meet you as soon as you land. If something happens and you can't leave after tomorrow, you wait for me, and I promise to come back for you."*

Sitting up straight, her chest heaved as her heart leaped. "I may have started out as part of his cover, but we made love, not just fucked." Hearing the words spoken aloud, she sucked in a long, cleansing breath before letting it out slowly. She had no idea what tomorrow would bring but hoped Knox would be in Norfolk to meet her. *Whatever we are or are not, I'll know tomorrow.*

Looking through the security hole again, she could see the pathway outside her door was clear. Opening the door, she rolled the cart just outside, then grinned as she snatched the platter still containing more crispy tortillas. Closing and locking the door, she felt as though she could breathe for the first time all day. Whatever she'd overheard at the hospital, she was unable to do anything about it on her own. She would see Dr. Neal tomorrow, and she would confide the overheard conversation to him before leaving. He'd been so kind to her and Roger, she felt sure he would take her seriously. *But my time in Belize is almost over, and I will have done all I can do.*

17

Knox continually checked his phone, but there were no other calls or texts from her. Sighing, he gathered his luggage, making sure to have Libby's with him.

The group had plied him with questions all day about Roger and Libby, and while he assured them Roger was going to be fine according to the cardiologist, it seemed to be Libby that was the subject of many of their questions. He was glad as the cruise ship approached Norfolk, giving the others something to do in preparation to dock.

The least I can do is help everyone since that's what Libby would be doing if she was here. After making sure the pursers had everyone's luggage to be taken to the claims area, he herded them to the deck to watch as they moved around Virginia Beach and into the Chesapeake Bay on their way to Norfolk.

Standing at the rail, his mind so full of Libby, Sally was able to walk up next to him undetected. She kept her gaze forward, but he had no doubt whatever was on her mind would soon be spoken.

"I told her she needed more spunk."

His brow lowered as he angled his head down to stare at her. "Sorry?"

"Libby. I told her she needed more spunk to get a man, but I'm not sure that was the right thing to say to her. Watching her over the last few days, especially with you, I think she always had spunk. She just needed to let it free with the right man."

"And you think I'm the right man?" The question slipped out, surprising him, but he wanted to know what she thought.

With her hands still gripping the rail, the breeze blowing her snow-white curls away from her face, she appeared almost youthful as she smiled. She turned and looked up at him, holding his gaze steady. "What I think doesn't matter. What do you think?"

"I think I'd like to be. I know I want to be—"

She released one hand from her tight grip on the rail to wave it dismissively in front of him. "Bah! You're too much of a take-charge man to give such a namby-pamby answer!" She wiggled her forefinger at him. "Are you the right man for her?"

"Yes." With that one-word declaration given without hesitation, his chest not only filled with the fresh ocean air but his heart pounded and his mind cleared. He fought the urge to howl into the wind, instead choosing to smile back at the small woman in front of him who was grinning up at him.

"You may as well know that Curtis has told some of

us what your job was. I figure you and she have got a lot to talk about when she gets here tomorrow. But you keep thinking about your answer to my question, and you'll be just fine." With that, she patted his arm and moved down the rail where several of the others were standing. He could see their heads bent together as they chatted and had no doubt that he and Libby were the center of their conversations and speculations.

He looked back toward the shoreline, ready to dock and help the others get on their bus back to Windsor Village and then head to the Norfolk International Airport. He planned to grab a hotel room at the airport so that he could be as close as possible while waiting on her to arrive. Anxious, he had a feeling the minutes would tick by slowly.

Much later, he was finally walking into his hotel room by the airport in Norfolk. He'd shepherded the group off the cruise ship and assisted in getting their luggage. Windsor Village had sent one of their large buses to meet them, and the seniors had invited him to accompany them home so that they could show him where Libby worked. Once there, the staff and nursing aides came out to assist, and Curtis introduced him to everyone who came up, including Libby's boss. Grateful that the man already knew about Roger and Libby, Knox assured him they would be flying home tomorrow.

Finally, shaking Curtis's hand as well as the others' and accepting hugs, back pats, and cheek kisses, he climbed into a taxi and headed to the Norfolk airport. Finding the closest hotel, he checked in after requesting a room with a view of the runways. It didn't make any sense, but he felt closer to Libby just seeing the place where she would land tomorrow.

He'd called several times, but she hadn't picked up. At least she'd answered his text when he asked if they were still on schedule to fly out in the morning. Her reply had been simple. **Yes. Roger's son will fly us both back.** It wasn't much, but he'd take anything from her.

After a long, hot shower and ordering room service, he climbed into bed, his back against a pile of pillows. With the remote in one hand, he clicked through a hundred channels on the TV, finding nothing could hold his attention. Finally flipping it off, he tossed the remote to the nightstand.

His phone vibrated, and as with each time it happened, he jumped in the hope that it was from Libby. Surprised to see it was from Curtis, he opened the text.

We've been sharing photos. Thought you'd like to have these. Thanks again. Sally says to tell Libby to hold on to her spunk. I guess she'll know what that means.

He chuckled, imagining Sally's grin as she passed that message on through Curtis. Seeing several pictures had been attached, he clicked on them, then gasped as the first one punched him in the gut. One of the others had taken a picture of the first night he and Libby had dinner at the table by themselves. He was leaning forward, his attention riveted on her, and Libby's smile was bright as her head was thrown back in laughter.

The next one showed the two of them still at dinner but bending their heads together, deep in their own world.

The third picture was of them standing at the San Gervasio ruins. He remembered keeping an eye on Curtis, distracted by Libby as she moved around. Someone had captured a picture of them standing near each other; she was looking at the ruins, and he was looking at her.

Another picture had been snapped when they were standing with their feet in the blue water at the resort in Costa Rica. In this photograph, they were close, their bodies almost pressed together, and from the angle of his head, he could tell it was snapped just before he kissed her.

The last picture was a close-up of him and Libby standing to the side of the whole group as their tour guide had taken the photograph in front of one of the Mayan pyramids. But instead of looking at the camera, he and she were staring into each other's eyes.

He sat quietly for several long minutes, flipping through the five pictures, one right after the other. His heart ached with longing, but his mind filled with resolve. What he'd told her was the absolute truth: *What we started as isn't where we are now. What we are now is a helluva lot more than what either of us expected.* Now, he just needed to get her back to him so he could prove to her every word came from his heart.

In the middle of the night, he woke with a start, his heart pounding and sweat pouring off him. Unable to discern what was wrong, he couldn't shake the feeling that something was happening. Climbing from bed, he checked his phone. No calls. No messages.

Pacing the room in an effort to dislodge the disquiet in his gut, he finally called Drew.

"Hey, man, what's up?" Drew asked, his voice rough from being woken up, but Knox knew his brother would be ready for anything.

"Just letting you know I'm renting a plane to have it ready for tomorrow if needed. Can't explain it, but I've got a bad feeling."

"What do you need from me, bro?"

"Nothing for now, but I wanted you to be prepared. Tell the others that I'll still be in Norfolk waiting for Roger and Libby, but I'll also be ready to leave instantly if needed."

"You got it. Try to get some sleep and call as soon as you hear anything."

"Will do. Thanks, man." He disconnected and then walked over to his laptop. Using LSI's secure information, he made arrangements for a small Cessna to be at the standby. He hoped it wouldn't be needed, but there was no way he was ignoring the tightness in his gut.

Deciding to brave breakfast in the food court of the resort lobby, she felt safe with other tourists around and enjoyed her coffee, fry jacks, scrambled eggs, and fruit. She figured it might be the last meal she had before they landed in the United States this afternoon, so she was determined to eat her fill.

As she sat and sipped her coffee, she wondered if Roger's son had already arrived. If so, she needed to hurry, not wanting them to wait on her. Calling the nurse's station number that she'd been given, she was glad to recognize the nurse who answered.

"Bethany, this is Libby Cook. I wanted to know when Roger Whitcomb would be ready to leave. I know his son was coming this morning."

"Libby! Roger's son came in the middle of the night, and he was discharged early this morning. They've already left!"

Her whole body jerked. "What? No, you must be mistaken. I'm supposed to be on that flight, also!"

"Well, hang on and let me see."

The food she'd just eaten sat in her stomach like a rock, and she closed her eyes and prayed that Bethany had the information wrong. *There's no way for him to be gone. There's no way!*

"Libby? I just double-checked. I'm so sorry that things got confused with Roger's son. But I have the notes in front of me. Doctor Neal is not in today, but he left discharge instructions for the doctor on call. I can only assume that Roger's son thought you must've had other transportation."

Still mentally stumbling with the idea that Roger had already flown out, she searched for clarification. "I was going to talk to Dr. Neal about something today, but you say he's not even there?"

"No, he's off today and tomorrow. Is there something I can help you with?"

Exhausted and overwhelmed, whatever was

happening at the hospital was too much for her to deal with alone, especially since she now had to get to the airport to book a flight back to Norfolk. Squeezing her eyes shut, she thought of the hit to her bank account and prayed the flight would not be too expensive. Realizing Bethany was waiting for an answer, she replied, "No, thank you. Goodbye."

Disconnecting, the desire to cry had her blink to battle back the tears. *Crying isn't going to get me home any faster.* Pushing herself to a stand, she stalked out of the food court and headed down the path to her room, determined to grab her bags, catch a cab to the airport, and hopefully, put what was turning out to be a disastrous vacation behind her.

Knox had been unable to go back to sleep and finally gathered his bags along with Libby's that he still had, leaving them just inside his room. Taking the stairs instead of the elevator, he headed directly to the hotel's restaurant to avail himself of their buffet. Piling his plate full, he ate heartily, not sure when he'd get a chance to eat while waiting for Libby to arrive.

He'd just finished and was walking out of the restaurant when his phone vibrated and he observed the call came from Drew. "What's up?"

"Have you heard from Libby?"

He jerked slightly, his senses on alert. "No, why?"

"Bray talked to Roger's son, Tom, yesterday, and he had contracted with a medical flight company to go to

Belize to pick up Roger. Tom was going with them to accompany his father back."

"Okay…" he prodded, his heart rate starting to climb as he listened to the serious tone of Drew's voice.

"When Bray called this morning, he didn't talk to Tom but Tom's wife, who informed him that another company could get there faster. So, Tom left last evening and flew the five hours to Belize, and they were on their way back already. The hospital released Roger as soon as the son came."

"That's good," he said, his heart now leaping. "That means Libby should be arriving or might already be here." He immediately began to think of how to meet up with her and prayed that she'd give him a chance for them to talk.

"No, that's what's wrong. Josh and Pippa checked on Libby's tracer… it's still in Belize."

"Maybe she left it there—"

"Knox, I hate to tell you this, but when Bray got hold of Tom just a few minutes ago, who was still on the flight… he left without Libby—"

"What the fuck?" Knox roared, not caring who overheard.

"Tom told him that he was told by someone at the hospital that Libby had made other arrangements to get back."

"Fuckin' hell. I knew it! I felt it in the middle of the night! Goddammit!"

"I know, I know, bro. That's exactly what I told the others. Tell us what you need. Cole and I are ready to fly down as soon as you give us a sign."

"Let me see if I can get hold of her and see what's happened. I'll be in contact." He almost disconnected when he added, "Tell everyone thanks… if you all hadn't been working on this—"

"You don't gotta say it," Drew said. "Give us a call when you get hold of her."

Disconnecting, he looked down to see the phone shaking in his hand. Drawing in a deep breath, he let it out slowly before dialing her number. Before he could finish, his phone vibrated with an incoming text.

18

Walking as though in a fog along the path to her room, she heard a crash and jumped, suddenly aware of her surroundings. She was near her room but stared in shock at the opened door. With her purse strap worn across her body, she slid her hand into the bag, wrapping her fingers around her phone. Glancing to the side, a thick grove of floral bushes with wide, waxy leaves was nearby. Carefully ducking behind them, she moved stealthily to see what was happening in her room. Voices sounded, and as she listened, a sense of déjà vu from yesterday in the hospital slid over her.

"Some things are here but not her passport. She must be close by."

"We were told to get her passport. Without it, she cannot leave."

"I can't get what I don't have!"

"Do you still have the picture of her?"

"Yes. From the hospital security cameras. That's how they knew she was the one there."

"She may have already headed back to the hospital. She won't know yet that the man is already gone."

She ducked down further as two men came out of her room, both wearing resort jackets that they pulled off and tossed into the nearest dumpster. *Hospital security camera! Whoever was in that room just had to follow me on the cameras!* Renewed fear clawed at her, and she worked to swallow down the saliva that threatened to choke her.

Waiting until they had left the area, she then raced inside. A lamp had been knocked over, probably what had created the crash that had alerted her to their presence. Thanking God for their clumsiness, she stood for just a few seconds of indecision, then knew she had to get out of there. She grabbed a cloth shopping bag and began stuffing the few clothing items and toiletries she'd bought into it. She raced to the door and peeked out, seeing no one. Hurrying in the other direction to circle around her building to the other end of the main building, she entered the lobby through a side door.

Uncertain where the men might have gone, she hoped they'd returned to the hospital. *But once there, they'd find out that she knew Roger had left.* Dashing into the same shop where she'd bought the clothes, she hurriedly grabbed a floppy hat and pair of sunglasses. They wouldn't make much of a disguise, but at least she'd have a chance of disappearing in a crowd. With no other plans but to get into a taxi to take her to the airport, she was sure she'd feel safe once she bought a ticket to anywhere and made it through security.

Darting into the ladies' room, she twisted her hair

up into a high ponytail, then pulled the hat on, completely covering the blonde. With the large sunglasses perched on her nose, much of her face was disguised.

Slipping back into the lobby, she glanced around, not seeing the two men but not wanting to wait around for them to return. Mingling with a group of tourists who were leaving the lobby at the same time, she made her way to the outside. The group was boarding a bus to Mayan ruins. Starting to go past them to the cabs, she halted, seeing the two men standing near the taxi stands. One was looking toward the front of the lobby, but she didn't think he'd seen her. Turning quickly, she had no idea how to escape. Moving back to blend into the group of tourists, she found herself climbing onto the bus. Hands shaking, she sat quickly, glad there was plenty of room and no one sat next to her. Completely out of her element and nearly out of her mind with fear, she pulled her phone from her purse and began to text Knox.

I need you.

Libby, I know about Roger. Where are you?

The air rushed from her lungs over the relief that Knox immediately replied. *Oh, Jesus, thank you!* Just knowing he was on the other end of the text made her feel safer even though he was far away. Typing quickly, she hit send.

Something happened. Can't talk. Have to text.

WTF? Are you okay?

Yes...

Libby, ur killing me. What's happening?

She knew it was a lot to type, but there was no way she could explain everything. Hoping he'd get the gist, she pecked at the keys and hit send. **Overheard something at hospital. Not good. Now someone is after me. Lied to Roger's son. Told him I wasn't going back with him. Was at resort. Someone broke into room looking for me this morning. I'm on the run.**

On my way. I have a plane – be there in 5 hours.

I won't be in Belize City.

Where are you?

Wanted to take cab to airport. Men were watching resort. Had to get on tourist bus to ruins.

What ruins?

She'd been typing so quickly, she had no idea where the bus was going. Looking at the pamphlet handed to her by the bus driver when she boarded, she typed **Lamanai. I don't know where it is.**

I'll find it. You stay in contact. Use this number if you need. It's the people I work with. They can help you, too.

She looked at the number he sent and quickly saved it to her contacts. She hoped she wouldn't need it but breathed a little easier having it. Looking out the window at Belize City moving past, she pressed her lips together, praying she wouldn't cry.

Knox had raced from the hotel with his luggage, still hauling hers, also. Glad that he'd made flight arrangements, he caught a cab to the private hangars at the airport and loaded his belongings onto the plane. Going through the necessary checks, he called Drew while the airport was readying everything for him.

"My premonition came true," he growled.

"Talk to me," Drew ordered. "I'm at LSI. Putting you on speaker."

He relayed what she had told him, hearing the curses in the background. "I should be taking off in about ten minutes. I need you to pull up everything you can about Lamanai. How best to get there from the air. If I need a helicopter, I need arrangements made for one to be available at the Belize airport."

"Do we know what she overheard at the hospital?" Mace cut in to ask.

"Not over texting. I'm going to contact her as soon as we hang up and have her text more info to you. Then you can send me whatever I need to know."

Gaining LSI's acceptance of his plan, he breathed slightly easier. Of course, it wouldn't be completely easy to breathe until he had her in his arms again.

"Bro?" Drew interrupted his thoughts. "Cole and I will fly down to Belize, also. We'll be available to assist and then can fly us all back when you get her."

Blowing out a deep breath, he said, "Thanks, man. Thanks to all of you."

"No thanks," Mace said. "But be safe and keep us informed. Have Libby get what she can for us. We can work it from here and then be ready for you, her, Drew, and Cole to work it from there."

"Will do." Disconnecting, he typed another message to Libby. **Call or text the number I sent to you. Give**

them details about what happened. I leave in few min. Will be in Belize in 5 hrs. Stay safe.

Not expecting a response, he felt his phone vibrate.

Ok. U be safe too.

With his flight arrangements complete, he climbed into the cockpit and rolled out of the hangar.

"Hello? Um…" Libby felt stupid calling the number Knox gave her but desperately wanted to connect with someone now that the bus had left the city and was heading out onto a smaller road.

"Libby, this is Babs, a coworker of Knox. Are you okay?"

Hearing a woman's voice allowed Libby to breathe easier. "Yes. I'm still on the bus… um…"

"You can speak freely. Knox has briefed us, but give us what you can."

Lowering her voice, she hated for anyone around her to hear what she was saying. "There are people around. Tourists."

"Okay, I understand. You don't want to say anything with other people around, right?"

"Yes," she continued to whisper even though her one-word reply wasn't whisper-worthy. She glanced around, but it didn't seem as though anyone was paying any attention to her as the other tourists were either looking out the windows, chatting with each other, or looking at the information the bus driver had handed to them.

"Is there anything you can tell us? Or would you rather text?" Babs asked.

Trying to discern how much she could say, she whispered, "I'll tell you what I can and then text the rest."

"Okay, Libby, that'll be fine. Just so you know, there are others in the room with me. We all work with Knox and are all security specialists. Everything you tell us we can get to him so that he'll have all the information when he lands there."

"Oh… um, okay." Lowering her voice even more, she said, "I was in the hospital but got lost… oh, that doesn't matter." Grimacing, she glanced around again, feeling foolish.

Babs' voice broke in, soft and gentle. "Libby? You can just give us the bare minimum, and I'll ask questions. Then you can text anything else. You're doing fine. Honestly, you are. The fact that you've kept yourself safe and have gotten away from the people after you tells me that you know how to handle yourself. So, take a deep breath and continue."

She closed her eyes and breathed deeply, feeling connected to the woman on the other end of the call. Opening her eyes, she didn't see anyone who appeared to pay any attention to her, so she began again. "I overheard something."

"Was anyone else around?"

"No."

"Was it people talking where you heard the whole conversation or one person talking on the phone and it was one-sided?"

"Two people."

"Okay, this is good. What they were talking about, was it illegal activities?"

"Yes."

"Was it drug-related?"

"No." She liked how Babs was asking questions but assumed there was no way Babs was going to be able to guess what she heard. Lowering her voice even more, she whispered, "Selling body... organs..."

There was no reply for a few seconds, but she thought she could hear people talking in the background. Uncertain if she should continue, she waited.

Finally, Babs came back on the call. "Harvesting body parts? Is that what you overheard?"

"Yes."

"We'll get more details later, but did they see you?"

"I didn't think so. But... um... cameras."

"Security cameras. So, they must have had a reason to think someone overheard them and watched the security cameras to see who it was."

She nodded, feeling foolish since Babs couldn't see her head moving. "I think so. I should... should have done something... but..." She closed her eyes and winced. "I got scared."

"You did the right thing. Never doubt that. Okay, Knox told us that someone was after you, and they gave Roger's son the go-ahead to leave without you. Libby, I want you to stay on the line for just a minute while I talk with the others."

Libby had twisted in her seat so that her back was to the window and she could keep an eye on the others. Still, no one seemed to pay attention to her, for which she was grateful. She looked back down at the pamphlet in her hand and skimmed over the tour information. Eyes bugging, she read that it involved a two-hour bus ride and then a twenty-six-mile boat ride. *Shit!* Her mind raced with the implications of the bus she'd snuck onto, and she fought to steady her breathing. *How will Knox ever get to me?* Another thought struck her, and she prayed it was enough to counterbalance the negative. *Surely, no one will try to follow me this far.*

Just then, Babs got back on the line, but before she gave her a chance to speak, Libby rushed, "I got on a bus, um, a tour bus to get away. But the tour is much longer than I thought. Knox can't—"

"Don't worry about that," Babs interrupted. "He'll be able to get to you no matter where you are. We have your location and will make sure he has that information so that as soon as he lands, he'll have a way to get to you."

Closing her eyes, her shoulders slumped in relief. "You know my location?"

"Knox gave you a lighthouse necklace."

Libby's eyes jerked open wide. "Yes." She couldn't imagine why he'd told them that, but her fingers flew to her neck where they clasped the lighthouse charm dangling from the silver chain.

"Keep that on you. He didn't explain what it was at the time, and I'm sure he had a good reason for that. But that charm is specially made with a tracer so that we can tell where you are at all times."

"What?" She winced at how her voice rose slightly,

then looked around, glad to see no one on the bus was looking toward her.

"He'll explain at a later time. But it's something that's given to only special people. Keep it with you so that we can tell where you are at all times. Then we'll be able to pass that information to him once he lands."

"Okay," she agreed. As her fingertips traced the lines and grooves of the lighthouse, her surprise gave way to warmth. *Given only to special people. We can tell where you are at all times.* She had no idea who Knox was working with, but these people were much more than just bodyguards. Suddenly, the subterfuge he'd used to get close to her initially no longer mattered. Whatever he did, he did it to protect Curtis, and now he was flying back to her to protect her. Sucking in a ragged breath, she let it out, waiting to see what else Babs would say.

"As long as you feel safe with the tourist group, we want you to stay with them. We pulled up the information and can see that you're in for a long journey. The good news is that by the time you reach your destination, Knox will almost be landing in Belize. So, stay with the group. Stay vigilant. And if you need to hide, then do so, and remember that we'll be able to find you."

"Okay," she agreed again.

"We'd like to know more specifics about what you heard at the hospital. Text that to us so you don't have to say it aloud on the bus."

"Okay."

"The last thing is to keep this number programmed in your phone on speed dial. Let us know if anything changes in what's happening. And Libby? You're doing fuckin' phenomenal, girl."

She had no idea who Babs was but had a feeling the woman was as badass as they came. While she'd never felt badass in her life, hearing Babs say that she was doing fuckin' phenomenal caused her lips to curl into a wry grin. "Thanks."

Saying goodbye, they disconnected. With the phone still in her hand, she quickly began typing.

People voluntarily selling their kidney. Then, harvesting organs from people with no relatives. Mentioned expatriates. Mentioned causing death to harvest organs. Worth millions.

She looked at the text, hoping it made sense, and hit send. Her phone vibrated almost immediately, and she looked down.

Got it. Stay safe.

Glancing at the time, she saw that only thirty minutes had gone by. She had another hour and a half on the bus before they got onto the boat. She hoped the men at the resort looking for her had given up and headed to the hospital. Then perhaps they'd head to the airport to discover that she wasn't there, either. She doubted they'd find her where she was going. *Knox will come, and I'll be safe.*

Refusing to close her eyes, she turned so that she could stare out the window. The scenery passed by, but there was no enjoyment. Her mind was filled with what she'd just told Babs. *People are being killed for their body parts. Someone at that hospital is making money from that.* It was as though the horror of what she'd overheard was finally sinking in. *But what can I do?* The answer hit her that by herself, there was nothing. But with Knox and the people he worked for, maybe...

Easing deeper in the bus seat, she realized it wasn't much, but it would be something.

19

Knox landed in the Florida Keys to refuel. Calling into LSI, Tate answered.

"Knox, we've heard from Libby. Babs talked to her and got a lot of info. Then she texted and gave us more. She's fine. Still on the tour bus to Lamanai ruins. Josh is tracing her."

"Good. I should have about three hours to get to the Belize airport. What will I need once there?"

"A bird. We're making the arrangements."

"Will she still be there?"

"The tour bus she is on will take two hours to get to the next leg, so she's probably just getting there. Then, there will be a boat ride for over an hour. By the time you land, the tour will still be at the ruins."

"Got it. Have the bird ready, send all directions and the tracer info to me through my GPS."

"There's more," Cobb cut in.

His stomach dropped, not liking the tone of Cobb's voice. "Talk to me."

"It's about what she overheard. Seems she stumbled onto a conversation between two people about harvesting organs… illegally. She overheard something about an expatriate and causing death to obtain their organs, and it would be worth millions."

"Goddammit! Fucking hell!" He ignored the airport employee currently filling his rented Cessna with gasoline, who stared at him in shock and probably a bit of fear.

"Babs says Libby feels guilty that she ran off and didn't do anything, but Babs also told her she did the right thing. Just letting you know that besides working to keep Libby safe and you down there, we're looking into the hospital from here."

Knox knew why they were doing this, a new mission that they'd never get compensated for, but Libby having information about an ongoing organized criminal activity that netted millions, even in another country, could leave a target on her back. The Keepers knew she meant something to him so they'd step up to do anything they could to keep her safe. With the phone still held to his ear, he dropped his chin and stared at his boots. The mission had now changed for him, too. Instead of just getting to Belize, traveling to where she was, and getting her out, they'd need to find a way to shut down the threat.

Cobb continued, "We'll keep you updated. For now, all you need to worry about is getting to her. Drew and Cole are on their way to Belize airport, also. They're about three hours behind you and will be your transportation back to the States, but whatever we find on the hospital, we'll send to them."

He looked over and saw that his plane was refueled, and offering a chin lift to the attendant, he finished his call. "Thanks, man. I'll be in touch." Disconnecting, he walked over and signed the requisite paperwork, then climbed back into the cockpit. Soon, lifting into the air, his mind had moved from meeting up with Libby to an active mission.

Libby followed the other tourists down the sandy path through palm trees to the edge of the river where there was a small dock. When she'd read that there would be a boat ride, she assumed it would be a larger boat, one that would be able to hold all thirteen people who had been on the bus. Instead, she was shocked to see that there were four smaller motorboats lined up at the dock, each with a man near the back at the controls. She'd hesitated and was now the last passenger to walk toward the boats. The first boat was able to take half the passengers, leaving her and the others to clamber onto the second boat.

Without waiting for anyone else, the boats pulled out onto the river, then their speeds increased so that she had to pull her hat off and hold onto it or it would have blown into the water. Sucking in a deep breath, she looked around, finally seeing the beauty of the land. She'd been so anxious on the bus ride that she hadn't appreciated the jungle terrain and lush forests.

Easing back in her seat, she clutched her hat, bag, and purse, which was still strapped around her, in her lap. At times, the motor was so loud no one spoke, but other times when they slowed, the driver pointed out sights of interest on either side of the river.

She learned that Lamanai means submerged crocodile, and they certainly saw several. Birds chirped and squawked. Snakes wrapped around tree limbs that overhung the water. They were told that manatee could be seen, but she never spied one. The boat sped along, slowing as they passed local fishermen. The thick jungle grew to the edge of the river, hanging over, hiding any shores. The ride was mostly smooth although traveling over wide, thick lily pads caused the boat to bounce. They began twisting and turning as the river became more curved.

At one point, he slowed the boat and guided it to the edge of the water where small monkeys clung to the trees, bending down to take a piece of proffered fruit from his hand. She could not help but laugh at their antics, and finally, as the sun beamed down, she found the cold fear that had slithered through her body ever since she'd stumbled onto the wrong floor of the hospital was now replaced with warmth and a feeling of freedom. Here, no one was chasing her, and she allowed the beauty of the tropical rainforest to fill her senses.

After a while, she reached into her bag and grabbed the bottle of sunscreen she'd purchased along with her other toiletries and swiped it over her face, arms, and legs. She didn't usually burn easily but had a feeling being on the river for so long, she'd soon be bright red.

The other passengers took pictures, laughed, and chatted amongst themselves. She wondered what it would've been like to have had Knox with her—just two travelers discovering the wonders. She knew he'd seen many places, but for her, this trip was probably going to be a once-in-a-lifetime occurrence. Glad the motor of the boat drowned out her snorting scoff, she was quick to decide that perhaps traveling wasn't for her.

The boat finally slowed, and she looked up to see they were coming to a wooden dock similar to the one they'd left from. She spied another boat already docked, much larger than the one she was on and filled with cruise passengers with life jackets. Chuckling, she realized she'd slipped into one of the super-economy tours.

Leaving the dock, she walked slowly along the shell pathway leading into the jungle. They continued as the path widened, the thick, green trees lining either side teeming with birds. Libby couldn't help but wonder what else they teemed with, shivering at the thought of snakes.

The jungle finally fell away on one side, exposing an expanse of lush green grass leading to one of the tall, gray-stoned Mayan pyramids. Even though there were a few tour groups, she was surprised at how uncrowded the area was. With a quick count, there were probably no more than fifty people milling around the large expanse of ruins. Out here, she felt completely anonymous, and the tension in her shoulders eased.

She listened to one of the guides as she walked around but didn't want to stay with any particular group too long, preferring to be alone in case her phone rang with either Knox or Babs. She looked at the time, and based on what Babs had said, she thought that Knox must surely be getting closer to Belize. Deciding to send a text, she walked to the side of one of the magnificent ancient structures and typed a message to Babs.

At Lamanai. Tour is supposed to last four hours. Do I stay or go back to hotel with them?

It only took a moment for her phone to vibrate.

Stay. You're safer out of Belize. We'll text when K has landed.

THX

Keeping her phone in her hand, she began to wander more, listening to the guides' speeches and snapping photographs of the ruins, all the while wishing that Knox was with her. Not as a rescuer. Not as a protector. Just as a man interested in her, enjoying a vacation together. Sighing, she wondered if that would ever be them.

Knox taxied into the private hangar at Belize Airport. Checking his messages from LSI, he read, **You will be met by Bruce Williams**

Climbing down from the plane, he stretched, cracking his neck before turning and grabbing the bags he'd brought with him. A man approached, and Knox stiffened, waiting to see what the stranger wanted. The man was just under six feet tall, wiry but muscular. He approached, his dark eyes locked onto Knox, no smile, but one hand stretched out with a photo ID and badge.

"I am Bruce Williams. Lead detective for the National Criminal Investigation Branch of the Belize National Police Department. And I believe you are Knox Drew?"

Carefully scrutinizing the identification, he looked up and nodded, then pulled out his own LSI identification.

Jumping straight into the heart of the matter, Bruce said, "I know you've been in the air for hours, but your team has been in contact with me."

"And you were chosen because...?"

Bruce smiled, his white teeth gleaming against his dark skin. "I was contacted directly by James Cellini of your DHS."

At this, Knox offered a chin lift in acknowledgment.

Continuing, Bruce said, "There are those even in the police who would turn a blind eye to illegal activity that would line their pockets. While it is not illegal for someone to voluntarily offer a kidney for money, it is illegal for someone to make that offer for another person. Unfortunately, in poor areas, a parent might volunteer their child or an older relative for that type of surgery for monetary gain."

"Jesus," Knox muttered, shaking his head.

"And it is even more disturbing to know that someone in the medical profession would cause another person's death so they could remove organs and get rich by selling them. I have heard of this but have not had the personnel to fully investigate. When James Cellini contacted me a few hours ago after having spoken to someone who might have information, I quickly agreed.

Right now, I can tell you that no one else in the police force, other than the commissioner—who is above reproach—knows about this."

"Just because a man is at the top of his law enforcement career doesn't mean he's not on the take," Knox warned.

"I don't take offense at that," Bruce agreed. "But I know the commissioner and trust him with my life." Knox did not respond, and Bruce held his gaze. "I also understand that you have no reason to trust either of us. But I hope you do."

"All I care about right now is locating the person I'm here to pick up."

"Your people have arranged for a helicopter to be at your disposal. I'll take care of any flight plan and assist in any way I can. I also understand that you have two coworkers who will be arriving here in a few hours. Accommodations near the airport will be arranged for them, so there will be no customs or any evidence they were here."

"I'll need a place to stow my luggage."

With a nod, Bruce waved his arm toward the door near the back. Walking with him, Knox kept his eye out, but his Spidey senses did not alert him to any danger. Bruce moved to the door first, and Knox observed a room with several large lockers, another door leading to a bathroom, and shower stalls.

Taking a few minutes, he grabbed his duffel and shifted his belongings between it and the suitcase, only taking what he might need for a day if necessary. Opening Libby's luggage that he'd carried back with them, he chose a few items of clothing, stuffing them into the duffel, as well. His fingers lingered for just a few seconds on the green dress she'd worn the night they had dinner the first time. Her clothes smelled like her, and the scent filled his nostrils. His fingers curled, fisting the material before he quickly closed her suitcase and stowed it alongside his in a locker.

A gun appeared in his peripheral vision, and he jerked around. Bruce smiled and said, "Your company knew you might need this." He handed the weapon to Knox along with ammunition.

Knox checked it, then looked up, offering another nod of appreciation to Bruce.

Bending to pick up another bag on the floor, Bruce held it out to Knox. "Your people had special requests that I was able to meet. You'll find these items useful if they become necessary."

Looking inside, he saw that it was filled with tactical equipment. Older than what he would have from LSI but serviceable, nonetheless. "I need to talk to my people, but how are you involved?"

"Once you retrieve Ms. Cook, then I'd like to talk to her... here, of course, and with you present. I want all details on where she was, what she heard, anything. She just might have information that allows me to narrow the focus on who in the hospital is running this heinous operation and allows me to shut down the black-market sales coming from Belize." He rubbed his chin, his jaw tight. "There is one more problem. I know you are flying to Lamanai, but there is an electrical storm approaching. You should have no problem getting there, but it might prove too dangerous to fly back until it passes. There is a small hotel at the ruins. It is nice accommodations but not luxury."

It was on the tip of Knox's tongue to growl that he'd slept on rocks more times than he could remember but thought of Libby and hoped the hotel was clean enough and comfortable enough for her to rest. "I appreciate it. If I think we can get back tonight, that would be my preference. I'll check with my people."

Bruce nodded, then walked him out to the hangar where the plane he'd flown in was already being prepped for another flight. A few airport employees moved around, ignoring the two. "Your helicopter is here," he said, walking through another door that led into another hangar.

Knox silently breathed a sigh of relief at the Robinson R22 that appeared to be in mint condition. He stowed his duffel and equipment, then turned back to Bruce. The two men shook hands, both seeming to take a measure of each other. Not quite trusting, but neither had a choice.

"Godspeed, Knox," Bruce finally said. "I'll see you tomorrow."

"Thank you," he replied, then moved over to the helicopter to begin his pre-flight checks. As soon as he completed the tasks, he climbed into the cockpit and called LSI. "Here and in the bird. Met with Bruce. Have equipment but was told a storm is passing through in a couple of hours and I might have to spend the night there. I need that confirmed."

"Roger that, and to let you know, we've heard from

Libby. She's safely at the ruins," Clay said, being the one who answered. After a moment, he came back online. "Severe storms will be passing over the area in about three hours. Not enough time for you to get to Libby and get back to Belize safely."

"Check out the hotel there."

While Clay worked on that request, Mace got on the line. "Pippa and Josh worked on Bruce's background before we talked to him. Married. Two kids. With the police force for twenty-six years. Owns his own house, but it's modest. His vehicle is six years old, and his bank account is what you'd expect from a policeman, even one who's the top investigator. He lives within his means and has no additional bank accounts, offshore accounts, or evidence of extra money. James Cellini had his contacts at the CIA check him earlier today. They say he's clean."

"Okay. I didn't get a bad feeling, I just wanted to know who to trust."

"Cobb's been working on the human organ black market information. It's everywhere as you can imagine, especially in poor areas. Chances are there aren't many who know what's going on. His guess is that the two people Libby overheard and possibly only a few more are actually involved. As long as you have a couple of people with medical knowledge and connections, they don't want too many hands in the pot."

"Okay, thanks. I've got the coordinates to Lamanai. I'll stay in contact. Let me know when Drew and Cole arrive."

Disconnecting, he lifted off and aimed the bird

toward the northwest. Blowing out a long breath, he tried to settle his mind. *Flown a lot of special ops. I know what the fuck I'm doing. It's not my first rescue. This is a piece of cake compared to what I've done in the past.*

And yet, no matter what he told himself, anxiety vibrated through his body. He couldn't wait to lay eyes on Libby again. They had a lot to talk about, including a future he hoped she'd share. *But first, I need to get her fuckin' home!*

20

Deciding to make the best of her time while waiting for Knox, Libby walked past the Mask Temple and stood at the bottom of the Jaguar Temple, listening to the guide.

"This temple is unique with the presence of two massive jaguar sculptures on the front of this building. While this temple is a little shorter than the High Temple, there is still much of it underground that is yet to be excavated. When that is complete, it will be much larger than the High Temple."

As the guide continued to speak, she looked upward and yearned to see from the top. She'd observed several people coming down who appeared quite winded, and she hoped she'd be able to make it. Starting the climb, many of the steps were no steeper than what you'd find in a modern building, but then she came to others where she was using her hands, almost as though climbing a ladder.

Stopping to take a look around, she was surprised to see she was only about half of the way up. Refusing to quit now, she continued to climb until she reached the mossy top and plopped heavily onto the ground. The site was beautiful. A large tree was growing nearby, the sound of monkeys screaming in the branches as they jumped and swooped. Looking to her right, she could see the river they'd traveled on to get here.

Above the tree line, she felt sure she could see all the way to Mexico. The rainforest was lush and green, starkly delineated against the bright blue sky. In the distance, the clouds seemed darker, and as the breeze blew over her, evaporating the sweat dripping down her back, she wondered if a storm was coming. That thought made her heart beat faster, praying that Knox would get to her safely.

Almost as though on cue, the sound of a helicopter in the distance met her ears. Leaping to her feet, no longer tired, she held the brim of her hat to cover her eyes and looked up, spying the approaching aircraft. She had seen no others arriving, and now her heart beat faster for another reason—excitement. *That's got to be him!*

Determined not to break her neck as she carefully made her way back down the pyramid, she discovered that going down was no easier than climbing up. The helicopter had disappeared beyond the trees, and by the time she'd made it to the bottom, she darted past the other tourists still mingling with their guides and tour books.

She had no idea from which direction he might come and was afraid to run around too much in case she missed him. She turned several times slowly, around and around, her gaze searching. Finally, along a narrow path through the jungle, she recognized the confident stride of the tall, dark-haired man, his eyes hidden behind his reflector sunglasses, but it was evident even from the distance that he was searching, as well.

She started running, slowly at first as though afraid he was a mirage that would disappear. She could easily tell the instant he recognized her, and she ran faster, one hand holding on to her hat as her bag bounced against her back. He raced toward her, too, his expression not smiling but as intense as the last time she'd seen him when he was pulling away in the taxi from the hospital.

Neither slowed as their bodies collided. His arms banded around her and lifted her, and she wrapped her legs around his waist, burying her face in his neck, breathing him in. She refused to wonder about the emotions crashing into her about a man she'd known less than a week, lost and found at the same time.

Elation at the sight of him. The feel of his body pressed to hers as though they could meld together. The way her heart pounded, knowing that he was holding her, making it obvious she was more than a cover.

When she finally lifted her face from his neck, she slid his sunglasses from his face and warmed under the intensity of his blue eyes that didn't waver from her. "Hi." The single word slipped out, barely a whisper. To some, it might have seemed ridiculously short compared to all the emotions she was feeling. Things like *I can't believe you came for me,* or *I'm so glad you're here,* or *My world hasn't been right since you left.* But with her simple greeting, his lips curved slightly, making her feel that he must have understood all the feelings that were tied up in that word.

"Hi, yourself," he replied.

She watched in fascination as his smile eased, not quite dropping, but the lines emanating from his eyes deepened as his focus narrowed on her.

"Are you okay?" His words were punctuated with a tightening of his arms around her.

She nodded. "Better now that you're here."

His gaze shifted behind her, then to the sides, and she now recognized signs of his scoping their surroundings. How many times had she seen him do that but just thought he was interested in what was going on around them, not dedicated to making sure everyone was safe? Now, filled with understanding, she remained quiet, allowing him to do whatever it was he felt that he needed to do.

He must not have detected anything suspicious because his gaze landed back on her face. She loosened her legs, and he held her steady as she slowly slid down his front until her feet were firmly planted on the ground. She noticed his arms stayed around her, but considering she clutched his biceps with one hand, it appeared neither of them wanted to let go. His sunglasses were still in her other hand, and she smiled as she lifted them to him.

"I should give these back. They keep people from seeing what you're looking at, but I needed them off so I could see your eyes."

He grinned, one arm banded around her back as he

took the glasses from her hand, but instead of putting them back on his face, he perched them on top of his head.

She met his grin with a wide smile. "That works, too." A breeze whipped by, and she twisted her head to look over her shoulder and up, seeing darker clouds moving over the area. Jerking her head around, she observed him looking upward, as well. "Should we be leaving?"

His attention fell back on her, and he shook his head. "I'm sorry, babe, but a storm is rolling in from the east off the coast. I can't take a chance on us trying to fly through it."

Eyes wide, her fingers gripped his arms tighter. "Then when will we leave?"

"Dawn. First thing, I promise."

She dropped her gaze, staring at his chest, and sucked in her lips, filled with uncertainty. She felt his biceps flex slightly, and she focused on the thick, corded muscles covered by smooth skin. Intelligent eyes that didn't seem to miss anything. Steady. Tall and strong, Knox could take on danger and defeat it but also knew how to avoid it when necessary. All these things came to her at once, and she was no longer afraid.

When she lifted her gaze back to him, he was staring at her intently. She loosened her grip and smiled. "Well, okay then." She looked over her shoulder to see the Jaguar Temple, an idea forming. Stepping out of his arms for a second so that she could dig into her purse, she pulled out her phone. Pulling up the camera, she held it toward them with the temple in the background.

His brow furrowed. "What are you doing?"

"Capturing the moment."

He held her tight as she clicked several pictures. Wanting to offer more of an explanation, she turned back to him as she tucked her phone back into her purse. "When you flew in, I was on top of that pyramid. I was looking around and thinking how much I wished you were with me. I realized that I didn't have a picture with you. I know that sounds silly with everything that's gone on. Running for safety, waiting for rescue. And yet, I just wanted a picture with you."

His face softened, an expression she loved seeing on him. It wasn't that he was always stern, more like always intense. And as he held her gaze, she felt as though it was a special gift he bestowed on her.

He looked beyond her and said, "We've got about half an hour before the storm hits. Want to show me a pyramid?"

For a brief second, she wondered if her legs would be able to do the climb again, but one look at Knox, and she knew she could do anything if he were by her side. "Sure. Come on." She took him by the hand, and they walked back to the base where the sculptures sat guarding the area. Most of the other tourists had left, and the ruins felt deserted. Perhaps all the world had disappeared except the two of them. And that thought didn't frighten her at all.

Knox climbed, needing the physical exertion to wipe away the fatigue from the flight as well as to clear his mind from the anxiety since leaving Libby's side at the hospital that had threatened to overtake his emotions. Seeing her in front of him, her body real, her touch electrifying, they hadn't even kissed, but their reunion was perfect. Two halves separated then coming together.

Now, as the wind increased, he wondered if it made sense to climb to the top of the pyramid when they would undoubtedly get wet on the way down. She panted, stopping on an outcropping of rocks near the top, and his hand darted out to hers. "Stop here."

She looked over her shoulder, her head tilted to the side, waiting. Waiting to see what he was going to say. What he was going to do. Waiting with trust in her eyes. Christ, he wanted to be worthy of that trust.

"I don't want you to overexert yourself with the storm coming. And I sure as fuck don't want you to fall on these stones."

She grinned and stepped closer. Being a tall step higher brought their faces to the same level. Placing her hands onto his shoulders, she leaned in, offering a light touch of her lips on his. Pulling back, her smile still in place, she jerked her head to the side. "Come on."

He nodded, and she turned, climbing up to the next level then scooting around toward the back, and he mumbled, "Babe, I'd follow you anywhere."

There was a slight overhang of stone, creating a place where they could stop and be slightly protected. She sat down, then patted the hard, gray stone next to her, and he gladly joined her. Wrapping his arm around her, he pulled her close, tucking her into his side before staring out over the view. The fuckin' spectacular view.

The lush green jungle below was sliced by the river cutting through. Even though dark clouds were rolling from the east, it didn't take away from the beauty of the vast greenery that lay before them, stretching all the way to Mexico.

"I'd made it to the top, but I'd seen this little place on my way up earlier. I know we don't want to get stuck when the rain hits because that'll make the stone slick, but I wanted to let you experience the view even if we couldn't go all the way up."

"For someone who's never traveled, you're quite the intrepid traveler."

She laughed and shook her head. "I don't think a luxury cruise that I didn't pay for and then a race against unknown bad guys makes me an intrepid traveler. More like a super-lucky person with the first part and an amazingly unlucky person with the last."

They both chuckled, then their mirth slid away as the reality of her situation moved to the forefront. He lifted a hand and cupped her face, his fingers yearning to glide along her smooth skin. "I've got you now." There was more he wanted to say but hoped she understood his words were all-encompassing.

She held his gaze, her pupils darting back and forth between his eyes as though searching their depths. She slowly nodded, the corners of her lips barely curving. "I'm glad."

He reached into his pocket and pulled out his phone.

Glancing up, he said, "I've got some pictures to share with you later, but it seems Cynthia and others were taking pictures of us."

Her chin jerked back in her eyes widened. "Really? I'm so glad!"

Just like she'd done earlier, his thumb flipped to his camera app, and he held the phone up. He snapped a few close-ups of her with the amazing vista in the background. Then he flipped the camera and held it on them, snuggling her closer. Looking at her, he said, "Life's too short not to capture every memory. So, here's to a lot more moments we have to capture." Snapping a few pictures with them together, he tucked away his phone.

He'd barely lifted his hand from his pocket when she grabbed his face and pulled him close. Her dark eyes were even blacker as she closed the distance, her mouth sealing with his. The kiss was as wild as the untamed jungle that crept to the base of their temple, as hard and unyielding as the ancient stone underneath them.

Their heads twisted and turned one way and then the other. Tongues delved deep, tasting as they swept the warm space, tangling together. Their bodies were crushed together, her soft form pressed against the hard planes of his chest. He wanted to strip the clothes from her body, worship each inch as he tasted every dip and curve.

Finally pushing back, his chest heaved as though he'd raced up the pyramid earlier, his breath struggling. Her lust-filled eyes were hooded, a small moan of protest slipping from her lips, and her fingers dug into his shoulders.

Doubting his sanity for a moment at stopping, he shook his head. "I want you, babe. I want this, right now, right here. But there's no way I'm gonna do you out here where anyone can come by and see us. I'm sure as fuck not going to lay you back on this hard stone in the middle of the storm that's almost here."

"Then where?" Her words were mournful, and if his cock wasn't so hard, he would've laughed.

"Let's get off this pyramid and get to the hotel that's nearby. It won't be luxurious, but I've heard it's clean. They'll have food and a bed."

A slight giggle slipped out. "Food, you, and a bed. What else could I ever want?"

Laughing as well, he stood and gently pulled her to her feet. Checking the approaching storm, he led her back to where they had climbed up and moved first so that he'd be able to assist her down. They'd had just enough time to make it to the bottom of the pyramid when the first splats of rain started to fall. Racing hand-in-hand to the cover of the thick trees overhead, they made their way down the path.

"Wait here," he ordered. "I'll be right back." They'd come to the small clearing used for helicopter tours. His was the only helicopter on the meadow. He quickly grabbed his duffel, having already carried his equipment in his backpack. Securing the bird and setting a special alarm that would notify him of any tampering, he jogged through the rain back to the wide-leafed umbrella of the trees. Turning down another path away from the ruins, they came to the lodge.

Going inside, he headed straight to the check-in desk. The dark-haired, dark-eyed, smiling woman wearing safari khakis greeted them.

"Welcome!"

"Hello. You should have a reservation for one night for Drew. Knox Drew."

She nodded with continued enthusiasm, her warm gaze moving between them. "Yes. But it looks like you were caught in the rain. I was going to suggest that you head to the dining room, but you might want to change into dry clothes first?"

"Yes, please." He pulled out a credit card, but she waved it away.

"Oh, no, sir. Your room has already been paid for when the special request came in."

He nodded, surprised that Bruce had taken care of the bill, but considering he was possibly going to get closer to nailing a major investigative case with Libby and LSI's assistance, he could afford to be generous.

A fresh-faced young man in safari khakis that matched the woman's bounded in. Reaching for Knox's duffel, he said, "I'll show you to your cabana!"

Knox waved his hand and picked up the duffel. "Thanks, I'll get this." His hand resting lightly on Libby's lower back, he guided her through the door as they followed the young man down a palm-lined path.

"Just behind the check-in desk is the dining room. The menu is set, but they can accommodate just about every request. And don't worry about the time. They'll serve you whenever you get there."

Libby turned and made wide eyes at him, and he wondered when she'd last eaten. Turning to their porter, he said, "We'll get cleaned up and then definitely be over for food."

They passed several small cabanas, coming to the last one that was overlooking a jungle view of the river just beyond the trees. Going through the open door, Libby gasped as her head swung around. He could understand her reaction. The cabana was built with walls of traditional hardwood and thatched roofs. The wood was stained a golden-red, and while the furnishings were minimal, a large bed centered the room with a desk, chair, and small cabinet lining one wall. A door led to a bathroom containing a large shower, toilet, and wide cabinet with a sink. The air conditioning had been turned on, but in their wet clothes, he watched Libby give a little shiver.

He tipped the porter well, then closed the door behind him. Turning, he spied Libby still standing in the middle of the room, turning around.

"This is so much more than I thought it was going to be!" she squealed.

Chuckling, he nodded. "To be honest, I thought we were really going to be roughing it. This is nice." She shivered again, and he stepped forward, wrapping his arms around her. "Hop in the shower and get warm. We'll go eat once you've got dry clothes."

Her arms wrapped around his waist, and her top teeth landed on her bottom lip as she looked up at him, a grin spreading across her face. "How about you join me in the shower and we'll both get warm together?"

He smiled. That was Libby. Not coy. No games. No pretending she wasn't interested just to lead him around. She *was* interested and laid it out there. *Thank fuck!*

He bent and kissed her lightly before lifting his head and holding her gaze. "I'm going to say no, but it's killing me." Seeing her face fall, he quickly added, "Not because I don't want to. But I want to get you warm, and I want to get you fed. If I get in the shower with you now, you'll get warm, but you won't be fed because I won't let you out of this room for the rest of the night."

Her arms squeezed, and she laughed. "Even though I'm hungry, that doesn't sound bad at all."

"I want you, Libby. And I hope tonight we'll get things settled, so I have all night to prove that to you. But first things first. You get warm, get dressed in dry clothes, and I'll get you fed. Then we need to talk."

He watched as doubt and a touch of fear moved through her eyes. Lifting his hands, he cupped her cheeks, his thumbs sweeping over the soft but chilly skin. "I've got explaining to do as well as apologizing. Once we get that out of the way, everything will be laid open. Then, and only then, when you know you've got me, the *real* me, then I plan on using that bed for a lot more than to sleep."

Her dark eyes warmed, and her smile returned. Lifting on her toes, she touched her mouth to his, swept her tongue over his lips, then settled back on her heels. "Then I guess I'd better get in the shower!"

Still feeling the touch of her tongue, his cock reacted. As she hurried into the bathroom and the water started, he remained in the middle of the floor, hands on his hips, head dropped back, staring at the ceiling fan, counting the rotations in an effort to ease his aching need for her.

21

Libby hurried through her hot shower, anxious to finish, eat, and get back to the room with Knox. She knew he wanted to talk, and she understood. After all, they'd started a relationship under false pretenses and assumptions. But between Curtis' attempt to explain and the fact that Knox not only had the resources and ability to come to her rescue but also the desire to do so meant that she was ready to move forward.

Stepping out of the steamy, glass-walled shower, her gaze landed on a pair of shorts, a T-shirt, and sandals that she had brought with her on the cruise. Next to them was her small toiletry bag. The realization that he had brought her things from the ship, obviously carrying some of them back to Belize just for her comfort, had her dance a little jig of happiness. Drying off quickly, she slid into her clothes and slathered moisturizer over her face, arms, and legs. Towel drying her hair, she braided it, not caring if it appeared neat.

Stepping into the room, she saw him lounging on

the bed, legs stretched out in front of him, ankles crossed, his back against the pillows. He'd changed into dry clothes, as well. His phone was in his hand, but as soon as she walked into the room, his piercing gaze raked over her, and he tossed the phone to the mattress. Swinging his legs over the side, he stood and stalked to her. Grabbing her hand, he pulled her toward the door. "We need to eat."

He continued to quick-walk with her hand in one of his and an umbrella in the other. Finally, she jerked on his hand and brought his gaze down to her.

"Knox! What's the big hurry?" she asked, staring up at him, wondering if she'd taken too long with her shower.

He stepped closer, looming over her, dwarfing her, but all she felt was protected. Tilting her head to the side, she waited.

Knox sucked in a deep breath through his nose, his chest inflating, then let it out slowly. "I'm sorry. I didn't mean to drag you along. It's just that the whole time you were taking a shower, I imagined you wet and naked. When I brought your clothes in, I didn't look. I knew if I did, I wouldn't have the strength to not strip and join you."

A soft gasp slipped from her, his words sending tingles throughout her body that had nothing to do with the heavy rain all around and the lightning in the distance.

He continued, "And then, when you walked out, smelling so fuckin' sweet, your skin pink from the warm water, and smiled at me as though I had given you the greatest gift by bringing you a few of your clothes, I knew if we didn't get out of there, I was going to say to hell with dinner, to hell with talking, even to hell with apologizing. I'd strip you and lay you on the bed." His eyes squeezed shut for just a few seconds before she was met with the beautiful blue again. "So, cut me a little slack, babe. I want to do this right by you. I *need* to do this right for you."

Every word he'd said had lashed her with a velvet ribbon, soft and sweet. Swallowing deeply, she nodded. "Well, okay, let's get some food!"

He threw his head back and laughed, and they continued to jog down the path until coming to the main lodge where the covered, open-air dining room was set up. Much like their cabana, the polished, golden-red wood of the floor, tables, and half-walls covered by a thatched roof was unique and beautiful. The servers brought out platters of food, starting with mango juice, freshly fried tortilla chips and salsa, conch fritters, and then tilapia with white rice and corn.

She couldn't believe how much food was placed in front of them, and like always, never minded eating heartily. They finished with thick slices of banana bread and cups of tea. Finally, leaning back in her chair, she looked over the scraped-clean plates and laughed. Catching Knox's questioning gaze, she shook her head. "I should be embarrassed for shoveling down so much food so fast."

He grinned and leaned over, taking her hand. "Never be embarrassed about that. I'd much rather see you eat what you want, when you want, how you want than to either pretend to not be interested or starve yourself to fit some image that you think you should be."

She leaned forward, meeting him in the middle, kissing him lightly. Holding his gaze, she nodded. "Good answer."

The blue of his eyes darkened, and she shivered—but not from cold.

"You ready to head back to the room?"

"Oh, yeah," she whispered. She had no idea what the evening might bring, but she was ready. No more guessing. No more wondering. Now was either going to be the end or the beginning. *God, let it be the beginning.*

They didn't speak again during their jog along the wet path back to their room. Stepping onto the covered porch, Knox shook the umbrella and left it outside the door before they entered. She waited as he quickly checked the room and bathroom before walking back to where she waited in the middle of the room. He stopped several feet away, and she continued to wait. This was his show, his need, and she wanted to give him control.

He hesitated, and she realized that for such a take-charge person, he appeared to feel out of his element. She reached forward and gently placed her hand on his. "You want to sit on the bed?"

Since there was only one hardback chair by the desk and the other chairs were out on the deck and probably wet from the rain, there really wasn't anywhere else for them to sit. He nodded and led her to the bed, where they both kicked off their shoes.

They sat facing each other, his legs stretched out in a similar manner to how he looked when she came from her shower. She mirrored his posture with her much shorter legs stretched out next to his.

He held her gaze for a long moment, then said, "In case you're wondering, my name is Knox Drew."

She blinked, realizing she'd never considered that he'd given a false name. Thankful she didn't have to re-learn his name, she smiled. "Good. I mean, I'd like any name of yours, but to me, you're Knox."

For the first time since they'd left dinner, he smiled, the tension in his shoulders appearing to ease. "I want you to know that everything I told you about myself is true. My family. My brother. Being a pilot for the Navy. Being a pilot for a private company. I live and work in Maine. All of that is true."

She closed her eyes for a few seconds, her nerves settling as she heard that the man she'd shared with, talked with, laughed with, and made love with was not fake. She hadn't realized that her own shoulders had grown tense until they, like his, relaxed. Opening her eyes, she held his gaze and smiled. "I'm glad."

He dipped his chin, then continued. "What I didn't tell you was the whole story. I work for a specialized private company. We work private and government contracts providing security although not basic body-guard-to-the-stars type of work. We also assist in inves-tigations, either local, national, or international." He dipped his chin, inclining his head toward her neck. "Lighthouse Security Investigations."

She gasped, her eyes open wide as her fingers reached up to clutch the lighthouse charm dangling around her neck. "Babs told me this was special."

He sighed, regret slashing across his face. "It is. You are. That was one lie I told you, when I said that I'd picked it up locally. We use those to give to someone special to help us trace where they are. I hated leaving you and wanted you to have that. But I couldn't explain at the time why." He lifted his hands palms up, sighing again. "As you now know, the company I work for was hired to provide security for Curtis. You know him as just a retired scientist, but he does work for DHS, and his knowledge of bioterrorism is important. This cruise was a vacation for him, and because he's a private citizen, the government couldn't provide their own security, so they asked us to. It was supposed to be simple. I'd pretend that my father had known him, and I'd be able to keep a closer eye on him. At first, meeting you was a bonus in my cover. Spending time with you gave me more of a reason to hang with Curtis, making it less obvious to anyone interested that I was there for him. I hadn't counted on finding you not only beautiful but also fascinating, interesting, and someone I really wanted to know. It didn't take long to realize that you were much more than a cover."

She bit her lip as she tilted her head and held his gaze. "So... you were interested? I wasn't just a convenient... whatever?"

"Yes. I told myself it worked for both of us at first. I could tell that you weren't interested in the attention of Andre, and I sure as hell wasn't interested in the attention of any other woman there. But by the end of our first dinner together, I knew I was in trouble. I struggled to acknowledge that my interest in you went far beyond convenience. By the time we spent the day at the resort, I knew I was all in with you."

"Was Curtis in danger?"

He rubbed his chin. "Our biggest area of concern was the excursions. For one thing, there was always the fear that he could come under a random act of violence which happens to tourists more than tour companies want you to know. There was also a slim chance that someone watching him could snatch him for his information. Honestly," he said, shaking his head, "I went into this knowing that it was mostly going to be a paid vacation for myself. But that didn't mean I could take my duties lightly."

"And us?" she asked, wanting to know the truth and yet fearful at the same time. Just because he'd come for her didn't mean he wanted anything more than what they had. But one way or the other, she needed to know. He leaned forward and reached out, linking fingers with her. Once again, his gaze held her captive, and she was pulled into the blue, knowing how easily she could drown in his eyes.

"Everything about us was real. Every feeling that was growing inside of me for you was real. Every kiss, every touch, every shared look was real." He shifted forward even more. "And when we came together, we made love, Libby."

She swallowed deeply. Just as she'd been afraid that she might drown in his gaze, his words threw her a lifeline. "And now?" Her words were barely whispered.

"Now, baby, if you can accept all that I've told you, and believe everything I've told you, and accept my heartfelt apology that I wasn't able to tell you every-thing on the cruise... then this, right now, right here, is the beginning of you and me."

Libby stood on a precipice, much like the top of the pyramid she was on earlier, where the wild jungle full of the unknown lay before her.

Her lips slowly curved as her decision was already made. Bending deeper toward him, she whispered, "I accept you. I believe you. I forgive you. And more than anything, I want the beginning of you and me."

A growl was pulled from deep within him, rumbling from his lungs, and she felt its vibration to her very core. He gently tugged on her hands, and she shifted forward as he fell to his back and she landed flush on his chest. She grunted, the sound swallowed as his mouth landed on hers. He rolled, and her back pressed into the surprisingly soft mattress. His hands clutched her cheeks as hers roamed over his back. She had the feeling he was taking it slow, but she wanted all of him now.

Angling her head, her tongue met his and danced wildly. His hands slid underneath her, and he shifted, moving back on bended knees while pulling her forward. He slid his hands to the bottom of her T-shirt, and she lifted her arms straight up as he whipped it over her head and sent it flying across the room. Her hands moved to do the same to him, but he was faster. Reaching behind him, he clutched a fistful of material and jerked it over his head, tossing it in the other direction.

Her gaze feasted on his thick, defined muscles, the

tight ridges of his abs, and the flex of his arms as he leaned forward, their chests almost touching as he reached behind her and unhooked her bra. Pulling the straps gently, she barely noticed the silk dropping over the side of the bed.

As though forcing himself to slow down, his hands landed on her shoulders and gently smoothed down her arms before gliding up her ribs to cup her breasts. He gently teased her nipples with his thumbs before bending forward to suck one deep into his mouth. She clung to his shoulders with her fingers while throwing her head back, offering herself to him, reveling in the sensations vibrating through her entire body. Outside, the storm raged, but it was tame compared to the lightning snapping between them.

He shifted back and held her gaze as he shimmied down her legs. She placed her hands on the mattress and lifted her hips, allowing him to slide her shorts and panties down her legs. Now completely naked, she didn't feel exposed as his gaze roved over her. Instead, she felt worshiped.

He swung his legs over the side of the bed and stood, his hands going to his pants. She didn't take her eyes off him as he kicked off his boots and shucked his pants and boxers. Bending, he snagged a condom from his pocket and tossed it onto the bed next to her.

With him now as naked as she, her smile widened. Carved from the purest marble, his Adonis body crawled back over hers. She reached down, curling her fingers around his cock, swirling the drop of pre-cum over the head, loving the hiss that left his lips and the way his blue eyes darkened.

He gently slid her hand away, murmuring, "As much as I like the feel of your hand on me, we've got plenty of time to play later. For the first time as a true *us*, I want to be buried in you when I come."

She had no objection when he settled between her thighs and lifted her legs, his gaze staring at her most private place as a man starved. His fingers parted her, gently dragging through the slick folds. Then, lowering his head, he dove in, licking, tonguing, laving, and sucking. If she thought the electricity had been firing earlier, it was nothing like what she was experiencing now. Her fingers clutched his hair as her back arched, and her hips thrust upward as though desperate for a closer connection.

He inserted a finger, and just like before on the cruise, he had no problem finding the magical spot that wound her body tight, and all it took was for him to pull her clit deep into his mouth, and she cried out, the coil inside snapping, and her orgasm had her entire body shaking before her arms and legs flopped to the side, boneless.

Uncertain she could move, she was fairly certain she didn't care. She heard him chuckle and would have accused him of being cocky, but the truth was he had every reason to be. She had no idea how many sexual partners he may have had over the years to have gained such talent, and she didn't care. To be the benefactor of such an experience was amazing.

22

Knox slowly kissed his way from her sex up over her soft belly to her breasts, moving from one nipple to the other before his lips landed on the lighthouse charm resting on her chest. For a few seconds, he closed his eyes, grateful that he'd given it to her and even more grateful that she'd continued to wear it even when she thought she'd been played.

As he continued to move his mouth upward, he pressed his lips against her fluttering pulse at the base of her neck, then the underside of her jaw. His cock reacted to every kiss. Lifting slightly, he looked down to see her lips curving, and he kissed her smile. It didn't miss his attention that with this kiss, he felt it in his heart.

Shifting slightly, he rolled the condom on then settled between her thighs, his erection pressing at her entrance. As he slowly entered, he linked fingers with her and lifted her hands, pressing them back into the mattress. There, he held her gaze as he slowly thrust, and she wrapped her legs around his waist. They moved as one, emotions laid as bare as their bodies. Acceptance mingled with forgiveness. Certainty overcame fear. And looking down at Libby's dark eyes, he prayed they'd have years to discover everything about each other.

He gently lowered to his elbows, her nipples now teasing his chest as his thrusts grew more desperate. Shifting his position slightly, his pelvis rubbed against her clit, and her body shuddered through another release. This time, he felt the vibrations to his core. He quickly followed, his fingers gripping hers as the thunder roared outside and the lightning flashed behind his eyelids. They rode their releases together before he wrapped his arms around her and rolled to the side.

For a long time, they lay in bed, bodies tangled, whispering stories and sharing laughs. They made love again, this time her on top. As he stared up at this beautiful woman riding him until they both came together again, he felt sure he'd died and gone to heaven. Tucking her in close, he felt her drift asleep and vowed that she'd never have another reason to doubt him.

Knox woke with a start, his gaze instantly going toward Libby, seeing her fast asleep. Gently, so as not to wake her, he rolled to the side and grabbed his phone. The alarm program he'd set for the helicopter had gone off. It was a less-than-optimum program, and he knew there was the possibility that wildlife might have caused the alert. Not willing to take a chance, he slipped from the bed, pulled on his boxers and camos, then jerked a tight, black T-shirt over his head.

Arming himself, he grabbed the equipment he needed and turned, hearing her stir. Libby propped up on one elbow, her other hand shoving her hair out of her face as she blinked in the moonlight.

"You okay?" Her sleep-filled voice was sexy, and he wouldn't mind hearing it at another time.

He leaned over the bed and kissed her lightly. "I've got something I want to check on. I'll be right back. Stay here, and stay locked in."

Her eyes widened, suddenly clear, and her hands snatched out to land on his arm. For a second, he tensed, expecting her to demand where he was going and why or demand that she didn't want him to leave.

"Honey, be careful," she whispered as though someone else was close by. "I'll be here, so don't worry about me."

The air rushed from his lungs, and his hand snagged out to cup the back of her head, pulling her forward, his lips landing on hers. She leaned into the kiss, and he wanted to take it deeper, make it last longer—hell, have it end with his cock sliding into her. But instead, he made it hard and fast. And when he pulled back regretfully, her eyes were hooded and her face soft.

"I'll be back," he vowed.

"I'll be waiting," she whispered.

Drew's comment came back to him. *They get us. They just fit into our lives without trying.* He didn't have time to explain to her how much it meant that she accepted what he needed to do. But sometime, he

243

would. With a chin lift, he slipped out the door, securing it behind him. Avoiding the main path, he moved through the jungle, the night vision goggles allowing him to see where he was going.

Coming to the edge of the clearing, he heard voices. Two men, one standing near a Jeep and the other walking away from the helicopter Knox had flown in. They climbed into the Jeep and left, and after giving several minutes for them to get down the road and ascertain no one else was around, he crossed the grassy field.

It didn't take long to see where they had clumsily tampered with the fuel line. *Fuckin' amateurs. But who were they? The only one who knew of my plans... Bruce Williams.* He rubbed his chin, then remembered Bruce had said the commissioner of police also knew. Eyes narrowed, he stalked away, his phone to his ear.

"You've got Blake," came the response from LSI.

"Someone knew what was going down. My alarm alerted me to visitors. Bird is disabled."

"Goddammit!" Blake cursed. "What's your plan?"

"Going back to the room and getting Libby. We'll take one of the boats here at the dock and get to a rendezvous point."

"Copy that." There was a brief pause, and then Blake added, "Fuckin' hell, sounds like you'll be doing for Libby what Sara and I had to do to get out of French Guiana. What do you need from us?"

"Send me the GPS of the river and all coordinates I'll need. Going south toward Belize, not fucking where the tour boats normally go to Orange Walk Town. Let Drew know what's up and where to meet us. And I want to know who the fuck set us up. Bruce said that the commissioner of police knew about this mission. I want to know if he's on the take or if Bruce is the one behind this."

"You got it. Josh is coming in now, and I'll fill him in. We'll get that sent to you in a few minutes. Good luck, man."

Disconnecting, he jogged the rest of the way back to the lodge. Stopping for just a minute on the front porch, he looked over his shoulder and saw the sky lightening ever so slightly toward the east, indicating that dawn would soon give them better visibility.

Opening the door, he stepped in and glanced toward the bed, his breath halting when he found it empty. Turning to check the bathroom, his heart pounded at the sight of Libby walking out, fully dressed and pulling her hair into a ponytail, securing it with the band wrapped around her wrist.

She startled as her gaze landed on him, then rushed over, her hands landing on his arms. "I got dressed in case something was happening."

"Smart thinking. We need to go."

She didn't waste time with questions but instead raced back into the bathroom, and he heard her move a few things around before she quickly came back, dropping her bag and purse onto the floor where he was gathering his items. "I'm ready."

"Good girl," he said. He made a quick trip around their room to make sure they hadn't left anything, then used the bathroom. Coming out, he said, "It'll be a while before we come to another bathroom."

Nodding, she rushed past him, and a moment later, he heard the toilet flush. As she walked out and grabbed her bag and purse, she grinned. "Thanks for the reminder!"

They stepped out onto the porch, the dark of night still surrounding them with only the barest hint of dawn to the east. "Stay right behind me and watch your footing," he reminded.

Together, they made their way down the path, staying toward the side where the branches created more cover. Nearing the field, he veered to the left, heading toward the docks. He felt her hesitation, and twisting to look behind him, he shook his head.

She nodded without question, continuing to follow him as they now jogged out in the open, down the long path, and onto the wooden dock where several boats were moored. He didn't pause but headed to the smaller one, tossing his bags and equipment into the bottom of the four-passenger boat. Turning, he held out his hand and assisted her into the vessel. "I'll be back here steering. Take one of the seats right in front of me."

By now, knowing that she would obey, he grabbed his bag and quickly pulled out another weapon besides the one he had tucked into the back of his pants. Hoping he wouldn't need them, he planned on being fully prepared. Pulling his phone from his pocket, he checked the coordinates that LSI had sent to him. He knew he'd be able to navigate the river, glad that it was going to be a smooth ride for Libby but also knowing that there were many twists and turns, making it difficult to travel quickly at times.

Unhooking the rope from the dock, he started the engine, and they maneuvered out onto the river. "Keep your phone with you, babe. There may be times I need you to call into LSI." Realizing he'd never mentioned the full business name to her, he added, "LSI stands for Lighthouse Security Investigations."

"Got it!"

He grinned. If she was scared, she didn't show it. And she sure as hell wasn't balking at anything he asked. Keeping his focus on the river, he gunned the engine where it widened and straightened, then pulled back on the throttle when navigating the curves.

Constantly aware that there could be someone on the river anticipating them taking this transportation, his concern eased slightly when they were almost to their destination and they hadn't had a problem.

Libby bent over to pull something from her bag, then shifted in her seat so that she was able to maneuver as close to his side as she could. Glancing down, he saw an opened bottle of water in her hand.

"I grabbed a few things from the room before we left, not knowing if we might need them."

Taking it from her, he tilted his head back with a swig. "Thanks, babe."

"I'm glad you know where you're going because if it was up to me, I probably would have us heading in the wrong direction on the river," she said, blushing as a wry grin crossed her face.

A chuckle slipped out, and he shook his head. "I'm

going in the opposite direction from where you came yesterday. It's a shorter, more direct route."

She looked around in the early dawn light and blinked. "Oh. I hadn't noticed." Turning back to him with her smile still firmly in place, she added, "But then, it all looks the same!" She settled back in her seat. "I thought I might have my first helicopter ride today. But I assume you operate on a need-to-know basis, or at least, that's how these things work in movies."

"I had an alarm set on the helicopter. It went off, and when I went out to check, someone had tampered with it—"

Gasping, her eyes flew open wide as she bolted upright again. "Oh, my God, Knox! Someone knew we were here! Someone is still after me! But how can that be?"

"I don't know. There was only one person I talked to outside of LSI that knew where I was going and why. He said the commissioner of police knew also. The man I talked to had been approved from our contact at DHS, who'd spoken to his counterpart at the CIA. They cleared this man. But the commissioner? Hell, there's no real way to know."

"But if organ harvesting and selling on the black market is worth millions, it would be easy to buy off the police, even the commissioner!"

She was right, but he didn't want her to worry. Just then, he glanced down at his phone, receiving a call from LSI. He maneuvered closer to the edge so they were under cover of the jungle overhang,

"Talk to me."

"Took a look at the security camera outside the resort where Libby got on the tour bus. We can see two men near the taxi stand that appear to be watching the crowd. They moved around, and then, after the tour bus left, they went over and talked to a man who had been selling tickets for the tour. We have no idea, but they may have decided that she left with them. But who they report to, we can't tell as of yet. As you can imagine, the police commissioner is on several committees and belongs to the Belize Country Club along with many of the doctors on staff at the hospital. Still looking into his finances."

He sighed, wishing there was more to go on, hating to have Libby exposed while still in Belize. "I want to get her out as soon as possible. Where will we meet Drew?"

"Continue in your direction for another two miles. Drew and Cole have landed at a small clearing near the river. They'll guide you in."

"Thanks. Update you when we make contact." He looked over at Libby, her upturned face holding his gaze. "Looks like you'll get to meet my brother and have your first helicopter ride today all at the same time."

"I suppose either one of those things should make me nervous, and the combination of both at the same time should really scare me." She wrinkled her nose as she looked up at him. "I guess that sounds silly, but do you think he'll like me?"

"Who? My brother? Why wouldn't he? After all, there's nothing to not like!"

She smiled, a light blush tinging her cheeks. Shrugging, she said, "But it's my fault all of you are in danger. That's probably not the best circumstances for us to meet."

Knowing they were coming close to the end of their boat ride, he slowed and veered toward the side of the river. Leaning over, he cupped her face, holding her gaze. "First of all, nothing is your fault. The fault lies with those who are trafficking human organs. Second of all, the only reason you were there was because you were taking care of Roger, something that you went above and beyond to help with. Thirdly, my brother will be thrilled to meet you because you're important to me."

Her smile returned, and he stood to face the front again, pulling up LSI's signal on his phone. In a clearing in the jungle on the east bank of the river and in the early dawn light, he could see the helicopter, recognizing the tall man standing nearby. Aiming the boat toward the riverside, he cut the motor and let it bump against the sandy bottom. Cole was already there, ready to grab the rope that Knox tossed him.

Once the boat was tied off, Libby scrambled to grab her bags, then stood to the side, waiting. Knox grabbed his as well, then held her hand as Cole leaned forward to steady the boat. "Good to see you, man," Knox said.

"Right back at you," Cole laughed.

Drew came from the side, his grin wide. "Bro, I knew those days in the Navy would pay off." He reached a long arm out and held his hand for Libby. As soon as she moved closer, Drew leaned forward and assisted her from the boat, making sure her feet were on dry ground.

She leaned her head back as he said, "You must be Libby. I'm obviously the more attractive of the Drew brothers. Most people call me Drew, but I have a feeling you'll call me Robert."

Laughing, she put her hand in his and nodded. "It's very nice to meet you, *Robert*."

Knox moved forward and wrapped his arm around her shoulders. "And this is Cole Iverson. And yes, this is Libby Cook." He looked beyond his brother and said, "I'll feel a lot better when we get out of here. The last I heard, the plan was to meet Bruce Williams at the airport."

"We've met him and been briefed from headquarters about your concerns. What do you want to do?" Drew asked.

"For now, we'll stick to the plan. But I don't want Libby unprotected."

She turned to look up at him, and he could easily see the questions in her eyes, but she remained silent. With a smile, he squeezed her shoulder. "Let's get airborne."

It didn't take long for them to squeeze into the small helicopter. He helped her put on the headphones and made sure she was strapped in securely. When called on for the checks from the pilot seat, she gave a bright-eyed, enthusiastic thumbs-up, and Knox laughed aloud. Catching Drew's laughter and wink, he reached over and took her hand, settling in for the short ride back to Belize City.

23

Libby sat in the hard plastic chair at a metal table in a bare, utilitarian room in the same hanger where Knox had brought her after they'd landed at the Belize City International Airport. He hadn't left her side except for her trip to the ladies' room, during which he'd stood sentry outside the door.

Her hands wrapped around the cup of coffee, empty plates that had been filled with breakfast items provided for them pushed to the side of the table. Knox sat next to her, Drew on the other side, Cole next to him, and across from her sat a tall, wiry, dark-eyed man who'd greeted them when they arrived.

Knox had introduced her to Bruce Williams, and from what she remembered from the introduction, he was the main investigator for the Belize Police Department. And while he'd been nothing but gracious to her, she knew Knox trusted him but not anyone else around him.

"And when you got off the elevator on the wrong floor, you continued down that hall, Ms. Cook?"

Her gaze jumped back to the detective. He'd already invited her to call him Bruce. "Please call me Libby. And yes. I didn't realize I was on the wrong floor." She thought she'd heard a strangled sound coming from next to her and shot her gaze toward Knox, seeing his lips twitch. Feeling her cheeks heat, she continued. "I'm afraid I don't have a very good sense of direction. The nurse on Mr. Whitcomb's floor told me that the cafeteria was on the bottom floor. When I got onto the elevator, there was a button for the first floor, but there was also a lower button for the ground floor. To me, when she said the *bottom* floor, I thought that meant the *very* bottom, therefore the ground floor. I know that might sound silly, but I didn't even consider that she actually meant the first floor."

Knox slid his hand over, wrapping his fingers around hers, giving a little squeeze. She sighed. He'd certainly seen her get confused enough times when they were on the cruise ship to know she wasn't exaggerating.

"When the elevator opened, I stepped off, and there was no one around. It didn't look like any of the other hospital floors with patients or the lobby. But I still thought that made sense, thinking that the cafeteria might be away from the other parts of the hospital."

"Which direction did you turn?" Bruce asked.

"Left. Actually, that was the only way you could go. As soon as I stepped off the elevator, there was just one room to the right, but there was a closed door, and no one was around. So, I continued to the left." She pressed her lips together, then closed her eyes, pulling up the memory of walking down the hall. Continuing to describe where she was while keeping her eyes closed, she said, "There were doors on either side of the hall, but none were open. Unlike other parts of the hospital, there was no hustle and bustle or people moving about. The hall turned left again. By now, I didn't think I was in the right place and started to turn around to go back to the elevator when I heard some voices."

"Voices coming from further down the hall you were in?"

Opening her eyes, she nodded toward Bruce. "Yes. I did pass by one door that looked like some kind of laboratory, but there was no one there. But the voices were coming from a room across the hall, and the door was barely cracked open. I didn't want to interrupt something important, so I hesitated just as I was ready to knock on the doorframe to see if they could help me find the cafeteria. I wasn't trying to eavesdrop, but in my hesitation, I clearly overheard what they were talking about. And I've already told you exactly what I heard, almost word for word."

He nodded and said, "The floor you were on held some labs but mostly some offices. It would be helpful if we knew exactly which one you were at. Was there any sign, room number, postings of any kind? Could you see an exit sign? Or signs for the stairs?"

She slowly shook her head, then squeezed her eyes tightly shut, blanking out everything but the memory of standing there with her fist still raised, ready to knock on the door. Suddenly, she gasped, her eyes flying open wide. "G-one-forty-seven!" She jerked her gaze around, seeing all four men staring at her intently. Looking to the side, directly into Knox's concerned face, she said, "There was a room number right next to the door frame. It just hit me when I was thinking about what I'd done. My hand was still lifted so that I could knock on the door as I was listening to what the men were talking about. The little plate next to the door frame was right at my eye level. G-one-forty-seven."

He squeezed her shoulder, his offered smile meeting one of her own. "Good job, Libby."

"Excellent!" Bruce said, tapping into his laptop. He turned it around so that everyone could see the image on the screen. "This is a floor plan of the hospital, and I've been following along on the ground floor as you were speaking, Libby. Not to test you, but let's just say to test your memory. So far, you were exactly right. Coming off the elevator, you had no choice but to turn left. At the end of that hall, you turned left again. The room number shows this was the office you were standing outside of."

"Couldn't you just take a look at the hospital security videos?" She hated to ask the obvious but was surprised the detective hadn't thought of that. His features immediately twisted, and she leaned back slightly in her chair, glad for the steady presence of Knox at her side.

"I assure you, Libby, I would if I could. I'm afraid my country's technological and investigative means are not nearly as advanced as yours. My assumption is that is how the people in the room discovered that you were the person who possibly overheard what they were talking about. Not willing to take a chance, especially when you disappeared so quickly and solidified in their minds that you did indeed overhear them, the security videos for that entire day were wiped clean." Bruce scrubbed his hand over his face and sighed heavily. "What you overheard about body parts being worth millions is true. There is nothing illegal about someone voluntarily donating a kidney for money. It is, of course, a different matter when a doctor simply takes what has not been volunteered. Who knows how many patients have gone in for surgery only to come away without one of their kidneys and don't know about it? Or a patient comes in and dies of *natural* causes and ends up on the chopping block."

She visibly shuddered, and he muttered an apology. "Please don't apologize, Bruce. It's a brutal business, and there's no need to sugarcoat it on my account."

"How many people would have to be paid off for that to happen?" Knox asked, drawing everyone's attention over to him. "I can't imagine everyone on an entire surgical rotation being paid off to turn a blind eye to someone coming in for an appendectomy and their kidney is removed at the same time."

Bruce's eyes flashed as he nodded with emphasis. "Exactly. That's been the angle that I've spent months looking at. While there are certainly people on the take in any business, I cannot believe that the Hippocratic Oath means so little to most of the hard-working, devoted medical staff at our hospitals."

"So, it would just be a few," Cole said. "A surgeon and

a few of his hand-picked, well-paid, turn-a-blind-eye surgical staff?"

"My investigation has been hampered by the fear of giving away too much, too soon," Bruce said. "The head of the hospital has always answered my questions, but I could tell he does not want to believe that anyone on his staff would do such a thing. But he has allowed me to take a look at some of the surgical rotation shifts. As I've pored through them, I can't find the same group in any consistent manner."

The group quieted for a moment, and Libby hesitated. With investigators filling the seats around her, she felt like an outside guest at the dinner table but decided to plunge ahead anyway. "What about the expatriate? The one they mentioned. The one they said had no family. Surely, it wouldn't be too hard to figure out who that is. In the end, if they're scheduled for surgery, you'd be able to be there and stop it. It needs to be stopped. I can't stand the thought of somebody being butchered for monetary gain."

"For all we know, it may have already happened in the past day," Bruce said, his dark eyes flashing and jaw tight.

She grimaced, hating the thoughts that filled her mind. Looking toward Bruce, he appeared to share her concern. "Then what do you need?"

Aware of looks being shared between Knox, Drew, and Cole, she jumped slightly when they said in unison, "LSI."

Bruce's gaze jumped to theirs, his expression hopeful. Turning her head to look at Knox, she whispered, "You guys are going to help?"

He smiled, and her heart melted a little. "Yeah, babe. Our people are already looking at the financial records of some of those in a position to be in charge. We're going to take some time to work with Bruce."

"I appreciate your trust," Bruce said. "I will not report anything to the commissioner. We will work this alone."

"While LSI is investigating which American expatriate might be the one they were talking about, I want to get into that office," Cole said, rolling his shoulders as though he were ready to jump into a fight. "Not all their records will be on the computer. Shit like that might be somewhere else."

"If we knew exactly who we were talking about, we could target their financials," Drew said.

Bruce called out as his gaze focused on his computer screen. "That office belongs to Dr. Jonas Southerland." He lifted his head to peer over the top of his laptop. "The physician in charge of the morgue."

"But he's not a surgeon, is he?" Libby asked.

Knox replied, "Yes, he is, but probably not the surgeon who's performing regular surgeries. He could be the one harvesting organs or directing the whole deal."

"We know he's working with someone else," she said, her heart racing. "The female voice I heard."

Drew tapped out a message on his phone. "Just told them to check his finances out. Bet we'll find he's a lot richer than the others."

A moment later, Cole looked up. "Josh is on the line," he said, putting the call on speaker.

"Pippa and Cobb will work on the finances of the surgeons on staff as well as some of the surgical nurses. It was easy to find the expatriate in the hospital records. Paul Gibbons. Sixty-three years old. Heart attack brought him in. Still on the fourth floor. No next of kin listed. His cardiologist is Dr. Neal, the same cardiologist who was treating Roger Whitcomb."

Libby jerked to attention at the name of the doctor she'd been in contact with when she was with Roger, then her heart ached, thinking of the man who lived as an expatriate in Belize with no family and was in the hospital alone. And might die alone. And then would be at the mercy of whoever was harvesting organs.

Josh continued, "Now, what I've discovered has to do with the security cameras in the hospital. Either they're a complete joke, the electricity goes on and off all the time in the hospital, or somebody is strategically turning them on and off at certain times."

Bruce's gaze shot over to the others, and he shook his head. "There's no way the electricity goes on and off that much, plus there are generators that immediately kick in."

"I was there for hours and hours with Roger and electricity never went off at all," Libby said.

"Most security systems are set up so that even breaks in the electricity won't interfere with them," Cole added.

Josh continued, "That's right. So, my best guess is that there's somebody who's messing with the cameras, probably someone or more than one in hospital security, so they'd have ready access."

"What sections are most affected?" Knox asked.

"Staff elevator near the back. And—ready for this? The ground floor."

Libby watched as the men's gazes jumped back and forth, but she wasn't certain she understood the implications of the news. She placed her hand on Knox's arm and mouthed, "What does that mean?"

Knox cut his eyes toward her and explained, "It means a patient can be taken into an elevator, and there's no camera visibility on them after they leave the floor."

"But surgery is not on the ground floor," she said, her brow furrowed.

"No, but the morgue is."

"But if they're removing extra organs during a regular surgery—"

"They could have a separate place... a place near the morgue for when the body needs to be disposed of."

"But..."

Knox turned to her and said, "Babe, we don't have to know exactly what they're doing or how they're doing it. We just need to find enough evidence that Bruce can get in and force an official investigation. Even the evidence of a room used for surgeries that's not part of the hospital business will be enough for him to step in."

She scrunched her nose, mumbling, "Sorry."

He chuckled, linking fingers with her. "Never be sorry for thinking through a problem. You do that all the time in your job, and your thoughts are perfectly good here, as well."

"So, how do we find out who might be the surgeon performing these illegal organ removals?" she asked. As soon as the words left her mouth, the table went silent, and she was met with four pairs of wide eyes.

Knox's hand on her shoulder flexed and curled her toward him until they were face to face. Just as mesmerized by his intense eyes as the first time, she sucked in her lips.

"The *we* I assume you're referring to is the four of us investigators. Not you as a part of this *we*."

Narrowing her eyes, she glared. "Do I need to remind you that *I'm* the one who overheard the conversation? *I'm* the one those men were after? I might not be a big shot investigator, but I'm not stupid."

"I didn't say you were stupid!"

"Well, then don't talk to me like there's nothing I can do to help."

"Considering you just admitted that someone is after *you* because *you're* the one who overhead something, then you should let us handle things while we work to keep you safe."

She opened her mouth, but the expression in his eyes halted her words. Sucking a deep breath through her nose, she pinched her lips together.

"Babe," he said softly, leaning closer. "I want you safe."

At that, her heart melted a little more. Then his lips touched her forehead, and she knew she was a goner.

24

Knox, Drew, and Cole slipped toward the back of the hospital, avoiding the area normally meant for food and laundry deliveries. Even in the middle of the night, there were a couple of trucks and employees milling around those entrances.

The back of the hospital had numerous angles based on various wings, making it easier to find other doors near the rear that were less conspicuous to anyone who might be watching from the outside. The three entered on the ground floor near the offices around the corner from the morgue since Josh and Pippa had the ability to tap into the security system of the hospital, disabling the camera while creating an alternate view for any security that might be watching.

Each dressed in tight, black, long-sleeve T-shirts and black cargo pants, pockets filled with equipment and earpieces always connecting them to LSI, they moved down the hallway. Heading past the service elevator near the back and with the spoofed security feed going to their phones, they were able to see that the coast was clear.

Bruce had stayed in the car with Libby, his face possibly too well-known to any security in the hospital, tipping off that an investigation might be occurring. Plus, Knox wasn't about to leave Libby in the airport or in the vehicle unguarded.

Following the path that Libby had taken, they turned to the left and walked down the hall, then made another left. The morgue was beyond the room they were aiming for, and with the area deserted, they easily slipped into G147.

The office was large and strangely empty of furniture other than a desk and a few chairs, a filing cabinet, and a bookcase. While Cole headed to the computer and connected it to his phone, allowing Josh to pull up any information and historical data from the computer, Knox looked through the files. Drew moved to the small closet but turned and shook his head. "Office shit in here, and that's it. I'm going to check the walls."

Knox, growing more frustrated, glanced over his shoulder toward Cole. "Nothing. Hope something comes on the computer, but I doubt he puts anything incriminating on that."

"Head to the morgue next?" Cole asked as he pulled out the drive from the desk computer.

"Yeah. Should be just down the hall."

Checking the camera views from their phones, making sure Pippa still had the security camera feeds altered, they left the room as they found it and walked to the double doors that led to the morgue. It was quiet tonight, dark inside the large room. Typical of most modern morgues, the room was divided into sections with multiple doors leading away. A records room, an office with several utilitarian desks that appeared to be available to anyone dictating or writing notes, and supply closets. Another room was set up for autopsies, and one of the side walls contained the storage drawers for the deceased until the bodies were removed for burial.

Another room led to a cold storage area to slow decomposition as a body awaited identification or autopsy. As Drew and Cole checked each room, they found nothing untoward. Knox followed afterward, mentally cataloging everything he saw. The two chilled rooms side-by-side caught his attention. Stepping into one and then the other, he could tell a definite difference in temperature. There was no one in the colder room, but a gurney with a single sheet-draped body was in the other.

Radioing LSI, he asked, "Why are the chilled rooms at different temperatures? One is significantly colder than the other."

Bray, their medic, replied, "The colder room puts the body at near freezing. They do this to slow the decomposition for a longer period of time, especially if they are waiting for identification. The other room is more refrigerated, slowing decomposition enough for someone awaiting an autopsy. Anyone else can be in the drawers which are also chilled, awaiting transfer to a funeral home."

Knox stood in the center of the room and slowly

turned around in a circle. A strange sensation moved over him, but no matter how carefully he studied the room, he couldn't see anything out of the ordinary. Swiping his hand over his face, he finally shook his head, ready to accept that what he really wanted was to get Libby back to the States so they could figure out the next step in their relationship and leave the investigation to Bruce.

After Knox, Drew, and Cole had left the car, Bruce chatted for a few minutes, then focused on his phone. Libby looked outside the window, but there was nothing interesting to take her mind off worrying about Knox and the others. Parked on a side street next to the hospital, it struck her how calm it was outside. Visiting hours were over and the daytime employees had left, leaving the parking lot virtually empty. The evening staff would be in the employee parking lot on the other side of the hospital, and where Bruce parked the car now seemed conspicuous even if it was in the shadows of nearby trees.

Her phone vibrated, and she jerked her gaze down, hoping she might have a message from Knox. Instead, she was surprised to see it was from Dr. Neal. Glancing back toward Bruce, whose attention was still on his phone, she read the message.

Received your voicemail but haven't had a chance to reply. Is all well with Roger?

Quietly typing, she replied. **He is back in the U.S.**

Your message indicated you had a concern about the hospital that you'd discovered.

She hesitated, wanting to know if he'd heard any rumblings of organ harvesting, but uncertainty filled her. She glanced up at Bruce again, tempted to ask him what she should do when another message from Dr. Neal came in.

Are you back in the U.S. also?

Without answering his direct question, she thought about the expatriate and hoped it wasn't too late to possibly save him. **Checking on another American. Paul Gibbons.**

My patient. I didn't think there was a next of kin.

Checking for a friend. She winced, knowing she was getting in over her head but wasn't sure how to get out of the conversation now.

Unable to give you specifics unless authorized.

Stifling a groan, she wondered why she'd begun this line of messages. *I'm not an investigator. I'm not even an amateur sleuth. I don't have a clue what I'm doing!* She had a feeling that if Knox knew what she was doing, he'd be furious. Hoping this would end the conversation but that it might give him pause if he were part of something illegal, she shoved her phone back into her purse, glad when it didn't vibrate another incoming message.

"Shit," Bruce said under his breath.

Libby bolted upright, guilt filling her until she realized there was no way he could know what she'd been doing. "What is it?"

"Visitors. I'll handle it."

Twisting her head to the side, she spied two hospital

security guards approaching the driver's window. Bruce rolled down the window and chatted, showing them his ID. They didn't seem upset, and he opened the door and stepped out, the three men continuing to chat. A tap on her window on the passenger side caused her to jump. Swinging her head around, she saw a female security guard smiling at her, asking for her identification.

She pulled out her passport and rolled down the window, holding her hand out with the documents. A loud grunt came from the other side, and she whipped her head around just in time to see Bruce slumping against the hood of the car, his body jerking before falling to the ground. She barely had a chance to gasp before her hand was grabbed and jerked further toward the guard, then a prick in her arm caused her to cry out in pain. As her head turned toward the open window, the world was already fuzzy before going black.

Pippa's voice came through the radio. "Libby is on the move. I can't get a visual right now, but she's not with Bruce—"

"Fuck!" Knox cursed as he looked up at the other two who'd heard through their earpiece radios as well, his stomach dropping. For the first time ever during a mission, his mind blanked for a few seconds, not knowing what to do. His body jerked as though punched, and he whirled around, racing toward the door.

Cole grabbed his arm, stopping him and checking

the hall before the three bolted out of the morgue. Racing through the supply door at the end of the hall that led to the outdoors, Drew reported to Josh to make sure their tracks were covered by the altered security feed.

"Send her tracer info to me now!" Knox ordered, his pounding heart racing faster than his footsteps.

"There's more," Pippa interrupted. "Libby just received a series of messages from Doctor Neal before she started moving. She didn't tell him that she was still in Belize, but she mentioned she was checking on Paul Gibbons. My guess is that she is trying to keep someone from killing him for his organs by making it seem like he has someone looking after him even if they're not next of kin."

"I'll get a lock on Doctor Neal," Cole said to Knox. Into his radio, he asked, "Is Doctor Neal a surgeon?"

"Negative. He's a cardiologist, but not a cardiac surgeon," Pippa replied. "Doesn't mean he's not involved, though."

Having burst outside, the three raced around the side of the building toward the car where they'd last seen Libby and Bruce. "Where the fuck is she?" Knox growled into his radio. By now, they were almost to the car.

"The signal is going in and out!" Josh cursed through the radio. "Shifting to a different program to pull it in."

Knox grabbed the door handle of the car even though he could see that Libby was not inside. Jerking it open, he forced his brain to catalog what he was seeing, not focus on the fact that she wasn't there. Her purse was on the floorboard. Her phone was on the seat. Bending, he grabbed her purse, having no clue what she kept in it but hoping something would catch his attention.

"Bruce!" Drew called out from the other side of the car.

With Libby's purse still in his hand, he raced around, anger flooding him, momentarily washing out his fear. He reached down to grab Bruce by the collar, ready to beat some answers from him, stopped only by Cole pulling him back.

"He's been tased," Drew said, helping Bruce to sit up, propping him against the driver's side door.

"Talk, man, and talk fast," Knox ordered, his body tight against Cole's hold, barely keeping himself in check.

"Guards," Bruce said, his breath raspy as he blinked rapidly, sucking in air. "Two guards, male, approached my side. Just checking to see why we were parked here. I showed them ID, they acted cool. I thought it was fine, then a female security guard came to the side and asked to see Libby's ID. I had turned toward them to see what was happening when I got fuckin' tased. Couldn't move, couldn't do anything, and I heard Libby cry out."

Digging through Libby's purse, Knox said, "Her wallet is still here, but her passport is gone."

"That doesn't make any sense," Drew said. "If they wanted to grab her and erase any identification left behind, why did they just take her passport?"

"My guess," Bruce said, struggling to stand with Drew's assistance, "is that the guards aren't very smart.

She had the passport in her hand when they took her, they didn't think about anything else."

"Where did they take her?" Knox barked, both at the others and into his radio.

"Signal has stopped!" Josh said. "I've managed to trace it to the back of the hospital, but then it stops. And the fuckers have shut down the security cameras in the entire hospital. Don't worry, we're going to get in through a different program!"

Mace came through the radio. "Everyone is here and working on the problem. Do what you've got to do."

Without waiting on the others, Knox shoved her wallet and phone into his jacket pocket, racing toward the back of the hospital. Anger coursed through his veins. The goddamn investigation that wasn't even an official investigation for LSI had gone fuckin' sideways, and all he cared about was getting to Libby and getting her safely home.

Drew caught up to him as they raced around the back corner of the hospital. Going in this direction, they came to other entrances than the one they'd used when they first arrived.

"Look," Cole bit out, pointing downward.

Knox dropped his gaze, his knees threatening to give out on him as he stared at the flash of silver on the concrete. Bending, he snagged the LSI lighthouse charm, clutching it in his palm as a painful vise squeezed his chest. "How the hell did we miss them?" he asked, disbelief and agony filling him.

"They couldn't take a chance on dragging her or carrying her. They must have had a way to get her in without arousing suspicion in the hospital. If they came around from the other side than us, we wouldn't have seen them," Drew said.

Bruce and Cole caught up to them, Bruce still wobbly as Cole made sure the policeman stayed with them. Knox glanced over at them, willing to let Bruce lie on the ground if that's where he fell. He had no reason to suspect he was behind anything, but allowing Libby to be kidnapped from under his nose didn't endear the man to him.

"That door is where carts of laundry are taken in and out," Bruce said, lifting his hand point.

On this side of the hospital, away from the morgue, there was more activity, and Knox could see a few hospital employees pushing deep, cloth carts filled with folded laundry through one of the doors. It wasn't much to go on, but with nothing else coming in from LSI, it was all they had. And right now, he'd take anything to get him closer to her. *Come on, babe. Where are you?*

25

Libby blinked her eyes open, but the desire to sleep made her want to give in to its pull. Her lips felt dry, her limbs heavy, and she was unable to focus on anything. She shivered, wondering who had turned on the air conditioner while her fingers moved slowly to grasp and pull the covers more firmly over her.

Each slow-motion movement had a delay in reaching her brain, but she finally realized that her fingers were not clutching her soft blanket. Forcing her lungs to suck in a deep breath of cold air, the intake of oxygen seemed to finally allow her thoughts to come more into focus.

Blinking her eyes several times again, the fogginess didn't lift until she recognized a sheet over her head. Drawing upon all her strength, she pulled the material down, continuing to blink as she looked around the small room. Cinder block walls painted a utilitarian soft gray. Fluorescent lights above although as dim as the room was, she wondered if they were all turned on.

Rolling to her side, she pressed down on the mattress and pushed herself upward, her vision clearing slowly as she continued to stare at the wall and solid metal door, trying to ascertain where she was and, more importantly, how she got there.

The mattress was hard, and looking down, she realized she was on a gurney, the metal railings lowered on each side. *What happened to me? Did I get sick or fall?* There were no sounds coming from outside the room, unlike any ER she'd ever been in. Shivering again, she couldn't understand why the room was so cold.

Her fingers fisted the sheet, and she pulled it up, wrapping it around her body. Glancing down at her arm, she noticed a dark bruise around a bloody prick point. She didn't remember someone treating her. Staring at the injury, she realized it wasn't in a place where an IV would be inserted. Unable to remember any more, she sighed. More concerned with getting out of the cold room and wondering how long she'd been here, she twisted her head to look behind her, hoping to see a clock.

Another sight met her eyes, and she gasped, bolting from the gurney. Her legs immediately folded underneath her, and she crashed unceremoniously to the floor.

She sat for a moment, her still-somewhat-foggy mind slow to process what was in the room. Licking her dry lips, she shifted forward and placed her hands on the floor, pushing herself to a stand. With still-shaking knees, she grabbed hold of the gurney she'd been sitting on. The room was small, but there were two gurneys side-by-side, the one she'd been on and one with a sheet-draped shape of a body lying on it. Her chest heaved as the air rushed out, but she found it difficult to suck in enough oxygen. Lightheaded, she wanted to close her eyes to focus on breathing but didn't dare. All the stupid teenage horror movies that her friends had watched at slumber parties came back to her, and as ridiculous as it might seem, she wasn't about to close her eyes in this place. Not with another body lying in front of her.

She moved her gaze to the area of the sheet-covered chest and watched but saw no discernable movement of breathing. *If they're not alive, then why am I in here, also?* The cold air finally seemed to cut its way through the mental fog, and memories rushed to the forefront of her mind. Knox. He and the others going into the hospital. Bruce in the front seat, then talking to the security men. *A woman at my door. My passport.*

Jolting as though her heart had had an electric shock, she remembered Bruce crying out and his body shaking before slumping over the hood of the car. She also remembered a sharp pain in her arm before everything went black. *Drugged! She drugged me!*

Emboldened with the memories, she steeled her legs and spine, standing straighter, determined not to fall again. Carefully skirting around her gurney while still holding on to it, she reached her hand out, her fingers skimming over the edge of the sheet hanging off the side. With bravery she never knew she had, she clutched the material and jerked.

Gasping again, more from the idea that a person

might suddenly sit up and come after her as her overactive imagination considered, she stared at the man dressed in a hospital gown. His eyes were closed. His face was pale. *He's dead.* Swallowing deeply, she realized he was no threat to her. Whoever put her in the cold room with someone who was deceased was the true threat. *I don't even know where here is!* Her hand reached up to clutch the lighthouse charm that Knox had given her, promising that he'd always be able to find her, but her fingers felt nothing but skin. Desperation filled her as she clutched all around her neck and chest, finding no necklace. *Oh, God, it's gone. Now he has no way to find me!*

A sound on the other side of the door was heard, and her heart leaped into her throat. Eyes wide, she prayed that Knox would step through the door. As it opened, she wasn't met with his familiar strong jaw, dark hair, and piercing blue gaze. Instead, two surgery-garbed and masked men walked in, their eyes immediately going to her standing near the now-uncovered man on the gurney.

She screamed and tried to rush past the first one but was quickly grabbed. Her arms held tight against her body, she kicked and screamed as she was dragged from the chilled room, not able to appreciate the slightly warmer room they brought her into.

"Shut her up!" a man's voice called out.

She looked toward the sound but only saw another man similarly garbed as the two who'd grabbed her.

"I've got her."

Another equally robed person stepped forward, and the only way Libby knew it was a woman was by her voice. Staring in horror as the woman approached with a hypodermic needle, she felt another jab despite her struggles.

Her arms and legs felt weak, but this was different. She didn't go to sleep. The world did not turn black. She could still see and hear what was going on around her, but she had no control over her limbs. She felt herself being maneuvered onto another gurney and, for the first time, glanced around with wide eyes at what appeared to be a small room set up for surgery.

The four people left her on the table as they busied themselves, each seeming to have a task. She tried to tell her arms to move or her legs to swing over the side, but they refused to obey her mind.

The woman spoke, her words snapping, her tone sharp. "This will take too long trying to do both of them tonight."

"Gibbons is fine where he is. We can do him tomorrow. This one needs to be taken care of tonight."

"I've got buyers for him," she bit back. "We just got him down here an hour ago, and I want to get him taken care of. He won't last long, you know that."

The man who seemed to be in charge glanced toward Libby and chuckled. "And you think she won't be worth more? Young and healthy?"

"Don't patronize me! Of course, she'll be worth more. But she's been here barely fifteen minutes. I can keep her on ice until tomorrow and take care of

Gibbons tonight. If he doesn't live through the night, then none of his organs will be worth anything. You need to prioritize."

Fifteen minutes? I must have only been in the cold room for ten minutes before waking up. Oh, God, please let Knox already be looking for me!

The man stopped what he was doing and stared at the woman before shifting his gaze to the two other men and then back down toward Libby. She could see the indecision on his face, wanting to beg for her life but unable to get her mouth to say the words that were in her mind. The horror unfolded before her, and she was unable to stop it.

He looked back toward the woman. "What do you suggest?"

"We prep Gibbons and take care of him today. We put her back on ice. I keep her drugged as she is now for at least twelve hours. Maybe longer. I don't have a shift tomorrow. I know you have an autopsy first thing in the morning, but unless something else comes in, you're free. Create a reason for why you must leave. And then come here." She glanced at the two others in the room. "What are your shifts tomorrow?"

The man who'd grabbed her shrugged. "It was supposed to be my day off."

"You'll be well-compensated," she said, her voice clipped. Looking toward the other, she lifted a brow.

"Early morning shift."

Her lips pinched, and she looked back to the first man. "We can do this with just the three of us."

The second assistant spoke up quickly. "I expect to get paid. It's not my fault you're going to do this when I have a shift."

As Libby lay, a silent spectator to the play going on in front of her, she watched as the woman's face hardened. Of everyone in the room, Libby knew she was the scariest.

"And since when do you call the shots?" the woman asked.

The first assistant stepped slightly back and away from the second man as though he wanted to put as much space between them as possible, uncertainty mixed with fear on his face.

The woman's lips curved upward, but there was no warmth in her smile. "You've been paid very well for your services." Inclining her head toward Libby, she continued, "But do not think for one moment that you could not be the one on that table."

The man rushed to say, "I understand, I understand!"

"Well, since that's settled," the man in charge said, turning back to the counter where he was working. "Get rid of her and prep Gibbons. I've got someone ready at the airport to transport everything I get from him."

Libby could feel a tear running down her face but was unable to lift her hand to wipe it away. Relief flooded her that she was being given a reprieve, but it wasn't the same as a rescue. And she couldn't imagine how Knox would ever find her.

They rolled her on the gurney back into the chilled

room, pushing her into the corner before turning and rolling the man she now realized was Paul Gibbons. His eyes fluttered before closing again. *Oh, God, he's not dead. At least, not yet.*

And another tear slid down her face.

26

No longer caring who they might run into, Knox raced through the door leading to the large room where supplies and laundry were delivered. Behind him, Bruce flashed his badge and barked out to the few employees standing around, asking about the last deliveries. They pointed to the other side of the room where carts were lined up, ready to be taken to various floors.

"Are they all here?" Bruce asked.

"Yes, yes!" answered one of the men standing there, eyes wide as he cowered in front of the sight of four large, angry men.

One woman began to shake her head. "No, one was taken."

Rounding on her, Knox growled, "Where? Where did it go?"

The woman, now visibly shaking, cried, "I don't know! It was a security guard who pushed it past the others and went out that door." She lifted her hand and pointed to one of the doors on the side of the room.

Without waiting, Knox and Drew rushed forward. Rounding a corner at the end of the hall, they quickly realized they were near the entrance that they'd come through earlier.

Radioing LSI, he said, "Have you got into the fuckin' cameras yet?"

"We just overrode their system even though the electricity was shut down. We've got it up now," Josh said.

"Can you go back for the past twenty minutes—"

"Knox, man, they're not able to do that," Cole said, his face holding regret as he shook his head.

Almost at the same time, Josh gave the same answer. "I'm fuckin' sorry. We're searching everywhere now on every floor."

Squeezing his eyes shut, he tried to block out the image of someone with their hands on Libby but couldn't move past the pain in his chest. Dragging in a ragged breath, he looked toward Drew, whose face appeared as ravaged as his own.

"The morgue. I can't tell you why. I just had a goddamn, fuckin', weird-ass feeling that something wasn't right there," Knox said.

"Good enough for me, bro," Drew said. The two raced down the still-empty hall, Cole and Bruce closely behind.

Rounding another corner, they rushed through the morgue doors, coming upon a man in a white coat who whirled around at the sound of their approach. He gasped, his eyes wide.

Knox's gaze dropped to the name stitched over the doctor's white coat pocket. *Dr. Ellison Neal.* Without hesitation, Knox stalked straight up to him and grabbed the doctor's collar in his fist, shoving the man's back hard against the wall. "You. Doctor Neal. You talked to Libby Cook tonight. Texted her. Where the fuck is she?"

"Knox," Bruce said nearby, his voice low. "Easy."

Jerking his head around, Knox growled, "Fuck easy." Spearing the doctor with a glare that could peel the paint off the wall, he said, "Answer the fuckin' question because you do not want me to repeat myself."

Dr. Neal's gaze jerked around to the men, and he shook his head. "I don't know! I swear I don't know!"

"Then what are you doing down here?" Drew asked as Knox continued to press his fist against the doctor's chest.

"I'm looking for someone. A patient."

"I need more," Knox bit out, his patience ready to snap.

"I... I... it was a patient that was in my care. I was gone yesterday, and when I got back, I was told the patient had died. The patient had no next of kin. I thought. That's what we were told. But Ms. Cook had left a message for me the other day, and when I messaged her back to ask about Roger, she happened to mention that she was checking on this patient. She stopped texting, and it dawned on me that if there was someone who knew this patient, then maybe there was next of kin somewhere."

"And you're down here... why?" Bruce asked. "What are you hoping to find at the morgue?"

"The patient. His name is... was... Paul Gibbons. I wanted to come down here to make sure that the hospital's medical examiner would let the funeral home know that there might be next of kin contacting them."

"Who did you talk to besides her?"

"No one. There was no one in the morgue, but I wouldn't have expected the medical examiner to still be here. I had looked in the drawers, but most were empty, and Mr. Gibbons wasn't there. I looked in the chiller room, and it had one man that wasn't him either. That man is scheduled for an autopsy tomorrow. There's no one in the freezer room."

"So, no one was in here, not even the deceased man that should have been?" Bruce asked.

Knox turned over the information in his mind, murmuring, "It's got to be here. They've got to be here. Whatever's happening, it's got to be here."

Dr. Neal's face turned red as he shot his gaze around. "What? I don't understand. Why are you looking for Libby? What's going on?"

"She was fuckin' kidnapped from your fuckin' hospital when someone—a security guard—tasered Inspector Williams."

"No!" Dr. Neal gasped, shaking his head, his gaze moving from man to man surrounding him. "Why?"

"That's what we want you to tell us," Knox raged, his fist growing tighter.

"Me?" the doctor squeaked, his hands now lifting slightly to the side as his face grew redder.

"What did Libby want to talk to you about? The first time?" Bruce asked.

"Um… she just said that she'd stumbled onto something concerning and she wanted to ask me about it.

That's all her voicemail said. Then, when I texted her back when I got the message this evening, she didn't say anything about it. I thought maybe she was talking about Roger Whitcomb."

"She got lost and was down here. Overheard a conversation about harvesting organs. Black market. Millions of dollars. An expatriate with no next of kin was mentioned. Sure you don't know anything about that?" Knox asked.

"Oh, God," Dr. Neal whispered, shaking his head. "I know that kind of thing exists… but… I never thought it happened at this hospital." He appeared lost for a few seconds, then stared straight into Knox's eyes and vowed, "I don't know anything about it. Nothing. But I'll do whatever I can to help you find out what's going on and find her."

Knox stared hard into the doctor's eyes, his heart pounding, blood rushing through his veins so loud he could swear everyone could hear it. But the more he looked at the doctor, the more he believed him. His fist loosened slightly, and he squared his shoulders as he stood straight. "If you're fuckin' lying to me—"

"I'm not! I swear I'm not. That… that horrendous act… I'd never. And I won't stand in your way of finding whoever's doing that."

"Something's going on here. In the morgue. I don't know where or how, I just know it's here." Calling on the LSI radio, he barked, "Send a schematic of the morgue. Include the entire floor. Stat."

A few seconds later, he glanced at his phone, peering

closely at the architect plans and schematic drawings Josh had sent.

"What do you need from us?" Mace asked over the radio.

"I need all eyes on these. Something's not right. Run them through and compare."

"What are you looking for?" Drew asked, coming over to Knox as Cole stepped closer to look over his shoulder, as well.

"I got a feeling when we were in here before Libby was kidnapped. I was turning around looking at the space but couldn't fuckin' figure it out then. The morgue is next to the office of the medical examiner that we were just in, but the space doesn't seem right."

"You're right!" Josh called out. "When the two grids are placed on top of each other, the wall to your left doesn't meet the medical examiner's office. There's a large space in between."

Bruce stepped closer and said, "I've called for my team to come in quiet, come in easy. No sirens. But if the security in the hospital is involved, I want the backing of armed police to be here."

Knox looked to the side. "Can you trust them?"

Bruce held his gaze. "With my life. I… I didn't report higher. Not until we know."

Knox understood what Bruce was risking and appreciated his support, but right now, his mind blanked of everything but finding the room that didn't exist—and then praying that he'd find Libby whole and well when he did. Glancing at the large clock on the wall, over thirty minutes had passed since she'd been taken. Swallowing down the bile that threatened to choke him, he stalked to the wall with the others at his back as they stared at the cinderblock wall. Spying no evidence of a hidden door, they spread out and began pushing on each block. *Solid. Goddammit.* "It's fuckin' solid!" he bit out.

"Other side!" Drew said, just as Cole exclaimed, "The ceiling!"

Swinging his head from one to the other, Knox called out, "Cole, get up there. We're going into the office." Looking toward Bruce, he added, "Get your team to surround this area. No one gets in, no one gets out."

"On it," Bruce spoke into his radio, barking orders to his captain.

Knox headed toward the door leading into the hall, glancing over his shoulder as Cole climbed onto a table, removing one of the ceiling tiles above him. Then he raced down the hall to the medical examiner's office they'd searched earlier

"The closet. The fuckin' supply closet," Drew growled, pointing to the single door on the wall they were looking at. "I searched it earlier. If I fuckin' missed something—"

Knox shook his head as he rushed into the closet. "Get your mind back on track, bro. We weren't looking for fuckin' secret entrances."

"That door is too wide," Dr. Neal said, drawing the others' attention to him. "This is not a regular closet door size. It's wider. Wide enough for a gurney to roll through."

Christ! Knox turned back to the shelves and knew there must be a way to get through the back without moving the supplies, but not knowing how it might work, he grabbed a box and passed it to Drew, who tossed it out into the office. Looking over his shoulder, he watched Dr. Neal shoving boxes to the side, as well.

Speaking into his radio, he said, "Cole, location? What do you see?"

"I can see ventilation pipes and refrigeration pipes going toward the space. Ventilation makes sense. Refrigeration doesn't."

"So, there can be another refrigeration room that's hidden," Knox surmised aloud.

"There'd be no reason for that," Dr. Neal said, then gasped as his eyes widened. "Unless someone is keeping a body cool. They'd have to have someone who's alive. You can't harvest organs if the heart stops beating."

Just hearing the word *harvest* sent chills through Knox, and his gaze searched the back wall of the supply closet.

Drew was just behind him and turned around, looking up. "Got it!"

Whipping around, Knox saw his taller brother reach up and flip a switch that was almost out of sight. The wall swung inward.

Pulling his weapon from his holster, he stepped inside, not caring who he might have to kill to get to Libby, but the sight that met his eyes nearly caused his knees to buckle. It was only the feel of his brother at his back that allowed him to charge forward, desperation and rage taking over.

A body was lying on a gurney in the middle of the small room with four people dressed in surgical garb in attendance. One man stood with a scalpel in his hand, his head turned toward the intruders, his eyes wide. A woman operating what appeared to be an anesthesia delivery system was standing at the end of the table. She screamed then froze as Knox's gun pointed directly at her head. The other two froze, their hands immediately lifting in defeat.

"Jonas!" Dr. Neal cried out as he entered after Drew and Bruce crowded into the room.

Knox was barely aware he was talking to the man with the scalpel as his gaze shot toward the gurney. *Male... Christ Almighty, not Libby.*

"Where is she? Where's Libby Cook?" he growled, shoving the end of his gun into the chest of the closest man. "I'll blow a fucking hole in your chest if you don't—"

The man jerked his head to the back of the room where another door was located. Just as Knox took a step, Cole radioed, "I can see there's another room with refrigeration. Back of yours."

"Got it," Drew acknowledged as Knox twisted the knob, finding it locked.

Growling, he turned with his weapon raised, and this time the two assistants didn't hesitate. "She has a key!"

Drew was the closest of the Keepers to the female doctor, but it was Dr. Neal that got to her first. With a movement so fast Knox knew instantly the man must have been former military, he wrapped his hand around her throat.

"Suzette. I want to say I'm shocked, but you were always a greedy bitch. Where's the key to that door?!" Dr. Neal bit out, his fingers squeezing.

She started to reach into her pocket, but it was the surgeon who, with a defeated expression, cried out, "Watch out! The key is around her neck!"

"Shut u—" she tried to say, her face now red with Dr. Neal's fingers tightening even more around her throat.

Knox leaned over and grabbed the chain around her neck, jerking hard enough to move her body as well as snap the chain. Whirling around, he unlocked the door and raced through, adrenaline mixed with fear clawing at him.

The small room contained two gurneys, one empty and the other with Libby. He roared her name, rushing to her side. Her eyes were open, but her body was deathly still. "Baby. Libby, I'm here." He shoved his weapon into his holster just before scooping her into his arms. Her cold body flopped around, limp in his embrace.

Noises could be heard from the other room, but he didn't look nor care what was happening. A ceiling tile was shifted to the side, and Cole's legs dropped through. Drew assisted Cole into the room, then they both turned toward Knox and Libby.

"Knox, brother, lay her down. We need to see what's happening to her," Drew said softly.

Looking at her slack face but opened eyes, Knox was gutted with tears stinging the backs of his eyes. He looked up to his brother. "I don't know. I don't know what to do," he groaned.

Dr. Neal pushed his way in, took one look at Libby, and ordered, "Lay her down. She's been drugged. Lay her back down."

Unable to get his body to respond, he continued to cling to her until Drew and Cole assisted her back onto the gurney. Dr. Neal jerked out his phone and began calling orders for someone. Looking up, he said, "The drug Suzette gave her renders her conscious but unable to move. Talk to her. She can hear you, but she can't control any of her muscles to respond. I'm calling for my assistant to bring what I need to counteract what Suzette gave her."

Leaning over her, placing his face directly in her line of sight, he began. "Baby, he says you can hear me. I've got you. I've got you now. You're safe. He's going to get the medicine to counteract what she gave you." He placed his hands on either side of her face, her skin cold. Looking up, he barked, "We need to get her warm! Get them the fuck out of the other room!"

Cole hustled into the makeshift surgical room, herding everyone out. Several minutes later, he came back and said, "All clear."

They pushed Libby's gurney into the outer room, and by that time, several nurses called by Dr. Neal had rushed down. One had several heated blankets in her arms and began wrapping them around Libby with Knox tucking them in tightly. "We're going to get you warm, Libby, sweetheart. Doctor Neal is taking care of you, and we got them. You're safe now. And as soon as we can, I'm taking you out of here. I'll take you anywhere you want to go, but babe, I want to take you to Maine. Even if it's just a visit, I want you to come. I'm not giving up on you, and I'm not giving up on us."

He felt a presence pressing in but didn't turn his face away from her. It was his brother's voice that sounded softly in his ear.

"Bruce and his team have taken charge of the investigation and arrests. They moved everybody out into the hall, and the hospital is essentially on lockdown right now. It's filled with hospital bigwigs, the police, and even journalists are starting to show up outside. But nobody's in the outer office, so we can roll her out there to give everybody more room and keep her warm."

Nodding his gratitude, they continued to push her gurney out into the medical examiner's office. He watched as Doctor Neal injected something from a hypodermic needle straight into Libby while the nurses began hooking her up to the monitors they'd rolled down.

Helpless, he stood to the side, continuing to hold her icy, cold hand, continuing to talk to her. Bending low, he murmured everything in his heart while praying that she'd come out of whatever the witch had given her. "I know you've got your job in Virginia, but as soon as we can, I want you to see the beauty of Maine. If we've got to do long-distance until we figure everything out, we will, babe. But you and me, remember everything we talked about at the lodge. This is you and me now, babe."

Dr. Neal grumbled, "I want to get her upstairs onto the floor—"

"Too much going on out there in the hall," Drew argued. "What can we do to make this work?"

Dr. Neal shook his head, sighing. "It's fine. Hell, I worked with a lot less out in the field."

Cole looked up. "Belize National Army?"

Dr. Neal nodded before looking over at Knox. "A few more minutes, and you'll start to see her coming around."

"Is she going to be..." his voice cracked, "okay?"

Dr. Neal grimaced, lowering his voice. "Physically, she should be fine. Emotionally? The trauma of being paralyzed while still being able to hear and probably know what they were planning on doing... well, she may need... help."

Hearing the words, Knox was barely able to take them in, his gut twisting before Libby's chest depressed as she sucked in a breath deeper than what she'd been taking. Her lips twitched as her fingers wiggled slightly in his. He kept whispering to her, warmth slowly seeping into her skin. Focusing his attention back down, he whispered, "That's it, Libby. Just keep breathing. One breath at a time, babe. We'll get through this one breath at a time."

Chest heaving, she stared into his eyes. "Kn... knew... you... wou... come... fo... me."

He wasn't sure, but he thought she was trying to smile. All he knew was that he was grinning through his tears.

27

Knox tried not to stare at Libby but was constantly aware of her sitting in the seat next to him in the airplane as they flew back to the United States. Drew was flying, and Cole was in the copilot seat. He and Libby had the two seats behind them. With only a little over a foot between their seats, they were close but not nearly close enough for him.

She was subdued, and while he might have only known her a short while, this was not his typical Libby. She'd pulled inside herself, barely talking, and her smile didn't reach her eyes. And after everything she'd been through, he was worried. As she stared out the window, Drew would occasionally glance back, and Knox spied concern on his brother's face, as well.

The hours following her rescue had been a nonstop, continuous roller coaster. Doctor Neal had finally gotten her into a hospital room where she was monitored closely for several hours. As soon as she was able to speak, she'd given a formal statement to Bruce and been visited by the CEO and head physician of the hospital. Drew and Cole set up security outside her room for her own protection until all the guilty parties could be rounded up and arrested. Plus, it was effective in keeping the journalists away.

During all this, Knox didn't leave her side, both reveling in the fact that they remained touching through it all and hating that she clung to him when she'd wince as fear moved over her face. He couldn't believe how strong she was, handling everything that had been thrown at her. But when she'd asked about Paul Gibbons and was told by Doctor Neal that he had died, she broke down. She'd begged to get out of the hospital setting, saying she couldn't stand the smell. The doctor had agreed, and she was discharged.

She'd held onto Knox and begged him to take her home, refusing the offers of a resort stay that the hospital wanted to provide as recompense. Drew had stepped close to them, placing his hand on the back of her head and pulling her forward to kiss the top of her hair. "We'll get you home, darlin'."

Knox was torn. Part of him wanted to insist that she rest, but the other part agreed that he just wanted to get her home. And the words that he'd whispered to her earlier were true... he wanted to take her home to Maine.

Her eyes finally closed, and her head rolled gently against the headrest. She'd fought sleep ever since she'd been rescued as though afraid to close her eyes. Now, he hoped the rest she was getting would not be filled with terrors.

"How are you doing?" Cole asked.

He softly snorted. Cole knew him, but there was a reason Drew hadn't asked that question. His brother would know that he was barely hanging on. Plus, with Drew having gone through what he did with Babs, he knew exactly what Knox was feeling.

Whispering so as not to wake Libby, he replied, "Okay. Awful. Terrified. Grateful. You name it, I'm feeling it. And I know it's nothing compared to what she's been through." There was a lot he needed to say to her, but for now, he just wanted her to find peace.

"I'll get you guys home, bro," Drew promised.

Knox offered a chin lift and leaned his head back, as well.

Yes, but where is home? Libby's mind raced as she pretended to sleep. She hadn't slept since she'd been found, first overcome with emotion at seeing Knox bending over her and then listening to his voice as he whispered words of comfort while she regained her ability to move and speak. Then, so much happened so quickly, and she coped by shutting down all emotions as she gave her statement to the police. But she couldn't let go of Knox's hand, and thank God, through it all, he never left her side.

She'd heard Knox and his brother talking softly when she was being checked out by the nurses. *"The medical examiner is already running his mouth, probably hoping if he cooperates, he'll get a reduced sentence. The female doctor was one of the anesthesiologists, and honest to God, it looks like she's as much a ringleader as he was. The two others were nursing assistants, and Dr. Southerland is already giving up the people in security that were helping."*

Dr. Neal had sat with her, his face kind as he thanked her for pursuing what she'd overheard. "It's brave people like you who have saved so many from a fate they didn't deserve."

She'd sucked in her lips, fatigue pulling at every muscle in her body, but too afraid to close her eyes, she'd simply nodded. The idea of staying in Belize for one more moment sent terror through her, and she'd barely managed to not fall apart, begging Knox to take her home. And, of course, he'd agreed. They'd left less than twenty-four hours after she was rescued.

But now, flying away, her pulse raced as fast as her thoughts were bouncing around in her head. The truth was that the drugs affected her memory as well as her ability to move. She remembered snatches of conversations and seeing Paul Gibbons on the gurney, but most of what happened before Knox came to her was so fuzzy that she didn't remember. And that was fine with her. She'd have enough nightmares to last a lifetime without more memories to haunt her.

But what was filling her mind now were all the words Knox had whispered.

"I'll take you anywhere you want to go, but babe, I want to take you to Maine. Even if it's just a visit, I want you to come. I'm not giving up on you, and I'm not giving up on us... I know you've got your job in Virginia, but as soon as we can, I want you to see the beauty of Maine. If we've got to do long-

distance until we figure everything out, we will, babe. But you and me, remember everything we talked about at the lodge. This is you and me now, babe... Just keep breathing. One breath at a time, babe. We'll get through this one breath at a time."

Words she'd longed to hear. Words that brought her back from the brink. But words said under extreme duress. Words that might not have meaning beyond the moment they were said. And since then, Knox had been by her side, attentive, conciliatory, and everything she needed. But he'd made no more reference to Maine or what would happen when they got back to the States.

Considering she had no idea what she was thinking, she could hardly blame him for not verbalizing definitive plans, either.

What do I want? I have a job in Virginia Beach. One that I like, but I would still prefer to work in a nursing home instead of a luxury independent living facility. I care about the people I work with, but in truth, they don't need me. And I don't love them the way I love Knox. But does he love me? Enough to repeat the words he said in the hospital, only this time not with the world crashing around us?

With no answer forthcoming in the silent plane, she pretended to sleep, hoping that even if her mind couldn't rest, at least Knox would be able to.

Hours later, she stood in a hangar at the airport in Norfolk, her arms wrapped around Cole as she said her goodbyes and offered undying gratitude. The big man held her tight, brushed away her thanks, and said, "Can't wait to see you again when you come to Maine."

She didn't reply but looked up and smiled before

moving over to Drew. He also wrapped her into his embrace, then bent low to kiss the top of her head. She hadn't had a chance to speak when he beat her to it. "Don't even start with that *thanks* shit."

Despite everything, a giggle burst from her lips, and she leaned back to look up at the giant whose features were similar to his brother's but didn't come close to pulling her in the way Knox's did. "You don't mince words, do you, *Robert?*"

He laughed and shook his head. His eyes remained bright, but his expression sobered. "What we do, we do because of a calling similar to yours. But for you, babe, no thanks are necessary among family."

She cocked her head to the side as she held his gaze. "Family?"

"Darlin', I'm not going to say what's in my brother's heart even though I know it. That's for him to say. But Babs and I'll expect to see you soon." He bent slightly, bringing his face closer, his voice low. "I know a lot of good men, Libby. Work with some. Served with others. Raised by one. But Knox is the best man I know."

She swallowed deeply, uncertain she could take a breath with emotions threatening to choke her. Nodding, she whispered, "He's the best man I know, too."

"Good," he continued, then straightened back to his six-foot-seven stature and peered down with another easy grin. "I also know some good women, most married to Keepers. Lord knows, I married one. And you, Libby, are right up there with them. Can't wait for you to come and meet everyone." With that, he pulled her back in, kissed the top of her head again, and stepped back.

Knox stepped forward, his brow lifted as his lips quirked. "Thought I was going to have to fight you for my girl, bro."

"Nah, man. Babs would have my balls."

"She's already got them," Knox laughed. "See you soon, guys. I'll buy you a beer when I get back." The three men shook hands, and then Knox wrapped his arm around Libby as they watched Drew and Cole head to the plane.

Jerking her head around and up, her mouth hung open. "Aren't you... I mean, why... you're not leaving with them?"

He dropped his chin to peer at her. "No."

She blinked. "No?"

"Do you want me to leave now?"

"Well, no, of course not. But I didn't... we haven't... you didn't say..."

He turned and wrapped his arms around her, so similar to Cole's and Drew's embrace and yet completely different. With her face pressed against his chest and his steady heartbeat against her cheek, she felt like she was home.

He spoke, and this time, she felt the words from deep in his chest. "I want to make sure you're okay. I can rent a plane and fly back in a couple of days. That is if it's okay with you."

She nodded, her head moving against his chest, and felt his arms tighten.

"Libby, it feels like a lifetime ago that you and I were

at the Lamanai Lodge, vowing that we were the start of us. For me, nothing has changed. I'm afraid of saying anything to bring up memories from yesterday, but you need to know that my feelings haven't changed. I know you have a job here. I know you have a home here. But I want you to visit me in Maine. I want you to meet my fellow Keepers. I want you to meet my boss. I want you to meet their women. I'm not saying that I expect you to uproot your whole life for me, but I want to spend more time together. Then we'll figure out what's best for us."

The words washed over her, cleansing away her doubt and confusion, but it seemed he wasn't finished.

"You were part of a mission for only a day. Since then, you've been part of my heart."

Finally leaning back and peering upward, a tear slid down her cheek, captured by his thumb before he kissed her lightly. "I want to be with you, but…"

"But nothing. We know what our hearts want."

Nodding, she smiled. She did know what her heart wanted, and even if she didn't have all the answers right then, she knew she wanted this man. "So… if you've got a couple of days to spend here, we can check in on the Windsor Village gang together."

28

THREE MONTHS LATER

"Surprise!"

Libby jumped as she walked into the recreation room at Windsor Village and spied the balloons, streamers, huge cake on the table, and most of the residents standing around clapping.

With her hand clasped over her heart, she looked around. "Oh, my goodness! What is this?"

"You didn't think we'd say goodbye without giving you a party, did you?" Cynthia laughed.

She rushed into the room and began offering hugs, blinking back the tears, knowing how much she was going to miss the residents.

Curtis patted her on the back, saying, "He's a good man, Libby. I'd like to think I had a part in bringing you two together."

She nodded and grinned, knowing Curtis was right. Roger was next in line, and his hug was just as warm as it had been ever since she'd gotten back from Belize. He considered her his guardian angel, a title she refuted but smiled at, nonetheless.

"Going to miss you, sweetheart, but I know your new clients will love you as much as we do."

Swallowing back her tears, she tightened her grip on him, also. After she made her way down the line of men, the women crowded around. Finally, Cynthia and Sally cornered her after the others had received slices of cake and were seated at the nearby tables.

"So," Sally began. "Is the man as hot in bed as we think he is?"

Jerking, her cheeks pinkened as heat filled her face. "I'm not... that's not..."

"Honey, if you think some of us don't have a love life anymore, think again," Cynthia chimed in.

Pursing her lips to keep from grinning, she nodded. "Let's just say that I have no qualms about moving to Maine. I'm sure Knox can keep me warm during those long, cold winters."

The women cackled, then Cynthia pulled her in for a hug. "For what it's worth, I think what you're doing is wonderful. It's not that we don't love having you here, but you were destined for more than just museum trips with us. There are others who really need your loving care and experience."

"And not just Knox," Sally quipped, drawing another round of chuckles.

Cynthia moved to the table to claim her piece of cake, and Sally stepped up, holding her gaze. "I once said you needed more spunk and you'd get a man. I was wrong, Libby, and for that, I'm sorry. You always had spunk. You just needed to meet the right man. And Knox... he's the right man."

She nodded, knowing Sally was right, and with another tremulous smile, she looped arms with her, and they headed off to get a slice of cake, as well.

One Week Later

"Where do you want this?" Drew called, rolling in a handcart loaded with boxes.

"Where do you think she wants it, Flyboy?" Babs called out, standing on her toes to kiss him. "They have *kitchen* written on them."

"Oh," he said, looking down at his wife. "Do I get a kiss every time I ask a dumb question?"

She leaned up and kissed him again. "How's that for an answer?"

The others laughed as Knox looked around his and Libby's new house. They had gone together to visit the Windsor Village residents when they'd gotten back from Belize, but other than that, they didn't leave her apartment for two days. And two nights. Time spent talking, time spent planning, and time spent making love.

She'd visited him in Maine, and he'd flown back to

Virginia Beach enough times that when they were ready to move forward, they were both sure. She'd met all the Keepers and their women, instantly discovering what he knew she would—a camaraderie that went beyond friendships. Now, they'd bought a house together, she'd found a new job that she liked even more, and today was move-in day.

All the furniture and most of the boxes had been moved in. Tate, John, and Cole were outside firing up the grill. Levi and Blake were hauling bags of ice in tubs to keep the beer cold. Rank, Walker, and Clay were setting up tables and chairs. Cobb and Bray were setting up cornhole and frisbee golf in the yard. Mace and Drew were bringing in the last boxes from the moving van.

Knox turned from the sliding glass door to look into the kitchen that opened into the dining room and large family room and smiled. Libby was surrounded by Sylvie, Helena, Julie, Sara, Nora, Claire, Christina, Pippa, Josie, Marie, Marge, and Lucy. The best group of women he knew, and she fit right in.

He'd surprised her yesterday by showing up at Brightwaters Assisted Living, not far from where they'd bought a house. He'd stood outside the recreation room and watched as she moved amongst all the residents, helping those who were trying to have their snack, assisting others with paints and colors, and leading a few others through sitting exercises. She did this while smiling, offering gentle touches, kind words, and heart-felt hugs. And he watched the faces of those she interacted with and knew this was her calling. Just as he and the other Keepers were protectors, she was the ultimate nurturer. And she was his.

As the women carried platter after platter out the door to where the party would take place, he stepped over to Libby as she gazed around the box-filled kitchen and dining room. Wrapping his arms around her, he kissed her crinkled forehead, murmuring, "Don't stress. It'll all get done."

She looped her arms around his waist and squeezed tightly, smiling up at him. "Moving is daunting, but I'm not stressed. Being here with you and our friends makes it all worthwhile."

"Not sorry that you've moved up here?"

She laughed and shook her head. "On my last day at Windsor Village, Curtis told me something that he said he'd mentioned to you, and that was life without taking some chances is hardly worth the life at all. And the worst thing was to reach their age and be full of regrets."

"Wise man," Knox said, bending to kiss her again. He angled his head to take the kiss deeper when he heard Drew calling from outside. Grinning, he shook his head, staring at her beautiful, smiling face. "Ready to go party with our friends?"

"I love you, Knox, so I'm ready to do anything as long as you're by my side."

Deciding his brother could wait, he sealed his mouth over hers, and they kissed, celebrating their new beginning.

Don't miss the next books in the Lighthouse Security - West Coast Series!
Next up is Home Port (an LSI West Coast crossover novel)
Leo (LSI West Coast)
Rick (LSI West Coast)

ALSO BY MARYANN JORDAN

Don't miss other Maryann Jordan books!

Lots more Baytown stories to enjoy and more to come!

Baytown Boys (small town, military romantic suspense)

Coming Home

Just One More Chance

Clues of the Heart

Finding Peace

Picking Up the Pieces

Sunset Flames

Waiting for Sunrise

Hear My Heart

Guarding Your Heart

Sweet Rose

Our Time

Count On Me

Shielding You

To Love Someone

Sea Glass Hearts

Protecting Her Heart

Sunset Kiss

Baytown Heroes - A Baytown Boys subseries

A Hero's Chance

For all of Miss Ethel's boys:

Heroes at Heart (Military Romance)

Zander

Rafe

Cael

Jaxon

Jayden

Asher

Zeke

Cas

Lighthouse Security Investigations

Mace

Rank

Walker

Drew

Blake

Tate

Levi

Clay

Cobb

Bray

Knox (LSI)

Lighthouse Security Investigations West Coast

Carson (LSI West Coast)

Leo (LSI West Coast)

Rick (LSI West Coast)

Hope City (romantic suspense series co-developed
with Kris Michaels
Brock book 1

Sean book 2

Carter book 3

Brody book 4

Kyle book 5

Ryker book 6

Rory book 7

Killian book 8

Torin book 9

Blayze book 10

Griffin book 11

Saints Protection & Investigations
(an elite group, assigned to the cases no one else wants…or
can solve)
Serial Love

Healing Love

Revealing Love

Seeing Love

Honor Love

Sacrifice Love

Protecting Love

Remember Love

Discover Love

Surviving Love

Celebrating Love

Searching Love

Follow the exciting spin-off series:

Alvarez Security (military romantic suspense)

Gabe

Tony

Vinny

Jobe

SEALs

Thin Ice (Sleeper SEAL)

SEAL Together (Silver SEAL)

Undercover Groom (Hot SEAL)

Also for a Hope City Crossover Novel / Hot SEAL...

A Forever Dad

Long Road Home

Military Romantic Suspense

Home to Stay (a Lighthouse Security Investigation crossover novel)

Home Port (an LSI West Coast crossover novel)

Letters From Home (military romance)

Class of Love

Freedom of Love

Bond of Love

The Love's Series (detectives)

Love's Taming

Love's Tempting

Love's Trusting

The Fairfield Series (small town detectives)

Emma's Home

Laurie's Time

Carol's Image

Fireworks Over Fairfield

Please take the time to leave a review of this book. Feel free to contact me, especially if you enjoyed my book. I love to hear from readers!

Facebook

Email

Website

ABOUT THE AUTHOR

I am an avid reader of romance novels, often joking that I cut my teeth on the historical romances. I have been reading and reviewing for years. In 2013, I finally gave into the characters in my head, screaming for their story to be told. From these musings, my first novel, Emma's Home, The Fairfield Series was born.

I was a high school counselor having worked in education for thirty years. I live in Virginia, having also lived in four states and two foreign countries. I have been married to a wonderfully patient man for forty years. When writing, my dog or one of my four cats can generally be found in the same room if not on my lap.

Please take the time to leave a review of this book. Feel free to contact me, especially if you enjoyed my book. I love to hear from readers!

Facebook
Email
Website

Made in United States
North Haven, CT
17 February 2023

32747614R00190